SEROWE
VILLAGE OF THE RAIN WIND

Bessie Head

HEINEMANN

Heinemann Educational Publishers
A division of Heinemann Publishers (Oxford) Ltd
Halley Court, Jordan Hill, Oxford OX2 8EJ

Heinemann: A division of Reed Publishing (USA) Inc.
361 Hanover Street, Portsmouth, NH 03801-3912, USA

Heinemann Educational Books (Nigeria) Ltd
PMB 5205, Ibadan
Heinemann Educational Boleswa
PO Box 10103, Village Post Office, Gaborone, Botswana

FLORENCE   PRAGUE   PARIS   MADRID
ATHENS   MELBOURNE   JOHANNESBURG
AUCKLAND   SINGAPORE   TOKYO
CHICAGO   SAO PAULO

ISBN 0 435 90220 2

British Library Cataloguing in Publication Data

Head, Bessie
  Serowe: village of the rainwind. – (African writers series; vol.
  220).
  1. Serowe (Botswana) – Social life and customs
  I. Title
  968.1'1   DT803.S4

  ISBN 0–435–90220–2

Printed and bound in Great Britain by
Cox & Wyman Ltd, Reading, Berkshire

94 95 96 97 10 9 8 7

Contents

Foreword

I felt as I came to the end of this unforgettable book that I had understood not only Serowe, the huge Botswanan village which Bessie Head describes, but for the first time certain things about Africa itself which had never before found their way into literature. A new light floods in on the scene when, early on, she quietly states that Africa was never 'the Dark Continent' to African people. From this moment I knew I was seeing and hearing things which made sense at last of much of what has occurred there this past century. Rarely has the cadence and the intelligence of the four generations which lived through these years been caught so accurately or so movingly.

These black voices tell of a remarkable transition from the ancient tribal culture to a British Christian culture, and cover the whole period between the setting up and the dismantling of white colonialism. It is not only what they say but the tone in which they say it which tell one immediately that here are truths and complexities which have escaped the usual records. Bessie Head writes quite undefensively and with vivid power. Those who have told her what they witnessed during the reign of Khama the Great, the days of Tshekedi, Seretse and his English wife, and the time when Patrick van Rensburg came to Serowe, have a way of speaking which bares the soul of their nation.

Via this exceptional ear and eye, the Christianization of the Batswana often struck me as being something akin to that of a Saxon kingdom by royal scholars — Alfred's Wessex, for example; and Bessie Head's account of how her adopted people were preserved from slavery by, of all historical incidents, the Jameson Raid adds to the unique quality of this African story. She says that the advance of the Serowans has been the reality of their village life and that their tale is a beautiful one. Her way of retelling it through their talk is certainly most beautiful — though tough and accurate too.

Ronald Blythe

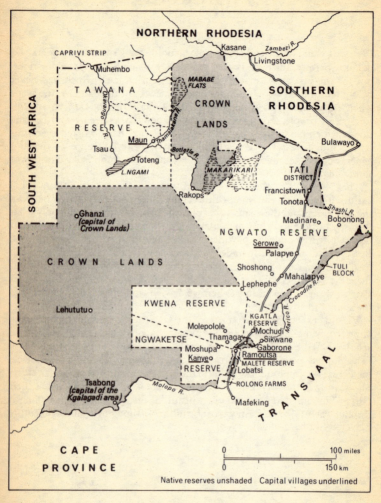

Map taken from J. Mutero Chirenje, *Chief Kgama and His Times* (Rex Collings, London, 1978)

The distribution of the tribes in Botswana

Map taken from Isaac Schapera, *A Handbook of Tswana Custom* (Oxford University Press, London, 1938)

Dedication

For
Jacqueline Alberti and Paddy Kitchen,
and the people of Serowe,
with love

Acknowledgements

The books and papers I have consulted, referred to and quoted from during the course of my work are listed in the bibliography (pp. 199—200). Special permission was granted by Sekgoma T. Khama to quote from the Khama Papers 'Khama's Exhortation to his People'.

My special thanks are due to Mary Kibel, Thato Matome and Bosele Sianana, who contributed advice and aid for all my work.

For permission to reproduce the photographs on pp. 1, 73 and 133, the publishers gratefully acknowledge the Botswana National Archives (Khama the Great); the Botswana Information Service (Tshekedi Khama); and Sandy Grant (Patrick van Rensburg).

Introduction

General Portrait of Serowe

His name was Harold M. Telmaque. His poem, the title of which I cannot remember, appeared unexpectedly in a magazine of the sort I used to read then — hoarsely and violently asserting blackness. I cannot survive in the heat of the moment, and I remember the peace with which my mind latched on to one line of Telmaque's poem. . . .

Where is the hour of the beautiful dancing of birds in the sun-wind?

All time stands still here and in the long silences the dancing of birds fills the deep blue, Serowe sky. Serowe people note everything about nature:

'The birds are playing,' they say, more prosaically.

And indeed there seems to be no sense at all in the bird activity in the sky, other than playing and dancing. And why is it always one bird-call I hear at dawn? It is always one bird that starts the day for me, outside my window, and he's not saying anything very properly — just a kind of hesitant 'peep-peep' as though he's half scared at opening his eyes. But the light outside, at dawn, is unearthly too — a kind of white light; an immense splash of it along an endless horizon. This white light quickly pulsates into a ball of molten gold and here in the sunrise, you can time the speed of the earth's rotation as the enormous fiery ball arises. It is barely a minute before it breaks clear of the flat horizon. It scares me. I say to myself:

'What the hell am I doing on something that moves so fast?'

At some stage I began to confuse Telmaque's lines with lines of my own, and I renamed Serowe the village of the rain-wind. We have more drought years than rain years. During my ten-year stay here, the two or three seasons when it rained for a whole month in one long, leaden downpour were so exceptional and stunning that I cannot even describe them. I am more familiar with the rain pattern of drought years. It rains sparsely, unpredictably, fiercely and violently in November, December and January. Before the first rains fall, it gets so hot that you cannot breathe. Then one day the sky just empties itself in a terrible downpour. After this, the earth and sky heave alive and there is magic everywhere. The sky becomes a huge backdrop for the play of the rain — not ordinary rain but very peculiar, teasing rain.

A ring of low blue hills partly surrounds the village; at least, they look blue, misty, from a distance. But if sunlight and shadow strike them at a certain angle, you can quite clearly see their flat and unmysterious surfaces. They look like the uncombed heads of old Batswana men, dotted here and there with the dark shapes of thorn trees. It is on this far-off horizon that all through December and January, the teasing summer rain sways this way and that. The wind rushes through it and you get swept about from head to toe by a cold, fresh rain-wind. That's about all you ever get in Serowe most summers — the rain-wind but not the rain.

Even so, summertime in Serowe can be an intensely beautiful experience, intense because with just a little rain everything comes alive all at once; over-eager and hungry. A little rain makes the earth teem with insects, tumbling out of their long hibernation. There are swarms of flies, swarms of mosquitoes, and swarms of moths — sometimes as big as little birds. Crickets and frogs appear overnight in the pools around the village: there is a heavy, rich smell of breathing earth everywhere.

It was by chance that I came to live in this village. I have lived most of my life in shattered little bits. Somehow, here, the shattered bits began to grow together. There is a sense of wovenness, a wholeness in life here; a feeling of how strange and beautiful people can be — just living. People do so much subsistence living here and so much mud living; for Serowe is, on the whole, a sprawling village of mud huts. Women's hands build and smooth mud huts and mud courtyards and decorate the walls of the mud courtyards with intricate patterns. Then the fierce November and December thunderstorms sweep away all the beautiful patterns. At the right season for this work, the mud patterns will be built up again. There seems to be little confusion on the surface of life. Women just go on having babies and families sit around the outdoor fires at night, chattering in quiet tones. The majority, who are the poor, survive on little. It has been like this for ages and ages — this flat continuity of life; this strength of holding on and living with the barest necessities.

Serowe is a traditional African village with its times and seasons for everything; the season of ploughing, the season for weddings, the season for repairing huts and courtyards and for observing the old moral taboos. In the traditional sense, it is not really a place of employment but almost one of rest. The work areas are at the lands and cattle-posts miles away. When people are in Serowe from about June to October or November, they are resting after the summer harvest and preparing for the next rainy season. During this resting period weddings take place, huts and courtyards are repaired. Most Serowans have three different homes; one in Serowe, one at the lands where they plough, one at the cattle-post where they keep their cattle. They move from home to home all the time. I have lived in a village ward which was totally deserted during the ploughing season. We are likely to keep this basic pattern of life for a long time.

Serowe is a village in the newly independent state of Botswana (formerly the British Bechuanaland Protectorate). It is young as far as dwelling places go. In 1902, during the reign of Khama the Great, it became the capital of the Bamangwato tribe who at that time were searching for surface water. Then two rivers, the Sepane and Manonnye, flowed through the village, but only the very old people remember this. The dry river-beds are there like huge gulleys running through the village but Serowe itself is stark, rocky, goat-eaten and soil-eroded.

Serowe has several arms and my book shuttles to and fro all the time, linking up the other dwelling places of the Bamangwato tribe. Shoshong, a village to the south and some hundred miles away, was the Bamangwato capital for fifty years, from about the time the first missionaries began to record southern African history. Then the surface water became scarce, and in 1889, Khama moved his village from Shoshong to Palapye. Palapye, some thirty-six miles away from Serowe, was the Bamangwato capital for fourteen years, then the water became scarce again and the tribe moved to Serowe. I think the problem of water shortages was caused by the huge number of people who lived in the Bamangwato capitals. As far back as 1889, the missionary, J.D. Hepburn, recorded a population of 20,000 at Shoshong, a large number of whom were refugees from the Matebele wars. Khama attempted a dispersal of the population in Palapye, but then he accepted another influx of refugees from the Anglo-Boer war of 1902. Another arm of Serowe is Pilikwe village, established in 1953 by Tshekedi Khama, not because of water shortages but because of the marriage of his nephew (the heir to the Bamangwato chieftaincy), Seretse Khama, to an Englishwoman, Ruth Williams, and the disruption to tribal life that the marriage caused.

Serowe is an historic village but not spectacularly so; its history is precariously oral. The monuments, like the Khama graves, are few, and even then a visitor might stare at them blankly, unaware of the drama and high purpose behind those silent stones. Serowe spreads in a wide circumference of eight miles and is one of the largest villages in Africa. Up until the time of independence in 1966, it had a more or less permanent population of 35,000 but the population has become so movable since the new mining developments that it is difficult to take an accurate census count. The 1971 population census had the figure of 15,723 for Serowe but no one believes it. A squatters' camp outside the new copper-nickel town of Selebi-Phikwe holds over a thousand people in shacks, but as soon as they have earned enough money they return to village life.

Today, the new independence towns of Gaborone, Orapa and Selebi-Phikwe have town planners and building contractors swarming all over them. Their construction does not involve their population who simply move into tedious arrangements of government housing schemes. But the construction of Serowe intimately involved its population. They always seem to be building Serowe with their bare hands and little tools — a hoe, an axe and mud — that's all. This intimate knowledge of construction covers every aspect of village life. Each member of the community is known; his latest scandal, his latest love affair. At first glance it might seem nearly impossible to give travel directions in the haphazard maze of pathways and car tracks. Everything goes in circles; the circular mud huts are enclosed by circular yards and circular pathways weave in and out between each yard. For ages, people and their names were the only means of locating one's whereabouts. But such is the nature of progress in a newly independent country that early in 1974, a road construction company abruptly descended on Serowe and carved up its centre into tarred ring roads and super highways. Serowans were so annoyed by the inconvenience this caused that they scornfully refer to the new development as 'government vote catching'.

Although we live by such an ancient pattern, no other village in Botswana is as dynamic as Serowe and no other has seen so much tangible change. This continuous change and upheaval was often brought about by spectacular and original leaders like Khama the Great and his son, Tshekedi Khama, because Bamangwato people have always had genius in their leadership and tended to identify genius or 'that something different' with traditional leadership. People will refer to eight such great leaders but, more relevant to the theme of my book, I have selected the names of two — Khama and Tshekedi — to make a point; that it seemed almost inevitable that they would one day be deprived of a traditional leader.* Tradition, with its narrow outlook, does not combine happily with common sense, humanity and a broad outlook.

In Khama's time and under his personal supervision, the old order of tradition, ritual and ceremony died and was replaced by a completely new order of things. In Tshekedi's time, the Bamangwato chieftaincy, and it had been the most powerful in the country, died, and the Bamangwato people became overnight people without a traditional leader; the older generation have found it hard to accept this state of affairs and they express unease about the future. An outsider cannot but appreciate the contradiction of these great rulers who unwittingly acted as liberators.

Serowans have never lacked direction — they have always been involved in causes and debates. I admit a love for those causes, so that my definition of the soul of Serowe may eventually be condemned as too one-sided and favouring the themes of social reform and educational

---

*According to Tswana custom, no chief or chief's son could marry without the consent and approval of the tribe. On the 28 September, 1948, Sir Seretse Khama (late President of Botswana, then an heir-apparent to the Bamangwato chieftainship) married an Englishwoman, Ruth Williams, without the consent of his uncle and guardian, Tshekedi Khama. Tshekedi Khama was at that time regent for the tribe, acting in place of Seretse Khama until the latter would be officially installed as chief of the Bamangwato. The marriage completely disrupted tribal life and resulted in conflict and rioting, with periods of exile for both men.

On the 26 September 1956, Tshekedi Khama and Seretse Khama renounced for themselves and their children all claims to the Bamangwato chieftainship. However, the older people have pressed for years to have a chief. On the 5 May 1979, Ian Khama, the son of Seretse Khama, was officially installed as chief of the Bamangwato. It appears to be a symbolic gesture of reconciliation.

advance which have been a reality of village life. The story, and it is a beautiful one, has a long thread.

This book is built around the lives and work of three men — Khama the Great, Tshekedi Khama and Patrick van Rensburg — and the story of Serowe is told through their contributions to the community and the response of that community to their ideals and ideas. One aspect of my original choice that seems to be sheer luck or coincidence, was that the time sequences in which the three men worked almost overlapped, presenting me with an astonishing record of self-help and achievement. The era of Khama the Great lasted from 1875 to 1923; the era of Tshekedi Khama from 1926 to 1959; in 1963, Patrick van Rensburg and his wife quietly appeared in Serowe.

I chose the three men for their responses to the adverse pressures of their times:

Khama the Great: When David Livingstone, the missionary explorer, first made his way northwards during the 1840s, Khama's father, Sekgoma I, ruled the tribe. But the white man had had some form of settlement in South Africa for over two hundred years. Africa was never 'the dark continent' to African people and they had passed through Shoshong long before Livingstone with reports of the white man's deeds, especially his land greed. With Khama, one continually gets the impression that he was deliberately reversing the tide that had swallowed up and submerged other black peoples in southern Africa. One of his laws, still adhered to in the land, reads: 'The lands of the Bamangwato are not saleable ... I say this law is also good.'

Khama's contribution to the community is not easily defined. He was too vast and rich a personality. I speculated deeply on his absolute commitment to Christianity because it was the basis for all his social reforms with which I deal extensively in the book. The traditions and taboos which all tribal people adhere to, I tend to regard as a kind of external discipline — rules of law and conduct created for people by generations of ancestors. People do not have to think about whether these disciplines are compassionate or not — they merely comply with all the rules. When I think of Khama's conversion to Christianity and his imposition of it on the tribe as a whole — it more or less forced him to modify or abolish all the ancient customs of his people, thus stripping them of certain securities which tradition offered. If his acceptance of Christianity was an individual and moral choice, then it meant that he carved out a new road for the tribe — the discipline which people now had to impose on themselves was internal and private. People might not have realized this, and this might account for the almost complete breakdown of family life in Bamangwato country, which under traditional custom was essential for the survival of the tribe.

Tshekedi Khama lived with two pressures. The British colonial authorities conducted a bitter feud with him all through his rule, and towards the end of his life he remarked: 'I am tired of this war.' The feud was of such a peculiar nature that I have set a question mark against it in the book and attempted my own explanation of it, against the background of Tshekedi's great contribution to the community. The second pressure Tshekedi created himself. Initially, he himself paid for the higher education of a small group of boys, whom he sent on to colleges in South Africa. The result of this was that the people wanted him to educate all their children and the best solution to this problem was to get people in Serowe to build their own primary schools, which they did, on a voluntary basis, and one college, Moeng.

Patrick van Rensburg was in the diplomatic service of the South African Government, so he was in the position of seeing the true hell of South Africa from the inside. The greatness of the man was that the day came when he simply said to himself: 'That's enough.' Then he came, seemingly quite accidentally, to Serowe. He seemed to step into Tshekedi's shoes and continued, at more creative levels, to stimulate an intense interest in educational progress. His educational theories are for everyone.

So, I shall attempt to tie three great personalities together and around their lives and work, draw a portrait of Serowe. The three men are all of the same kind. They wanted to change the world. They had to make great gestures. Great gestures have an oceanic effect on society — they flood a whole town.

Some Notes on the Main Themes

I chose the main theme of the book myself — that of social reform and educational progress. The other themes of the book people of Serowe developed themselves during the year I moved in and out of their homes. A number of people would repeat the same story, for instance the pattern of tribal movement and migration, and I learned to hold on to these stories as they vividly evoke the ancient African way of life.

The self-help theme goes back to 1875 when Khama the Great abolished *bogwera*, the initiation ceremony for men, which formerly grouped them into age regiments or *mephato*. Apart from circumcision, *bogwera* involved the ritual murder of one of the initiates and it was abolished by Khama on these grounds. Khama simply christianized the ceremony with a few prayers and lectures and almost absent-mindedly ordered the newly called *mephato* to go and build a portion of the mission church wall; the regiments were always building mission schools, houses and churches in an unorganized sort of way. By these means Khama prepared the groundwork for the massive explosion of highly organized self-help activity which the tribe contributed under Tshekedi Khama. When Tshekedi was faced with the pressure of providing his people with schools for their children, he turned to the *mephato* or age regiments and forced out of them incredible feats of service and endurance. Tshekedi in turn paved the way for the advent of Patrick van Rensburg in the village. Although Pat van Rensburg was able to draw on aid money from a number of donor countries, a lot of the projects he initiated in the village also needed contributions of voluntary labour from the community.

The migration theme was the favourite story of the old men of the village, and they repeated it so often that bits and pieces of the story appear all through Parts One and Two of the book, culminating in the move made by Tshekedi Khama and his followers to Pilikwe village. An old historian, Mokgojwa Mathware, in his recounting of the *Founding of the Bamangwato Nation,* vividly illustrates the simple brutality of the early conflicts which arose out of polygamous marriages in royal households — the senior brother in the royal line often ousted his junior brothers for fear that they might have more charisma for the people. A theme of high principles developed out of this very basic story during Khama's time. He was involved in endless struggles of this nature, with his father, Sekgoma I, with the brothers of his father's polygamous household, and with his first son, Sekgoma II. Tshekedi never betrayed the high standards set by his father, Khama; so that in the culminating story there is no power lust nor anything else of that kind, but only a kind of confused sorrow.

An intimate knowledge of construction is one of the major themes of Serowe life. Traditionally, people had to produce all their own household goods and clothing; thus, they had to have total knowledge of how their goods were produced — from gathering roots in the bush for tanning leather, to the completion of a final article, perhaps a Tswana mat or blanket. This theme continues to this day on modern self-help projects, like brigades and village co-operatives. Factories and specialized skills are unknown in the village. Brigade students, out of necessity, learn along the production line the whole of a new skill they are acquiring.

Things Unique to Village Life

The 'Green Tree' or Rubber Hedge or Tlharesetala

At first glance, especially from an aeroplane, you would think Serowe was a green valley. The proliferation of dark green foliage surrounding each wide circular yard is made by a rather unattractive plant known as the *Tlharesetala,* which means 'Green Tree', commonly used for hedging. The plant has an amazing ability to reproduce itself. From planted cuttings, with little or no water, the Green Tree sends out new roots and starts a new life for itself. A waxy coat effectively prevents water-loss by evaporation and milky sap gives it a bad enough taste to deter goats from eating it. The sap also congeals on exposure to air, so water losses through damage to stems and leaves are kept to an absolute minimum.

It is the cheapest, easiest and most effective form of hedging. In the old days trees were chopped down and stacked close together to hedge a yard. A rough count of poles around an old yard showed me that nearly a thousand trees were needed to fence a single yard. How many trees must have been felled to fence the yards of a population of thirty-five thousand? In any case, the poles were soon eaten through by white ants and had to be replaced. The labour of fencing must have been exhausting.

Then, in 1923, into Serowe came Hendrik Pretorius and his wife, more widely known by their local nicknames, *Seatasemadi* and *Mma-Seata.* Hendrik Pretorius was a hunter in the old days and invariably, when he came back from hunting he had blood on his hands, hence the nickname *Seatasemadi,* which means blood-on-the-hands. With him, he brought the Green Tree.

Village people said: 'We first saw the Green Tree in the yard of *Seatasemadi.* When it was high he pruned it and threw away the branches. We took these branches to fence our yard. Then Chief Tshekedi noticed that the Green Tree was good for fencing. He called a kgotla and encouraged people to use it. Once it was seen that Chief

Tshekedi liked the Green Tree, a woman, Mosarwa Aunyane, decided to do a little business. Her village was Serowe but she was married to an Ndebele man in Bulawayo. He had a business there. People in Bulawayo had been using the Green Tree for their yards for a long time. She brought the Green Tree from Bulawayo in their truck and sold it to the people. Once it grew all over the village, it was no longer sold. It was free for a new yard.'

Mrs Katherine Pretorius or *Mma-Seata* said: 'My husband and I came to live in Serowe in 1923. I went to visit a married sister in Maun and found the Green Tree in her yard. She told me it was a good windbreak. I brought back to Serowe a sugar-pocketful and planted it around my yard. It was so fast growing that in about two months it was three feet high. Once I pruned it I gave the cuttings away.'

The Village Dogs

As pups, they fetch a high price and people pay because dogs are useful to them, but you can't find a good dog in Serowe. The following recipe for dog's diet was given me by a sympathetic village woman. She said: 'People do not prepare special food for dogs. When food is dished up there is always a little at the bottom of the pot. The pot is then rinsed out with water. That porridge and water is dog's food.'

You often catch pathetic glimpses of them, all skin and bone, wearily and devotedly trailing after their owners' donkey carts and bicycles, unaware of other worlds where dogs are regularly shampooed and fed on chicken. It is his devotion to man in all circumstances that makes a dog such a wonderful animal and the Serowe dogs are a living example of it. Dogs are kept to guard the yards at night against the *baloi* or witch-doctors who have been known to creep into the yards and maybe put a mark of blood on the door, pee on the doorstep, put down a bottle of evil medicine, or a bunch of dried leaves or a bone tied with cow sinew. Also, when there is nothing to eat in the house, people turn to the bush for food. Dogs are taken along as assistants in hunting wild rabbits and other animals. They are given little in return for these services.

The Old-Style Calendar (translated by Martin Morolong)

A young American teacher said to me: 'I was out one night with some local people. I looked up at the stars and tried to engage them in talk about the southern constellations. They thought I was crazy. Talk about constellations, moon time and star time meant nothing to them. What sort of calendar do people go by here?'

In reply to his question, I stumbled upon what must be one of the most poetic calendars in the world filled with vivid observation of nature — its changes, its trees, wild fruits and flowers and the everyday work of man as he ploughs his fields. The old people were not star-gazers or fatalists. They concentrated on the real world and so worked out their own time scale.

The old-style calendar had thirteen months. As it was a seasonal calendar, it seemed easy to adapt it to the Julian calendar brought in by the missionaries. One of the months, Powane, was omitted for convenience. The old Setswana new year began about August and coincided with the approach of summer:

PHATWE (August)
'*Thare di tloga*' ... 'The trees are budding,' the old people said. There is an abrupt separation between the very cold days of winter and the heat of summer. This sudden approach of summer occurs about 15 August. There is a stirring movement in plant life. The sap rises in the trees.

LWETSE (September)
'*Maru a lwala*' ... 'The clouds are sick,' the old people said, expressively, of the low dark rain-clouds which gather in the sky at this time. They are the first hoped-for signs of rain. The Makoba tree, which is insect-pollinated, bursts into bloom. The air is filled with a deep, heavy, rich perfume from its yellow, weeping-willow-like flowers. The Mimosa thorn-bush turns green

POWANE (This month was eliminated from the Setswana calendar)
Powane means a young bull. During this month, the young bulls sharpened their horns to prepare themselves for the fights of the mating season. After a few showers had fallen, they thrust their horns into the wet ant-hills to sharpen them.

PHALANE (October)
'*Di phala diatsala*' ... 'The young impala are born,' they noted. Phalane is a baby impala. In this season they are born.

MOSETLHA (November)
'*Mosetlha wa thunya*' ... 'Mosetlha bears flowers.' The Mosetlha tree

flowers during this season and if the rains have been early, the children feed themselves on wild bush berries.

MORULE (December)

The Morule tree bears fruit. The fruit is eaten while still green. It is about the size of a small plum and within its thick, green coat it is all nut really, covered by a thin film of delicious, slimy jelly. The skin is broken open, the jelly sucked off, then the nut is cracked and the kernel eaten. Children and adults eat it, cattle and goats eat it and housewives gather basketfuls to make Morule jelly jam. While cooking, the vapour the fruit gives off is the same intoxicating odour as the bush, so the jam could also be labelled: Bottled Bush. The fruit is also fermented for Morule wine.

HERIKGONG (January)

'*Re loma ngwaga*' ... 'We are biting the new year.' People begin to eat the first crops of the summer from their lands. These are melons, pumpkins and a local squash, Leraka. In the old days, before people were allowed to eat anything from their lands, they took the first fruits to the chief who had to have the first bite. The eating of the first fruits was a time of ritual and ceremony.

TLHAKOLE (February)

'*Tlhakole*' literally means 'Wipe your plough.' It's too late for ploughing now, the corn will never ripen, so give it up. For those who have ploughed with the early rains, the corn stands high in their fields, the pollen has disappeared on the sorghum plant and its seeds have begun to form.

MOPITLWE (March)

'*Ngwaga wa pitle*' ... 'The year is narrowing.' The sun rises later; the first sign of winter.

MORANANG (April)

'*Moranang wa dinawa*'... 'The bean crop is ready.' Our bean crop is spreading over the land. Sometimes a pest, the Thanang worm, appears at this time. If we don't hurry and harvest, the Thanang worm will damage our crop.

MOTSHEGANONG (May)

'*Motshega di nonyane*' ... 'Laughing at the birds.' The corn is dry. The birds perch on the sorghum heads and try to eat them but the dry seed falls to the ground. The birds can only peck it out of the sorghum head when it is still milky and green.

SEETEBOSIGO (June)
'*Seetebosigo*' literally means ... 'This is the month when the cold winds blow. Do not go out at night. There is no room for you around my fire.'

PHUKWI (July)
'*Pukula di thare* ... 'The trees are naked.' The month of June stripped the trees bare of leaves.

People's Names

People's names evoke stories of events which took place at the time of their birth. I will recount a few of the stories told me, indicating the general pattern of naming children.

Kemotho means 'I am a person.' A young man was very poor and on the day of his marriage, village people passed scornful remarks to his wife's family along the lines of: 'How can you let your daughter marry such a poor man?' Though hurt, the young man kept quiet. When his first son was born, he called him *Kemotho* and quietly remarked: 'I may have nothing but I am still a person.'

Kgotodue is a wild flower of the bush. This flower springs up overnight after a little rain, is seen for a while, and then is gone again. A young mother had lost many children at birth. Then she had a son and thinking he would die like the others she said in despair: 'Here's another *Kgotodue*. We'll just smell it and it will be gone again.' The child survived to become a man.

Rebatho means 'Now we are people.' The grandparents had seen no grandchildren in the family for a long time. Then a young grand-daughter married and gave birth to a son. This caused joy and relief to the grandparents. They exclaimed: '*Rebatho*, now we are people again.'

Mma-Haile and Rra-Haile. When a foreigner earns great respect in the village an enormous number of children may be named after him or her. Such was the case with a Miss Evelyn Haile, a missionary, who ran the first maternity centre in Serowe at the London Missionary Society's mission centre in the village. The baby girls she delivered were called *Mma-Haile* and the boys, *Rra-Haile*.

Kgwathiso means 'to be lashed'. Any self-respecting man likes his pint of beer at the end of a hard day of labour, and one of the laws of Khama the Great that never quite succeeded was his abolition of beer-drinking. People continued to brew mabele beer in secret, so Khama was forced to send regiments into the village to arrest offenders. Villagers responded with humour and named their children after the trials they endured under this impossible bit of legislation. An old man, *Kgwathiso*, was born at the time some people were being lashed at the kgotla for drinking beer.

Children are also named after historical events. In 1902, when the tribe moved from Palapye to its new capital, Serowe, the children born at that time were simply named *Serowe*. Then, in 1952, the tribe was leaderless. Their chief, Tshekedi Khama, was in exile. The heir to the chieftaincy, Seretse Khama, was also in exile, due to his marriage to an Englishwoman. Rioting broke out in Serowe and the children born at that time were called, *Mokubukubu* — children of the riots. So, no one has a meaningless name and often the word combinations that make up a person's name are quite new and original. Anything is grasped upon in the surroundings by which to name a child — a year of good rain and a plentiful supply of corn; a touching history of suffering or struggle or quarrels and strife between relatives. The older people, who do not know their age due to the fact that there was no registration of births in their time, often have names referring to some national calamity, like a plague of rats which destroyed the corn. They talk of their names and age in these terms: 'You know when the plague of rats came? Well, I am *Rra-Dipeba*, Father of the Rats. I was born just at that time. . . . '

Marriage and Death (by Thato Matome)

Marriage and death ceremonies are a combination of traditional courtesies and Christian rites. The same crowds, the same faces are often seen at both ceremonies, the same cooking pots come out and beasts are slaughtered. But one is a riot of joy, movement and dancing; the other, a deathly silence, broken only now and then by mournful hymn-singing or prayer.

Marriage. Long before the actual wedding, relatives move in and out of a yard to smear and decorate the courtyard and walls of the mud huts with brightly coloured soil mixtures. On the afternoon before the wedding, the preparations for the wedding take place. Corn is stamped, beasts are killed and bread baked in pots. A portion of the meat which will serve as the wedding-breakfast is cooked at this time and the helpers stay up the whole night preparing the feast.

Diphiri is the wedding-breakfast for the bride and groom and all the guests. It takes place just before sunrise. *Seswaa* (pounded meat) and samp are eaten and in the dim light the relatives of the bridegroom approach. They bring with them the gift of an ox, the wedding-dress and the wedding-ring. As they enter the yard, the women break into shrill, high-pitched ululating as an expression of joy. They keep up this permanent commotion of ululating for the whole of the wedding-day as streams of guests arrive with gifts. The relatives of the bridegroom seat themselves in the yard and formally ask for the bride. They say: *'Go kopa metse'* which is literally to 'ask for water' — the bride is supposed to go and carry water at her in-laws' home. This done, and agreed to, the bride is dressed, ready to be taken to church.

Several ceremonies may take place, all at the same time. The ox has to be killed and traditionally apportioned. Different relatives get different parts of the beast according to their status: the paternal aunts get the intestines; the maternal uncles get the head; the mother gets the breast bones or ribs; the bride gets the loins.

If a first-born child is getting married, the parents fast for the whole day and eat in the evening. By contrast with all the joy, dancing and ululating in the yard, the Christian church ceremony appears very staid. On the bride's return from church, feasting begins. There are guests who just come and eat, then leave. There are guests who are invited traditionally — they are all the maternal aunts and relatives and they have to be specially catered for the whole day long with tea and bread and anything they may desire.

At about 2 p.m. the bridegroom's people come again to ask for the bride. They form a long column a few yards from the bride's home and walk ceremonially into the yard. They generally look solemn in contrast to the ululating that greets them, because from the bride's family there are often complaints about any traditional practices that have been ignored, and this is the time to express these complaints. If all is well, the bride is taken away accompanied by some of her own relatives. On arrival at the bridegroom's home, the bride is made to sit on a mat. She is divested of her wedding-veil, a *doek* (kerchief) is placed on her head and a shawl on her shoulders — the symbol of a married woman.

Death: people spend a lot of time on funerals as death is a communal responsibility. As soon as there is a death, a fire is lit in the yard and people start moving around to inform relatives and friends, who all make their way to the home of the deceased. This is where all families meet and relatives are expected to spend the night there — the closer the relationship, the longer the stay. Mourners also come from far and near and a lot of food is needed to feed them. Everyone in the surrounding area or village ward is expected to help. People bring along a gift of a goat, a bucketful of corn, wood for the fire or a bucket of water for cooking and washing up. A few men will volunteer to dig the grave; others will bring a wagon-load of wood for the fire.

The full burial rites, with a church service, are rare. Mostly, a burial service is performed at home by the priest of the church to whom the deceased belonged. The cemetery is an open, unfenced area of land outside the village. The soil is soft, red sand and easy to dig but it is a desolate, bleak and uncared-for place. Each grave is marked by a heap of stones. Now and then a name is etched out on a flat, smooth stone at the head of the grave, with dates of birth and death. But once people are buried, that's that. More attention is paid to the living than to the dead.

After the funeral itself there is work to be done. Clothes and any belongings of the deceased have to be washed, packed up and put away for about a year, after which time they are given away to relatives. Traditionally, there were no legal arrangements about property. A conflict has arisen about this. People's personal goods have become more costly and of a wider range. Relatives have been known to be greedy and have made off with the bulk of the goods, leaving nothing for the children of the deceased.

'When my mother died,' a woman told me, 'we only managed to claim teaspoons. The relatives took everything else.' Therefore, in present-day Serowe, the goods that may be handed out to relatives have been restricted so that the children of the deceased get a larger share.

Then there is the custom of *Go Tshedisa* — the paying of sympathy calls. This can be of indefinite duration but immediately following the death there must be relatives in the yard to receive the sympathizers for about one month.

PART ONE

The Era of Khama the Great (1875—1923)

'I am not baffled in the government of
my town, or in deciding cases among my own
people according to custom.'

From the Protectorate document of 1885 drawn up by Khama

1
Khama the Great

Wherever there is a spark of genius or true greatness in a man, mankind pays its homage. And so it is with Khama. All the missionaries, travellers and administrators who passed through his town took due note of his striking personality and achievements, and there are innumerable such records of his life. Unfortunately, all this material is as yet uncollected in one complete biography. Unfortunately too, according to the language and values of the Victorian era, he is treated as an exception to the rule and hailed from all sides as the one 'kaffir' or 'native' who somehow made it straight to God amidst the general 'savagery', 'abominations' and 'heathendom' of his land. Overlooked is the fact that all men are products of their environment and that only a basically humane society could have produced Khama.

Khama's was to be a long life of great fascination and drama and the story has about it a chain of absolutely logical, unbroken sequences as though the man moved steadily from one experience to another and always knew what he was about, what his next move would be. We get the first and very full portrait of Khama in John Mackenzie's masterpiece, *Ten Years North of the Orange River.* Khama was then a young man of about twenty-four years of age, who had recently, on the 6 May 1862, been baptized a Christian by a Lutheran missionary, H.C. Schulenburg. Due to mission difficulties, Schulenburg had to retire from the Bamangwato capital of Shoshong, and was replaced by John Mackenzie and Roger Price of the London Missionary Society. Initially, all was well, and Mackenzie and company, according to

African custom, were the guests of Khama's father, Chief Sekgoma I, who at that time ruled the tribe. The drum of 'heathen' and 'savage' was to be beaten loudly each time the name of Sekgoma I appeared in the history books. However, at this early stage, it was the great pleasure of Sekgoma, when the work of the day was done, to make his way by a secret footpath to Mackenzie's home. They would hold humorous dialogues about the relative merits of what they represented — Christianity versus African custom and tradition. Sekgoma had no intention of becoming a Christian, but he expressed deep satisfaction with his sons, five of whom were involved in the mission work in the village. Khama and a younger brother, Kgamane, were teachers at the two mission schools run by Mackenzie and Price.

Very little detail is given of the actual teaching work. It appears to have been of a christianizing and biblical nature. Each day Khama rode out with Mackenzie to the village school.

'His manner was very quiet,' Mackenzie records. (A number of other biographers were to record this extreme quietness which was a Khama characteristic.) Apart from that, Khama is at first almost incidental to the story. Mackenzie takes his time, and as the drama unfolds, he examines Bamangwato society with the eye of a sociologist. On a journey to Matebeleland, Mackenzie had acquired some insight into the brutal military dictatorship of Mzilikazi and much preferred and admired the legal, orderly and democratic ways of Bamangwato society. He peppers his book with the word 'heathens' all right, but it is not his aim to mock and despise black people and his observations of all the rituals and ceremonies of the people are recorded with stunning accuracy which makes the book extremely valuable.

Then, in April 1865, Sekgoma called an age regiment or *mephato* for one of his young sons. A number of young lads had at this time to be put through the initiation-into-manhood ceremony, *bogwera*. Previous initiates, of whom Khama was one, had to attend the ceremony of the new initiates. The five Sekgoma sons refused to attend. Mackenzie writes:

Each man mustered his retainers, and, surrounded by his own sons and near relatives, marched daily to the camp of the neophytes. Proud is the Bechuana father who is surrounded by a number of sons on these occasions. There is an honour connected with this which no distinction of rank can supply. Sekgoma's mortification was therefore very great when he found himself marching to the camp alone — not one of his five eldest sons accompanying him. They were all at our school instead, and every Sunday they were in their places at church.

This was the signal for the start of a complicated conflict between Sekgoma and his eldest son, Khama. Almost all the old men knew by rote the brutality of African power struggles which sent whole tribes into exile, which unleashed violent forms of jealousy and greed, in which a weaker man could be abruptly assassinated. But a new factor had been introduced into the conflict between Sekgoma and Khama — that of Christianity and its principles to which Khama adhered. It wasn't merely a question of Khama succeeding to the chieftaincy, but a question of all the new values he had acquired.

Sekgoma swung all the old African warfare tactics into operation, openly terrorizing the population into support for himself against his son. He also succeeded in breaking down and winning the support of two of his sons, Raditladi and Mphoeng, while the other three, Khama, Kgamane and Seretse stood firm in their opposition to their father. Three-quarters of the population of Shoshong were 'heathens' at that time, but what admirable 'heathens' they were! Mackenzie, whose very life was in peril at this time, noted that the people awakened and silently and intently began to watch the conflict, trying to suppress their liking for Khama. Khama was born with the sort of austere discipline of character that commits little or no error. An indication of Khama's popularity was shown when Sekgoma, soon after the *bogwera* incident, walked up to Khama's homestead and attempted to assassinate him but the gun was abruptly pulled out of Sekgoma's hand by a tribesman.

Then Sekgoma seemed to lose his head. Khama had not so long ago married a Christian woman, Elizabeta or Mma-Bessie. Sekgoma now ordered his son to take a second wife, according to the custom of polygamy, which was the prerogative of the chiefs. This Khama refused to do.

There followed a whole year of tension. Sekgoma was a thorough sort of torturer. During this period he hurled custom after custom at Khama, defying him to transgress. Khama had little support. He had to endure the torture alone, and the tortures he endured at this time were to lead to all his subsequent social reforms. He abolished *bogwera*, he discouraged polygamy, he abolished witchcraft and rain-making ceremonies. The psychological terror of witchcraft was one of Sekgoma's prime weapons; he was reputed to be the greatest sorcerer in the land. Khama systematically took the terror out of it by surviving all the incantations and charms prepared by Sekgoma. One can only

5

speculate on his extreme distress in the light of Khama's later utterances. Was this why he could declare with such extraordinary clarity to the British some years later: 'I am not baffled in the government of my town, or in deciding cases among my own people according to custom.'?

The climax to all the tensions came in March 1866. Sekgoma ordered warriors to surround Khama's home, and Khama together with all the Christian population of Shoshong was forced out on to the mountains, while Sekgoma held the village in a state of siege. 'When Sunday dawned,' writes Mackenzie, 'I had a sad prospect before me. Almost all my congregation were on the mountain.'

Sekgoma held the village for six weeks. During that time he despatched a message to an exiled brother, Macheng. Macheng, he said, was to take on the major task of assassinating Khama. He himself feared to do so as the people favoured his son. Macheng, on arrival, quietly turned the tables on Sekgoma. He immediately saw his own chance and how low Sekgoma had fallen in the estimation of the people. Macheng made a public declaration that he was not going to assassinate Khama. Defeated, Sekgoma fled and in the years 1866-72, Macheng ruled the Bamangwato tribe. Macheng allowed Khama to stay in Shoshong, possibly because Khama's popularity with the people would ensure support for himself.

It is at this point that John Mackenzie's absorbing record ends and the story is then taken up by J.D. Hepburn who replaced the departing Mackenzie family. *Twenty Years in Khama's Country* begins in a storm of hysteria. When Hepburn and his wife arrived in Shoshong in 1871, they encountered an entirely unnatural state of affairs under Macheng's rule. Macheng had a complicated history of his own. As a youth he had been captured by Matebele warriors and brought up in their dictatorial ways, which were quite foreign to the Bamangwato tradition. Macheng had decided that Christianity was undesirable and was in the process of stamping it out when the Hepburns arrived. The first two chapters of Hepburn's book are very misleading. The *whole* society is damned as consisting of 'heathens, abominations and savages' overlooking the fact that it is the dictatorial Macheng who has ordered continuous day and night drum-beating and wailing so that there is not a moment's peace and quiet. Macheng also abolished Sabbath observance. Moreover he hatched a little plot to kill Khama by poisoning him, but the plot failed.

In 1872, Macheng was ousted in a *coup d'état* by Khama, who very briefly assumed power. Khama recalled his father, Sekgoma, from exile, and handed back to him the position of ruler. Despite this gesture, within five months after his arrival back at Shoshong, Sekgoma cut Khama off from his inheritance and recognized his second son, Kgamane, as his heir. Khama deliberately withdrew to Serowe, which was at that time his cattle-post and, in doing so, split the nation in two. Hepburn writes:

> The movement began to be felt in the town and soon became a general one. For weeks long strings of people — women with baskets on their heads; men, some with bundles, and others driving pack-oxen — filed up the kloof. The stream flowed steadily on until the town of Bamangwato proper became almost deserted, and only a few old men and servants remained with Sekgoma.

On both sides a year of preparation for war followed, and Sekgoma rallied the tribes of the south to his aid. On the 3 February, 1875, Khama again approached Shoshong. Hepburn writes an on-the-spot description of this war:

> But that Khama was so near I had not then the least idea . . . I looked up at the mountain and could scarcely credit my senses. Men appeared to be throwing themselves from its crown headlong and to be coming down its sides as if they had wings . . . and I felt the very sides of the kloof vibrating with volleys of musketry. . . .

This battle, which lasted one month, established Khama as the chief of the Bamangwato when he defeated his father, Sekgoma. One can almost feel the peace and order which fell abruptly upon the village of Shoshong, reflected in J.D. Hepburn's letters to his London Missionary Society headquarters. Hepburn no longer resorts to those Victorian clichés 'heathens, abominations, savages'. But the victory had not been won easily; Khama told Hepburn that 'At one time, I thought there was nothing but death in front of me. I told them they could kill me, but they could not conquer me.'

Like most dictators who bedevil human society, Sekgoma and Macheng had had little to offer the people except a programme of power. But Khama had been dreaming of his new world all his life and he further confided to Hepburn: 'When I was still a lad I used to think how I would govern my town, and what kind of a kingdom it would be.'

The dream, as it was to unfold, was mainly to make his society more compassionate. Large social courtesies surrounded each ritual, ceremony and custom practised by his people. All the courtesies were retained, while the harmful or brutal aspects of each custom were neatly sliced away. His own experience had been so lonely — it was he as an individual who had been made to suffer for his principles — that all Khama's reforms are touched by personal insight into human suffering as opposed to group acceptance of tradition. One of his first actions on assuming power was to abolish the initiation ceremonies, *bogwera* for men and *bojale* for women. There are uneasy stories about *bogwera* for men. An elderly Serowe man told me:

> Not only was the foreskin cut and the youths put through endurance tests, but one of us had to remain behind. He was killed in a painful way, in the secrecy of the bush. When we came home, it was made out that the youth had died because he could not stand up to the tests. Everyone knew the truth but it was treated as a deep secret. That was why Khama abolished *bogwera*.

But the age regiments or *mephato* continued. Simple prayers and lectures were given without the ritual, and the social courtesy surrounding the event was retained. It gave men a sense of social responsibility and from Khama's time onwards the *mephato* began to volunteer for the construction of community projects like schools and churches.

The same compassionate insight is evident in the abolition of *bogadi* or 'bride price' for women. In his *Handbook of Tswana Law and Custom*, Isaac Schapera records:

> Khama deliberately abolished *bogadi*. His main reason for doing so ... appears to have been the fact that when a woman's husband died, she could not, under the old law, leave his home, and any children she subsequently bore were still regarded as those of her late husband. Even if she had been divorced and then gave birth to any children, these were also regarded as those of her former husband. Khama now said: 'Every man should be the father of his own children.'

Surely it is rare to encounter a situation of such vivid contrast. With Sekgoma I, the old order died a complete death. With Khama, a new order was born which was a blending of all that was compassionate and good in his own culture and in the traditions of Christianity. An historian, Douglas Mackenzie, writing during the 1920s, observed of Khama that he produced a history as yet unsurpassed anywhere in Africa. The reformer at village level was only one aspect of his complicated career. His life did not only benefit the Bamangwato. It reached out and benefited Botswana as a whole, for he was the founder of the British Bechuanaland Protectorate which, so people firmly maintain, prevented Botswana from becoming another South Africa or Rhodesia and resulted in independence for the country in 1966.

It might be said that the Protectorate owed its being to Khama's reputation in Victorian Britain as a wise, compassionate *Christian* ruler. Without the backing of missionary and philanthropic interests in Britain — aided by the fortuitous failure of the Jameson Raid — he might not have been able to present his case against Rhodes' British South Africa Company successfully.

In 1885, Khama drew up a lengthy preliminary document for British protection. There had been threats from the Boers and other enemies like Cecil John Rhodes to seize his land. Initially, the principles outlined in the document concerned only the Bamangwato. They were later to apply to the whole country, in so far as the British felt inclined to honour the document. I quote a short extract:

I, Khama, Chief of the Bamangwato, with my younger brothers and heads of my town, express my gratitude at the coming of the messenger of the Queen of England, and for the announcement to me of the Protectorate, which has been established by the desire of the Queen, and which has come to help the land of the Bamangwato also. I give thanks for the word of the Queen which I have heard, and accept the friendship and protection of the Government of England within the Bamangwato country.

I am not baffled in the government of my town, or in deciding cases among my own people according to custom. I have to say that there are certain laws of my country which the Queen of England finds in operation, and which are advantageous to my people, and I wish these laws should be established and not taken away by the Government of England. I refer to our law concerning intoxicating drinks, that they should not enter the country of the Bamangwato, whether among black people or white people. I refer further to our law which declares that the lands of the Bamangwato are not saleable. I say this law is also good; let it be upheld and continue to be law among black people and white people.

2
Traditional History

Mokgojwa Mathware

Age: about ninety-six
Occupation: traditional historian

Mokgojwa Mathware was born at Shoshong, during the early reign of
Khama the Great. His family moved with the tribe to Palapye; then in
1902, to Serowe. In the old days, the movement of a tribe from place
to place was a common occurrence. They moved when there was a
chieftaincy dispute, threat of war, or, as in the case of the founding of
both Palapye and Serowe, a search for surface water. Traditional
historians count these movements as 'ruins'. They say the tribe left six
or seven 'ruins' or abandoned villages behind them. A mud hut, with
poles and thatch, was easily replaceable in another area so they usually
packed their belongings on the backs of oxen and moved on foot to the
next settlement. The huts of abandoned villages were washed away
down to their foundations by countless storms, and forgotten. In the
traditional sense then, Mokgojwa Mathware should have counted two
ruins behind him during his lifetime — Shoshong and Palapye. But his
birth coincided with the arrival of the white man in Botswana and
map-making. Shoshong, which was the Bamangwato capital for fifty
years, is still on the map and by the time the tribe moved to Serowe,
the railway line from the south extended as far as Bulawayo, and

Palapye station became one of the main railheads of Bamangwato country. But Palapye itself is divided into what people refer to as 'New Palapye' and 'Old Palapye', and in the latter the ruins resulting from the move to Serowe can still be seen.

It can only be estimated that Mokgojwa Mathware might be ninety-six. There was no registration of births and deaths in his time and he might be well over a hundred. One of his eyes has closed completely with age, but not, he says, his memory. I was a little uncertain of this at first and showed him a picture of Khama. His face lit up.

'That's Khama,' he said, delighted.

We communicated through an interpreter. He spoke no English and I, no Setswana. My interpreter said teasingly:

'You are mistaken, old man. That's a picture of a white man.'

'I might only have one eye,' Mokgojwa replied, indignantly. 'But I can still recognize Khama. He was good. He was kind.'

'Why did Khama abolish *bogwera*?' I put in tentatively.

He kept silent for a while, then said abruptly: 'There was nothing wrong with *bogwera*.'

'But that started the quarrel with his father,' I persisted. 'Remember, he would not attend the *bogwera* of his younger brother.'

The old man turned suddenly and went into a brief, whispered conversation with the interpreter, striking him urgently on the knee. At last he burst out:

'I am a man who had great respect for the chiefs! To talk about them is like an insult!'

He can tell you endless tales about the long, dim past, which is a pain to no one, but nothing about the near present, which is a pain to everyone. I have included two of his historical tales which concern the founding of the Bamangwato nation. He did not mind talking about his own life. When he described new tools, new ways of living, he had an enchanting way of saying: '*Thakaa!*' which means: 'I'm surprised!'

*

Following the old custom, my father had nine wives. And I am the son of the seventh wife. Only four of his wives had sons and I was the last son born to him. I've been married three times. I married according to Khama's religion. My first wife died. When the trouble broke out between Tshekedi and Seretse, my second wife became a supporter of Seretse. I divorced her and married again.

My father, Mathware, was very wealthy, well-known and important. Although he was not a headman or of royalty, he was adviser to Chief Sekgoma. In our custom, if you are rich, many people surround you and respect you for wealth. He also felt pity for the poor and took eight poor people to live with us. It was a customary thing for the rich to help the poor.

Khama could not have called his father a moloi (witch-doctor). The name of moloi for Chief Sekgoma came from the tribes of the south who were very afraid of him.

When I was young I lived at the cattle-post and looked after my father's sheep and young calves. Later, my father gave me a dog to help me herd the sheep. I did not attend school. At the cattle-post we lived with older men, and in the evenings we sat around the fire and listened to the older men talking. That was where I learnt about the history of my tribe. They talked about the past of the Bamangwato; their chiefs and the battles they fought with other tribes. I have remembered every word to this day.

I was about eleven when the tribe moved to Palapye. I am not sure. We never took note of age. I don't know how old I am but I might be ninety-six. It was at Palapye that Khama gave us the iron-hand plough. Before that we had used a hoe for ploughing. It was a pole with a piece of iron at the end. The piece of iron was made by the Bathudi — all craftsmen were called Bathudi. The Bathudi took the iron from the Tswapong hills. The piece of iron was flat, with a sharp end. We heated the sharp end in the fire, then pierced it into the end of the pole and so we ploughed. That iron was called *mogoma*. We paid the Bathudi one goat for one *mogoma*. When Khama gave us the iron-hand plough, we called it *mogoma*, too.

Our way of transporting goods began to change too. I remember that my people did not use sledges. It was introduced by the Europeans. Before I was born my people only used oxen for transporting goods. When the Europeans brought wagons, we bought them. Khama bought me my first wagon. The second wagon I bought for myself. Another thing we copied from the Europeans was a new way of thatching. Some people had started working for Europeans. When they returned to the village they thatched in a new way. People came to stare at this. They said: '*Thakaa!* What's this now?' In the Tswana way of thatching we used the same grass the cows eat. For the European way of thatching we had to find a stiff, hard grass near the river or in sandy places. We all copied this way of thatching. We copied European clothes too but when I was young the men put on their *tshega* (a loin-cloth) at the lands and cattle-post. Before European clothes women wore skirts made from goatskins.

At Palapye there was an outbreak of *seakhubama* (outbreak of rinderpest in 1896) and a lot of cattle died. It was different from foot-and-mouth disease. The cattle just died. My father lost all his cattle but he still remained rich on sheep and goats. At about this time I was called to join my age regiment, Mathogela. It was called for the son of a younger brother of Khama and it was called according to Khama's religion. Three age regiments before mine had been called this way. We no longer went apart from people, into the bush. When Khama called us we went a little way outside the village with the chief, our parents, and headmen. We were given a speech by the chief and elders, then we were sent to build the wall of the London Missionary Society mission school. My father died before the whole tribe moved from Palapye to Serowe.

I was never involved in kgotla affairs like my father. When the tribe settled down at Serowe, I started to work for Europeans. A certain European of Palapye, Paul Jousse, built a shop in Serowe. Four Europeans worked in the shop for him and I served them with food in their home and also cleaned the windows of the house. After a while I resigned and started work for a German, Alfred Hoffman. *Thakaa!* I found a strange business in his house! He had made Khama a gift of a cup of tea every morning. Every morning I filled a big cup with tea, covered it with a saucer and took it to a special servant girl who took it in to Khama. This I did for seven years. Khama had tea in his house but this tea was especially appreciated as it was a gift. Alfred Hoffman was a trader who owned a shop. Soon Khama saw that I was sent about by Europeans. He took advantage of me and also sent me here and there, with his messages.

There is only one thing I would like to say about Khama. He thought about the man who was nothing. At the head of each ward was a headman. This headman was really a chief but when he lived under a chief like Khama, he was called a headman. When a headman died, his wife sometimes chose a commoner as the second husband or man friend. The people of that ward would then deny her children because they were not of royal blood. Khama changed that custom.

When Khama died four wards in Serowe were chosen to guard his grave. They were Bashimane, Maaloso, Maaloso-a-Ngwana and Diti-ma-modimo. My ward was Diti-ma-modimo and I was one of those chosen. They chose six people from each ward for a day. During the night three would patrol and three rest. During the day all six would be on guard. This order was given by Khama's son, Sekgoma. The grave was guarded for one and a half years. No reason was told to us for this order. The grave was in an exposed position at the top of Serowe hill, and during the time we guarded the grave they were building a wall around it. We seemed to be the wall because we were only relieved when the wall was complete.

Children no longer know the Tswana way of life. They go to school first and only know modern things. I don't like modern governments and chiefs losing their powers. One day we will get a bad ruler and all the people will leave the country.

Ngwato Creates the Bamangwato Nation (told by Mokgojwa Mathware)

Long ago we were all one tribe, the Bakwena, and Malope was our chief. Malope had three sons — Kwena, Ngwato and Ngwaketse. Now Kwena always quarrelled with his brothers, Ngwato and Ngwaketse, and so when he became chief of the Bakwena, Ngwato moved with his people to a village to the north of Kwena's village, and Ngwaketse moved with his people to the east.

One day Ngwato lost a brown cow. He went to his brother, Kwena, and asked him to help look for it. Chief Kwena agreed to help. But a few days later, Ngwato's herdboys saw the lost cow among the stray cattle in Chief Kwena's kraal, and as you know, in those days the stray cattle always belonged to the chief.

'Look, there's the brown cow we lost,' said one of the herdboys. 'Let's get her and take her back to Ngwato.'

'But she's among the stray cattle,' said another. 'We might get into trouble. Let's go home and tell Ngwato.'

So they went home and told Ngwato. Ngwato could not understand it. He went straight to his brother and said:

'Chief Kwena, my herdboys have found the brown cow I told you about among the stray cattle. I don't understand this because you said you would help me look for her.'

'It's not my job to look after your cattle,' Chief Kwena said, quietly.

But Ngwato did not hear this. He went closer and spoke again.

14

'Chief Kwena,' he said. 'The cow that I lost is among your stray cattle.'

Then Chief Kwena was angry. 'I'm not your herdboy, Ngwato!' he shouted.

Ngwato stepped back in surprise. He saw that his brother was angry with him, and so he said nothing and went away. But on the way home, he thought to himself: 'Chief Kwena is no longer a friend. The time has come for me to leave the tribe, for trouble is coming.'

When he got home, he told his people to prepare to leave. They took their corn and packed it in sacks made of skins. They filled their large clay pots with water, put them in skin bags and hung them across the backs of their oxen. They packed all their things onto their oxen and then waited for the night to come.

Ngwato sent a messenger to Ngwaketse. When Ngwaketse arrived, Ngwato said:

'Our brother, Chief Kwena, has stolen my cow. I am afraid that more trouble is coming because he often quarrels with me. Tonight I am taking my people away from the tribe.'

Ngwaketse replied: 'Chief Kwena often quarrels with me. I will not stay behind alone. I will also take my people away.'

And so it was agreed between them. Ngwaketse went back to his village. He called his men to the kgotla, and together they made a plan. That night, when everyone slept, Ngwato's people secretly left the village.

In the morning, some of Chief Kwena's men passed through Ngwato's village and found it empty. They hurried back to tell their chief. Chief Kwena called his warriors and set off immediately to bring back Ngwato's people. They followed the path to Khale for that was the only way Ngwato could go with all the cattle.

Now, early that morning, one of Chief Kwena's tribesmen had gone into the forest to hunt. He knew nothing about what had happened. He walked back carrying two jackals he had killed with his dogs, and on his way he passed through Ngwaketse's village. To his surprise, he found that all the people had packed their belongings on the backs of their oxen as though they were setting out on a long journey. He greeted them and asked where they were going, but no one replied. The Kwena tribesman could not understand this and he wondered what had happened.

As soon as he reached Kwena's village, he saw that all the warriors had gone and only the old men remained behind. He put his two jackals

15

in his yard and hurried to the kgotla to ask the old men what had happened.

'The warriors have gone to find Ngwato and to kill him,' they said. 'Ngwaketse has gone with them. Chief Kwena called Ngwaketse and said to him: "Our brother, Ngwato, wants to be chief. Let us go together and kill him." Ngwaketse's warriors have gone with Chief Kwena to kill Ngwato.'

When the Kwena tribesman heard this he was worried because he remembered the people he had seen in Ngwaketse's village preparing to go on a long journey. So he took his spear and followed Chief Kwena. He walked all day and when the sun set, he came to a place where Chief Kwena had camped. Warriors stood on guard all around in case Ngwato's men attacked. That night the Kwena tribesman slept alone in the forest, but when the sun rose he hurried to join them. Chief Kwena and Ngwaketse were together. Chief Kwena was busy dividing his warriors into groups ready to look for Ngwato.

'Ngwaketse!' called Chief Kwena. 'You lead your men that way and I'll take mine this way. We'll catch Ngwato today and kill him because he wants to be chief.'

When the Kwena tribesman heard this, he called Chief Kwena. But the chief would not listen. The tribesman called again, and kept calling until at last Chief Kwena stopped to listen. The warriors gathered around to listen. The tribesman came up to the chief and said:

'Chief, the Kgori bird is watching her eggs and does not see the trap.'

For he remembered Ngwaketse's people preparing for their journey and he knew that Ngwaketse must secretly be on Ngwato's side. When Ngwaketse heard this, he understood the warning and quickly said to Chief Kwena:

'Chief, don't listen to this man. He is wasting our time. Let's set off immediately and look for Ngwato.'

So Chief Kwena laughed and told his warriors to go.

But as soon as Ngwaketse and his men had left Chief Kwena, they hurried back to a place where their own people were waiting for them. There they found the old men, the women and the children with everything packed on the backs of the oxen. When Ngwaketse and his warriors arrived, they all set off towards the east. For Ngwaketse had also planned to leave Chief Kwena that day. His warriors were only pretending to look for Ngwato. Secretly, they too were leaving the tribe.

Ngwato travelled a long way with his people and Chief Kwena did not find him. He reached a place called Modikela and built his village there. When Chief Kwena returned home, he found that Ngwaketse had also gone.

And that is how we, the Bamangwato (people of Ngwato), parted from the Bakwena and the Bangwaketse, for ever.

How the Phuti* Became the Totem of the Bamangwato (told by Mokgojwa Mathware)

When the Bamangwato were settled and living at Modikela, the Bakwena attacked them. But because in those days warriors never fought inside the village, Chief Kwena sent a message to Chief Ngwato telling him to meet the Bakwena at a certain place outside the village. In that battle warriors were killed on both sides. They fought each other until at last the Bamangwato ran away. Ngwato then moved his village further north. But the Bakwena came again and fought them, and so Ngwato moved north once more.

When the Bakwena warriors came for the third time, the Bamangwato were living at Mochudi. They fought outside the village, and during the battle the Bakwena warriors saw Ngwato and chased him. They knew that if they killed Ngwato, all the people would then come back to Chief Kwena's tribe.

Ngwato was a fast runner. He ran for many miles with the Bakwena warriors following him. But at last Ngwato grew tired, and could run no further. He crept into some thick bushes to hide, and as he lay there he saw a phuti right in the middle of the bushes. The phuti lay there quietly and didn't run away. Soon the Bakwena warriors ran up.

'Ngwato is hiding in those bushes,' they shouted to the men behind. They crowded all round the bushes and looked inside. Ngwato lay very still. They pushed their spears into the bushes, and suddenly the phuti jumped up and ran out.

'Look!' they cried. 'There was a phuti inside the bushes. Ngwato can't be there. He has escaped.' And off they ran to look for him.

That evening Ngwato did not go back to the village. His people thought he had been killed in the battle, and his warriors looked for him

Phuti is a small buck.

all night long. In the morning Ngwato came home. He called all the people to the kgotla and said:

'Bamangwato tribesmen, from now on you shall never kill the phuti. I am only alive today because of the phuti. The phuti saved me from the enemy.'

And this is how the phuti became the totem of the Bamangwato.

3
Early Primary Education under the Trees

Rannau Ramojababo

Age: about eighty
Occupation: head of Seetso village ward and retired school-teacher

He calls himself one of the forerunners of primary school education in Serowe. Like so many other community services, primary education was first initiated under the control of the London Missionary Society. In about 1918, with three other untrained Batswana teachers, Rannau Ramojababo taught in the first schools opened in Serowe. Their classrooms were only the shade of a big tree. They were paid no salary and had to live on the proceeds from the sale of their cattle and goats. The first salaries teachers ever received were in 1929 when the colonial government took control of the schools.

Rannau Ramojababo was educated at Tiger Kloof in Vryburg, South Africa, up to Standard Six. Tiger Kloof was founded in 1904 by the missionary, W.C. Willoughby and this college particularly served the needs of Batswana students. Like all the old men, Rannau lives in the past and cannot reconcile himself to the present political changes in the country which have come with independence. The government is most disturbing to him. He prefers the personal and known rule of their former great chiefs, like Khama, to the impersonal rule of a government

miles away. Anxiety, coupled with literacy in English,
[...] to keep daily tabs on the activities of this removed, aloof new
[...]nt. So his day begins thus: at 10 a.m. he rises and attends to
his [...]s as headman of Seetso ward. Then he has his midday meal
and sets off, his walking stick firmly tapping the ground, to the homes
of young people likely to be in possession of the government papers, *The
Botswana Daily News* and the magazine, *Kutlwano*. His eyesight is
now so poor that he holds his reading material barely an inch away from
his eyes and reads out loudly to himself. He is extremely proud of his
ability to read and communicate in English.

'I don't know whether my English will sound quite proper to you,'
he said, with an engaging, toothless smile. 'The words don't come out
so well, as I have no teeth.'

*

I think I'm eighty years old. I was born about 1892 at Palapye. That
was during Khama's time and all the people were prosperous. We could
not say we were starving because we gathered our food freely from the
bush for all our needs. Our forefathers were hunters and lived on wild
animals during winter and the dry season, when we did not plough.
Before the first rains, a man used to return from the bush with a lot of
dried biltong and wild fruits to feed his children, while ploughing.
Today, if I want to kill a wild animal I have to pay for a licence. Today,
it's different. We are told at the kgotla: 'It is prohibited to shoot wild
animals without permission,' so we starve.

I spent my childhood at the cattle-post of my grandfather. When I
was about ten, Khama removed the tribe from Palapye to Serowe but
I did not see this removal as I was at the cattle-post. The reason for
the removal was that we only had a spring in Palapye and the water
became scarce. The spring was called Photho-Photho — that was the
sound the water made as it poured down from a rock in the hill. There
was plenty of water in Serowe, from three big rivers, the Sepane,
Manonnye and Motetshwane. The Sepane and Manonnye flowed right
through the town. About 1916 all the rivers dried up and people made
shallow wells on the river-beds to draw water.

When I was about twelve I was called by my father from the
cattle-post to attend school. I attended the primary school in Serowe
run by the London Missionary Society. During this time my father died
but I was elected by the missionaries for further education for which
they paid. They sent me to Tiger Kloof for two years where I completed

Standard Six. I then returned to Serowe and started teaching at the mission school, though I was not trained to be a teacher. The schools were under the control of the missionaries at first and we were not paid a salary. It was the rule of Khama that teachers should not be paid. That old man killed us. The chief's word said: 'You are working for your country to improve it, not working for money. All teachers must live on their own cattle, goats and ploughing of corn.'

There were few of us at first — Miss Sharp, the missionary principal and four Batswana teachers. At Christmas time Khama gave us an ox to slaughter and once, when the 'flu broke out, Miss Sharp gave us one pound for three months to help with medical expenses. We were the forerunners of education in Serowe, but later our services were forgotten. We managed to follow Khama's rule at that time because we did have cattle and corn but later on I became poor through serving the community. My cattle died during a drought and we teachers suffered a lot. We had no classrooms. We used to teach the children under the shade of a big tree. On rainy days there was no school and also on very cold, windy days. We had a blackboard, easel, box of chalk and duster — those were supplied all right — but we had no textbooks. The children had slates. We taught them the alphabet, arithmetic and scripture stories from the Bible.

In 1929 we received our first salaries because then the government had taken over the schools. It was very little pay — two pounds ten shillings a month. I was sent to teach at several places like Tswapong, Shoshong and Palapye but all the time I taught, it was always two pounds ten shillings. During my teaching time I was only once given ten pounds as gratuity. I began to feel a grudge at the low salary because I was a married man with children, and I left teaching in 1940 when I was about forty-eight years old. Cattle were very cheap those days and I had bought a few with my salary. From then on I lived on cattle and ploughing. I was married only once and had six children. My wife died in 1947 of sickness. I felt disinclined to take another wife but I regret it now because I am an old man and have no one to take care of me. According to our custom, it is a shame for a man to draw water for himself, like I do. Only when I talk and talk and talk angrily to my children do they go and draw water for me.

I have always lived a peaceful life. I've no serious record for any fault at the chief's kgotla. My father was headman of Seetso ward, where I live. When my father died, I took his place. A headman in my case means I am the leader of a particular ward or area. In this area we are all brethren, like uncles, brothers and so on. My duties are to listen to the complaints of the people and if a quarrel breaks out, I must settle it. If I don't settle it, I take it to the chief's kgotla. If any of my people are wanted by the chief's kgotla, I must produce them. The headman is expected to keep peace in his area. The quarrel that most often happens is trouble in early marriage between young people. A young man usually has other girls; when his wife is beaten severely or not kept in food and clothing, she will come and report to me. So I keep in touch with everything in my ward. Also, if it is known that a person of my ward has stolen goods, I must take the report and do something about it. When a case is too difficult for me I take it straight to the chief's kgotla. I say to the chief:

'There is a case at my place and I am unable to settle it.'

'Bring it,' the chief says.

The chief then hears the case and my judgement. If he agrees with it, all is well. If he does not agree with my judgement, he can make a new judgement. In my father's time, headmen were allowed to fine people, but not now. If a case is so serious as to deserve a fine, it must go to the chief's kgotla. Our kgotla is not like the police camp. Many people come freely to a kgotla, but only men, not women. When a man goes to kgotla, he is going to listen to news about all the affairs in the country and he is also going to listen to a case where someone is tried for any fault.

I don't think they like me at the chief's kgotla. During the quarrel with Tshekedi and Seretse, I became a supporter of Seretse and from then on, I was not liked. It was a simple matter for me to support Seretse as he was high in Khama's houses, but he refuses to be chief. We have no chief and it is ill for us because in our custom, we always had a chief. We hate anybody to be appointed as our chief; it can be forced on us but we don't like it. The young say to us: 'We don't like people like you who are not educated,' but we had good hearts. We could not only think of ourselves, we had to think of others as well. The young are very selfish; they only care for their own ideas.

I don't like the government and independence because originally I was Ngwato but today I am just an ordinary person and controlled by someone who is clever and comes in from other tribes, but he may be someone we don't like. Why can't Seretse rule us in kgotla like Tshekedi and his grandfather, Khama? It is the custom of most of our race.

Tsogang Sebina

Age: eighty-three

Occupation: retired school-teacher

I have no doubt that the father of Tsogang Sebina stood among those Sunday morning church crowds of Khama's time, in their Victorian top hats. The aura of that world still lingers about him, from the little Victorian knick-knacks in his small dining-room — the gilt-framed pictures and the folding desk — to the gentle courtesy of his voice and manners. Unfortunately, we had no Charles Dickens to record that era of African life, that extraordinary transition from one culture and its rituals, to another culture of quiet Bible study and foreign mores and manners. I was startled when gently inclining his head towards me, he asked: 'Would you like a cup of tea, Mma?' The tone of his voice was so beautiful, like something from an ancient world, long forgotten. Near the gilt-framed pictures, and starkly out of place, is a modern item, a framed certificate of merit bearing the following words:

Presidential Order of Meritorious Service

Awarded to Tsogang Sebina in recognition of exceptional services to Botswana. Given under my hand at Gaborone this thirtieth day of September 1969.

(*Signed*:) President of the Republic of Botswana

*

'What are all these "exceptional meritorious services"? I asked.

Well, he said, I was one of the pioneers. I was the first qualified teacher in the whole of Bamangwato country. I taught for thirty-five years and at first, during Khama's time, I worked for the tribe with no pay. I can't remember so far back all the details of my life during Khama's time, but Khama was a gift of God to the people. He was not educated, you know; he only had a Tswana education but he was in religion and rule what they call a sage.

I was born in Palapye in 1890. I was twelve years old when the tribe moved from Palapye to Serowe. I still remember how Khama called the people together in Palapye and told us that we were going to remove the village from Palapye to Serowe and that Serowe would be our permanent home and I remember very well that the Manonnye river was running — I used to take my father's cattle there for a drink. There were two other rivers and the Motetshwane was a spring. After a few years the rivers dried up and people had to dig open wells. Always in those days when a population settled near water, the human settlement seemed to be an interference with the surface streams and they dried up. I had had my Tswana elementary education in Palapye at the mission school and by the time the tribe removed to Serowe I could read a little. In 1905 I left Serowe to further my education in the Cape Colony which was then ruled by the British. I had my primary and teacher training at Healdtown Normal College. Healdtown College was named after a Wesleyan missionary, James Heald. I took the train for six years from Palapye to Fort Beaufort in the Cape. By then the railway had already extended as far as Bulawayo.

My father paid for my education with his cattle. He continued supporting me when I started teaching as I was doing voluntary work. To make sacrifices for the community did not disturb my heart but it was very difficult work. We taught the children under the trees with little or no equipment. We gave them an elementary education — but things always progress. Our first brick building was Khama Memorial School, which was built by the tribe during Khama's time — though the missionaries had built one school in the village.

It was during Tshekedi's time that education developed, from elementary standard to higher primary. Then those parents who were able, sent their children on to colleges in South Africa as we had no colleges here. It was also during Tshekedi's time that I received my first salary — just a meagre salary of R12.00 a month. That was increased later. When I retired I was getting R24.00 a month. The salary was just like a living allowance.

When I retired from teaching I took up tribal work for two years as a grain organizer. Tshekedi had organized something like co-operative marketing. It was planning for drought years when the crops fail. Each village ward was given a piece of land to plough corn. When harvested, this corn was taken to two big grain silos Tshekedi had built near the kgotla, for times of need. When they brought the grain in, I used to take a record of it. People produced the grain voluntarily, then anyone could purchase it again at a very low price. We used a traditional method of protecting the grain from weevils — we buried it in ash. When this scheme was operating, people never bought imported grain. It came to

24

a stop in 1949 during the time of the misunderstanding between Tshekedi and his nephew, Seretse.

I have done a lot in my life-time. I was a member of the finance committee and the finance committee was set up to collect tax — formally people's tax was paid to the District Commissioner. It benefited the people because they now had a say about their revenue. Tshekedi wanted greater control of tax money to establish things like boreholes and schools. Tshekedi was also at that time creating the Bamangwato Tribal Administration, which at independence lost most of its significance to the Central District Council.

I like independence because when I look back to my young days and compare it to the present there is a hundred per cent development at this time. I've never been actively interested or involved in politics. My whole life was devoted to teaching.

4
Religion

A history of the London Missionary Society Church

Nothing happens here that is *not* political, that is to say the Church and State are of necessity — on account of the outstanding nature of Khama's life and faith — one connected whole. Khama is the State — and the State means Khama. Khama also means church and it is natural that in the eyes of both Church-members and heathen, the Church means — Khama! He and I both agree that it is not so, but the popular idea prevails. We live very much as in the days of Constantine I should say.

An extract from a letter of the missionary A.E. Jennings to his London Missionary Society headquarters

... I govern by means of the Church

Khama, in his Jubilee address, 1922

The London Missionary Society was in an unusual position in the Ngwato country. Khama had given them the monopoly and had refused admission to other societies and sects. As a result they had become virtually a state church and both Khama and Tshekedi developed an attitude not unlike Henry VIII's towards the Anglican

Church.... (but) in 1956 a decision was taken by Tshekedi, Rasebolai and Seretse that henceforth any denomination would be welcome provided its representatives built schools or hospitals.

Mary Benson: *Tshekedi Khama*: A Biography

The London Missionary Society Church was opened in Serowe on the 9 June, 1915, thirteen years after the tribe had moved from Palapye to Serowe. Like all the churches and schools of that time, this Serowe 'cathedral' had been paid for by Khama and built by the tribe. It is Serowe's one great landmark and can be seen for miles around. It isn't spectacular — in fact, it is a rather big, ugly squat building of brownish sandstone blocks, with an austere interior of plain wooden benches, a small pulpit, and a bronze plaque of Khama in a corner near the pulpit. In Khama's time, all pathways on Sunday led to what people call the 'L.M.S. church' door. Despite this, a long and tortuous relationship existed between Khama and the London Missionary Society. In their pamphlets and books, the missionaries have a courteous way of explaining it: '... relationships between Khama and the current resident missionary were often badly strained....'

God, whoever he is, is unfortunately often badly represented by his earthly spokesmen. In Khama's time, God was both white and British and violently intolerant of 'heathens'. There was an inner conflict going on all the time — Europeans despised black people and yet wanted to embrace them in salvation at the same time. The missionaries had another distinction — they produced the first written records of African history, and one is forced to refer to them when doing any research into the past. This hurts, because their writings are a desecration of human life. They keep an eye on the audience back home who will be titillated by the sensational material. Khama was not blind to this, in spite of his preference for the London Missionary Society, and at a certain stage one begins to keep a joyful tally of all the missionaries Khama expelled from his country after reading such books as *Native Life on the Transvaal Border* by W.C. Willoughby and *Three Great African Chiefs* by Edwin Lloyd.

John Mackenzie's *Ten Years North of the Orange River* stands quite apart in quality and value from the general run of missionary writings, for in Mackenzie, God and humility were wonderfully blended. His humility drives him into a defence of anything considered lowly or despicable. 'Heathen customs' are common to all mankind and he

27

generously exposes all the heathendom of his own land. There had been a mingling of everything in Mackenzie's Scottish Highlands and as a young lad, he had unconsciously participated in both 'pagan' and Christian rituals. His 'Chapter of Bamangwato History' is riddled with footnotes comparing initiation ceremonies like *bogwera* and *boswagadi*, the ritualistic cleansing of widows and widowers, to similar customs practised in his own land.

For more than eighty years the people's love of their own wisdom had been smothered and suppressed, for fear no doubt that they would appear to be 'dirty heathens' in the eyes of the missionaries. But since Tshekedi's death and the lifting of the ban on other religious sects, a great number of churches have arisen in Serowe. They are not necessarily 'respectable' churches like the four or five Congregational, Anglican and Roman Catholic churches, but are offshoots of two hundred or so 'Faith Healing Churches'. They are certainly not considered respectable by the other churches, as their ministers tend to ordain themselves, but the conventional churches tend to lose their membership to them. Serowans often strike an observer as an intensely conservative crowd, and it is only in matters of religion that they reveal a side of themselves that is extremely unpredictable and creative.

The 'Faith Healing Churches' command the greatest popular following and in the year 1973, the Ngwato Land Board received 117 site applications for 'Faith Healing Churches'. These churches are established by Africans for Africans and, unlike the established churches, they make allowances for ancient African customs to be observed side by side with Christianity. The usual prerequisite for the start of a 'Faith Healing Church', is that a fairly ordinary, illiterate or semi-literate man has a vision, sees a flash of light, or hears a Voice. He then communicates his vision to a few people, and a small following gathers around him in his own backyard. The main focus is on the miracle-performing side of Christianity, and the man, by his vision, is said to have acquired the power of healing people by touch and become a 'prophet'.

The independent church movement first started in South Africa around the turn of the century and slowly took hold on African people until it has become one of the most massive movements in southern Africa.

*

Sego Mpotsang

Age: eighty
Member of the L.M.S. church

My grandfather lived in the days when the gospel was still new in the country and he was a polygamist with ten wives. It wasn't possible for the word of God to reach all the people at the same time, so those who were termed heathens had not yet heard the word of God. It is not as though anyone knows who God is. That is a mystery, as all life is and there has never been much difference between those who were called heathens and those who had heard the word of God. Our forefathers, who were heathens, prayed to spirits and so do we, because God is a spirit.

We were all marching up to the L.M.S. church during Khama and Tshekedi's times. Khama made that the rule for the unity of the tribe, which he needed then. If we had all been going in different directions, it would have split the tribe and caused disputes. All the new churches in Serowe now have our members who broke away from the L.M.S.

I have been in church every Sunday, all my life, because I was born into a Christian house. I believe in God with no questions, simply because every Christian does.

Thato Matome

Age: forty-six
Member of the L.M.S. church

You could say I was born into the L.M.S. church. I am still a staunch member of the church but the L.M.S. church is a dying world in Serowe today and I have watched it dying before my very eyes and am worried. It is the young of today who are critical of the L.M.S. church and you will find none of them there, only the old people and some of my generation — it attracts no new members.

I grew up during the time Chief Tshekedi was ruling and the whole atmosphere was very strict and filled with the life of the church. It was compulsory for us, especially as school children, to participate in church activities. We were all at Bible class once a week and Sunday school

29

every Sunday. Our old people had prayers at home every evening and if we fell asleep early, we were dragged out of bed, still half-asleep to attend evening prayers. It made its mark on us. Many of my friends have not broken the habit of Bible study and all the old people do not drink or smoke. So, in all this I wasn't capable of any criticism of the church.

I think the missionaries were allowed to impose too much on the people, but they gave little of themselves in return. People never experienced any closeness to the white ministers and this mostly affected the illiterate man — he was never attended to; the missionaries paid attention to those who were high up in society. If it was an illiterate man who was to be buried, they would send one of the deacons to his house and he'd never have a burial service in church. But there they were burying all the important people with full rites, in church!

Today, this very illiterate man is off to the Faith Healing Churches because these churches make him feel important. All the ministers are black and maybe closer to their flock. In the area where I live there are ten Faith Healing Churches, conducted in the yards of their priests and services often go on all through the night with singing and dancing. It is a pity though that so many people have left the L.M.S. church for the Faith Healing Churches. I feel that the Faith Healing Churches do not provide people with the principles of Christ. They are a lot of drama and very superficial — all the stress is on Jesus walking on the water, healing people in miraculous ways and turning the water into wine. They want to imitate Jesus. We never had anything like this. Later, when I was older, I had a chance of going deeply into the teachings of Jesus, and you find something there very great. It makes your life good and orderly.

Segametse Mpulambusi

Age: thirty-five
Roman Catholic

Like everyone else, my whole family attended the L.M.S. church up till the time my grandmother wanted to get married. Grandfather had already been married and his wife died suddenly. When he proposed to my grandmother he told her that he had married his first wife under Setswana custom and he was going to marry his second wife under

Setswana custom too. My grandmother was one who believed in God all her life and the church was a big thing to her. She went to report this matter to the L.M.S. people and they said that was one thing they could not allow.

'Tell him to come and marry in the church,' they said.

My grandfather refused. He said he would only marry under Setswana custom and my grandmother could choose what she liked — the church or Setswana custom. She chose to marry grandfather under Setswana custom. The next thing was that the L.M.S. people forbade grandmother to attend church. She was chased away. The whole family came together to talk this matter over. They could find no fault with grandmother, who was a good woman and they could find no fault with Setswana custom, which was also good. So they said: 'We shall all no longer attend L.M.S.'

That was what I found when I started to notice the world — the whole family was not at L.M.S. But there was no other church in Serowe. All those years we had no other church until 1956 when the Roman Catholic Church came to Serowe. Again, it was my grandmother who decided: 'Let us try this church,' she said.

At first, we had no church building. The church service was held in the yard of a church member and I was baptized that same year, in 1956, when I was twenty-one.

One day I became very ill with fever and my grandmother happened to report this matter to the priest. I was surprised to see the priest, who was a white man, come into the hut. I was sleeping on the floor on mats. The priest knelt down beside the mats and said some prayers for me. Then he asked if there was anything which I needed. My grandmother said L.M.S. never never did this for poor people and my heart decided that it just liked this church. Since that time I have attended church regularly.

William Duiker

Age: fifty-seven

Occupation: Anglican Archdeacon of northern Botswana

I really grew up in South Africa, though Botswana is my country. I was born in the Barolong area in southern Botswana in 1917. When I had completed high school, I had a bit of a job — I was apprenticed to an optical firm in Johannesburg, the sort of job a black man can't do there. It got to the ears of the government and the manager got rid of me. I went on to theological college from there. From 1941 to 1956, I worked for the Anglican church in South Africa; then in 1956, I came directly to the Bamangwato reserve because that was the time Tshekedi Khama relaxed Khama's rule that no other church than the L.M.S. could function in Ngwato country.

There's been a very amusing situation here. A lot of foreign tribes at one time eagerly sought the protection of Khama. That was all very well, but Khama also had his own conditions whereby foreign people might stay in his country, the two most severe being that they give up drink and accept the L.M.S. as the only church. Some members of my congregation, like the Bakhurutshe tribe for example, came this way with the Anglican denomination and settled in the north of Ngwato territory at Tonata. For many years they experienced great difficulty in practising the Anglican faith. It was forbidden for people to be anything other than L.M.S., so the Bakhurutshe used to cross the Shashe River on to what was known as the Tati Concession or Crown Land and hold their services on the farm of a certain Mr Haskins. To this day, they like to beat their breasts and say: 'Man, I'll die an Anglican! I've suffered for this faith!' They further say that when Tshekedi lifted the ban on other denominations, the Bakhurutshe made a special crossing of the Shashe River into Bamangwato territory singing: *Onward Christian soldiers!*

The Anglican church is a small church in Botswana and our membership is not so large. To complicate matters, we lose a lot of our membership to the 'Faith Healing' churches. Oh, there are so many of them and new ones spring up overnight! I missed a member of my congregation for some time and happened to encounter her in town one day. I said: 'I haven't seen you in church for some time. Where have you been?' And she replied: 'I've joined the "Jerusalem Jordan Church".'

'What!' I said. 'I've never heard of that before.'

'It's something very recent,' she said.

The names these churches go by! There's one called 'The Jesus Look Intently Church of God'. The most popular of all the 'Faith Healing' churches, and one that has the largest following is the 'Zion Christian Church'. It is also one of the most secretive of all the independent churches. I've often tried to find out what they are up to and have been put off by a sharp rebuff. They refer you directly to their dead founder, Lekganyane, and now his son who carries on the movement.

The independent or 'Faith Healing' movement started in South Africa at the turn of the last century and slowly took hold on people. I feel they are something established by Africans for Africans. There hadn't been a question of anything but the L.M.S. in Serowe but over a long period many of our people left the country to find work in South Africa as domestic servants and miners. There they encountered Lekganyane of the Zion Christian Church. He was very popular as he offered people good luck charms which would secure them in their employment and ensure that they were given the best salaries. In the 1960s, when the borders were about to close, the South African government ordered back to Botswana all the Batswana who had been working there, and on their return they brought back with them the 'Faith Healing' churches. That's the main reason we have so many of them in Serowe — they were imported back by our own people.

I am sorry to say it so frankly but I don't like them. 'Faith Healing' churches exist to rob the poor of their last penny. For all their secretiveness, word comes to us of their doings. They will perform all the old African ritualistic cleansings, at a high fee. They know the people believe in spirits and they go in for the chasing out of spirits a lot. If a man or woman is ill and goes to a 'faith healer' for treatment, he'll end up paying something like R5.00 before he is through. The patient sits in a bath and candles are lit all round. That costs R1.00. Then his body is bathed. That costs R1.00. Then the priest will suggest some internal cleansing like an enema or vaginal douche and this will be R2.00 and he may throw in another R1.00 for the effort to consult the spirits about the patient's ailment. As far as illnesses go, people never are assured of a cure and it costs only 40c to be examined at the hospital by a doctor and supplied with medicines. But will people ever be sensible? Thousands of people have left the established churches and joined the 'faith healers'. I find nothing Christian in them. They're there to make money.

We have such a muddled situation in the church world here, I think, because Khama's conversion was the only real conversion and the people followed after him, rather than Christianity, simply because he was their chief. Now that the leadership at the top are not committed Christians, like Khama, the 'faith healing' churches hold top sway.

Mr Quiet

Age: forty-two

Occupation: priest of the Galilee Christian Church

I was born blind. Although I cannot see with my eyes, I see from the inside, with my heart. I live a very active life and apart from my work as priest of the Galilee Christian Church, I also take on jobs in the village. I can erect the *dithomeso* and *lebalelo* (the wooden rafters of the hut) of the mud hut and dig pit toilets for people. Each day I find my way around the village with the help of God, so I have no fear of falling into holes or losing my way.

I was born in Serowe but I have been away for a few years. I went to Johannesburg to look for work. It was in Johannesburg that I met Lekganyane, who was the leader of the Zion Christian Church. Lekganyane's church is the biggest of all the churches who heal people by the power of holy water and it has many members. I went to Lekganyane, not for a cure — my parents had tried to find cures for me, but no one could help — but to be taught about God.

I remember my first visit to Lekganyane. I had a request. I wanted to be a priest of his church. He lived in a big house at the top of the hill at Moria and there he lived with twelve servers of the church. Down at the bottom of the hill was a gate and there stood another twelve servers on duty. Lekganyane was very good but he would never talk directly to people. When people approached his house with worries and requests, they told them first to the twelve servers at the gate. They would then decide if you could proceed to the house. Once at the house, you would again tell your troubles or requests to the twelve servers in the house and they would take your problem to Lekganyane. He was always sitting alone in a special room in the house. Although I became a priest of his church, I was never allowed to approach Lekganyane at his home. I always talked to the servers at the gate. The only times I directly approached him was at the church, where I was first a server.

My training period as a priest of the Zion Christian Church was two years. Lekganyane taught me the Bible and how to believe in God. He taught me how to heal people with the power of holy water and coffee. He treated all the customary sicknesses people have and also treated women who had barren wombs. The only things we use in treatment of people's ailments is holy water and coffee. When we pray, the power of God enters the holy water and coffee. The holy water is used both for drinking and bathing, and the coffee for drinking only.

There is a great difference between the Zion Christian Church and all the other churches who heal by the power of holy water. In those other churches men wear dresses like women, but in the Zion Christian Church men are dressed in their own clothes. Only Lekganyane wore a crown like the Pope, a special suit with special badges on the shoulders, and buttons on his coat which differed from the badges and buttons of the other priests and servers. And he carried a staff in his hand. All church members have a special uniform for church attendance and funerals. The women wear a green skirt and yellow blouse with a badge near the left shoulder stamped Z.C.C. The men wear a khaki shirt with a police cap, in the front of which is attached the Z.C.C. badge. The badge is of special significance. Attached to it is a piece of green cloth, under which is concealed a piece of blue cloth. This is in accordance with the law of Moses in the Bible, given to him by God — *Numbers* 15, verses 37-8:

> And the Lord spake unto Moses, saying, Speak unto the children of Israel, and bid them that they make them fringes in the borders of their garments throughout their generations, and that they put upon the fringe of the borders a ribband of blue: And it shall be unto you for a fringe, that ye may look upon it, and remember all the commandments of the Lord, and do them; and that ye seek not after your own heart and your own eyes, after which ye use to go a whoring.

We have the blue cloth concealed under the green cloth because the blue cloth is sacred and we do not want it damaged by the sun. It is our daily reminder to keep in the right path. The police cap worn by the men is just a mark of our church so that our members are known apart from the members of the many other churches who heal by holy water, and who also have their mark — sometimes a red string tied on the hand or a headband of stars.

Lekganyane died in 1967. When he died, his position was temporarily taken by all his servers. There was a lot of quarrelling on his death as a lot of priests were fighting for the chief position which Lekganyane had held. The day has yet to come when the full power of the church passes to Lekganyane's senior son, Barnabas. But Barnabas is consulted on all church problems.

When Lekganyane was still alive, he one day said to me: 'God has given this man power. He is different from us in the way God has made him. I can see that he will not stay long with me. He will one day have his own church.' In spite of these words, I stayed in the church and learnt from Lekganyane. It was only in 1973 that I started my own Galilee Christian Church. All the rules of my church are the same as the rules for the Zion Christian Church. I have only chosen a new name and shall choose a new uniform.

As soon as I had decided that I wanted my own church, I went to the police camp to register it — we all register. We register because there are a lot of quarrels and disputes in the churches and if a priest gets into severe difficulties, he can appeal to the law. I am just a beginner. I have eighteen members in Serowe and thirty in another village outside Serowe. My church service is held every Sunday at 3 p.m. in my own yard. During the week I am occupied by people who need treatment for their ailments. My usual fee for treatment of all kinds of ailments is R5.00. People have to pay because this is my work. I have to support myself and pay tax to the government. So some of this money which I take from people goes in tax and some of it goes in savings. The money which I keep for savings, I use to help people. Some of my members are very poor and sometimes they have no food in the house. I take this money and buy food for them or cover any emergency which they may have. Sometimes a member of their family suddenly dies and, being poor, they cannot afford the coffin. I must buy the coffin. I cannot say that this money belongs to me. I do not handle the money by myself. I have a treasurer, and in cases of need, the treasurer and I decide how the money can be used for the person who is requesting help. If I can help people and give them either good luck or good health, and it is successful, the person will be very grateful and give me a large gift of money, a goat or clothes. This I may take for myself. Lekganyane used to always get gifts of R10 or R20.00 from people.

All the decisions for my church come to me in my dreams at night. I dream about the uniform for my church. I dream about the correct treatment for ailments. A voice talks to me all the time. I believe it is God.

5
The Chief's Kgotla

This is the custom everywhere followed in these regions — strangers on arrival invariably proceed to the chief's courtyard and tell their news.

John Mackenzie: 'Austral Africa.'

Four more other people arrived and then the chief followed. There was silence; not that silence of fear, but that silence of respect; real respect which comes from a man's inside. There were greetings; not those greetings which come only from a man's lips; but from a man's inside. When the chief started talking, they listened, not with their ears; but with their insides.

From an article by 'C.G. Mararike, 'Things Are Happening', in the Botswana magazine, *Kutlwano*.

The above two quotations indicate the supreme position held by the chief's kgotla in the everyday administrative affairs of the people. But it was more than an administrative centre — the older people say the kgotla was the central part of their moral life, the sort of moral centre that was only paralleled by the instruction of the Christian church. In Serowe, the chief's kgotla is in the central part of the village, beneath Serowe hill and marked out by a wide, semi-circular arrangement of stout poles. It is now surrounded by the administrative buildings of the Bamangwato Tribal Administration and the offices of the Central

District Council. Today, breaking in on ancient tradition are the clickety-clack of typewriters and a huge army of clerks, but during Khama's time men listened 'not with their ears; but with their insides' and so they were governed.

The Bamangwato had the good fortune to be governed by a sage. The following extracts from a kgotla address by Khama show the width and depth of his intellect — if he moralized to the point of boredom about drink and beer, this was more than balanced by his brilliant management of the economic affairs of the tribe. This particular 'address to the nation' touches on everything — from prohibition and polygamy, to trade and cattle dealing.

The Chief Khama's Exhortation to His People: Laws and Regulations which have been disobeyed

My people of the Bamangwato: I am beginning to speak with you about the laws and regulations which I have passed ever since we settled at Serowe. Having noticed that my tribe was in an awful state of neglect, I was induced to hold, at different occasions, big kgotla meetings, in which I passed the following laws and regulations respectively according to the occasions:

I said in one of the meetings, that you could drink native beer but moderately and on condition that you would avoid drunkenness, further added, that you should drink it everyone in his own house without inviting friends so as to gather around you pots of that hateful drink. Gatherings for native beer, I said, were the source of fights, disturbances and quarrels common among my people.

You neither opposed the law or said anything in favour of it, at that meeting; but afterwards I saw you heedless of my law, carrying about invitations for friends to gather around at beer at different places.... Some time afterwards I said that total prohibition for beer to young men was necessary. I then passed a law forbidding young men to use beer.... To my disappointment I saw that drunkenness was common to both young and old....

Later on I said that your young men were perpetually in the habit of divorcing their wives, and that a remedy against this habit was to prohibit them marrying many wives. Polygamy, I said, was unavailable to young men of the present day, because after their divorce their fathers-in-law have to meet great inconveniences in providing the divorcees and their children with all the necessaries for living. This law also was not opposed at the time but you continually married them with the reason that you fully appreciated the necessity of polygamy, for in the case where a wife is barren, there is always the opportunity of having children with any of the other wives.

Not very long ago, I passed a law* forbidding the sale of cows. The object of that law was, as I told you, to avoid a decrease of our stock. I also pointed out to you that if white people buy breeding stock from us they would sweep them out of the country and they would export them to foreign and far remote countries beyond the reach of most of our people where they would increase immensely, while we here are left destitute of any stock. Further I said, white people were buying cattle for the purpose of keeping them in farms where they would breed them in order to sell them. Then we will always hear that a certain white man has visited the farms and has bought some cattle to send to either Transvaal or Bulawayo. Thus farmers will have intercourse with the buyers while we here are not dealing with anybody. I also recalled to your memory that breeding stock were the sole and chief dependence for our living, and if we had to sell them we might expect sooner or later, lamentable poverty in the country. The law, just as the preceding ones, was not obeyed. Breeding stock were sold in the same way as before, and I had to undertake to buy sold stock myself of which I bought 680 goats and sheep; 200 of which are at Shashane and 400 at Mmokwe.

And on one occasion also I said: 'No livestock of any nature should be sold at the railway or at any of the unauthorized places,' and I also said that you were only entitled to sell your livestock in the well-known towns where you are known and cannot be suspected of having stolen the property ... cattle which have been sold at the Railway ... have always presented many difficulties, because among them the majority are those which have been stolen by people, who either found them straying or actually took them away from the posts. Then in many cases people could not recover their cattle for the buyers generally took them away into some other countries. You did not obey this law also. . . .

*This law of Khama's, forbidding the sale of breeding stock in precarious early settler/invader times, has created modern problems of cattle marketing as most of the older generation still refuse to sell their beasts.

I hope this will do for the time being although I should have said much more of your misconduct. . . .

Khama papers, Serowe.

The Role of the Old Men at the Kgotla

Lekoto Digate

Age: eighty-six
Occupation: retired cattleman

The occupation of all old men like me, is to visit the chief's kgotla every day. This is something deep in our custom. We are now old and unemployed and it is not good for us to sit at home with our own thoughts. It is thought that if a man is alone with his thoughts, he may think of some mischief he can do.

There are so many small village wards in Serowe and each small ward has its own kgotla. This means that the number of small kgotlas in the village cannot be counted; there are too many. But there are four senior wards in Serowe and these first hear the cases from the great number of small kgotlas in Serowe. If the president of one of the senior wards cannot manage a case, he refers it to the chief's kgotla, which is the main kgotla in Serowe.

The functions of the chief's kgotla are many. Here public announcements are made from higher authority. Here meetings are called for the whole tribe and each year it is the duty of the chief's kgotla to annouce *letsema*, that is the time for ploughing, and permission is then given for the whole tribe to start the ploughing season. The chief's kgotla and all the small kgotlas, ensure that the people are well informed of all the events that are taking place, here in Serowe and in the whole country.

There are certain things which must be observed by all people attending kgotla. It is very necessary to be polite here. The people who have a case must address the president and the court politely in case their very manner helps them to lose the case. People brought to kgotla are not necessarily criminals as we think of it in a court of law. They are brought there by people who want their grievances redressed. These grievances arise over the sharing of property between relatives, the use of impolite words to somebody, a loan of money to somebody who is taking a long time to repay the loan or trespassing on a man's home or land. This is something that everyone hates and it is a grievous wrong to commit; each man's home or his land is a sacred thing to him. These are the daily problems the kgotla deals with.

Now, here is how we are very valuable to kgotla life. All we old men sit near the chief and people who have complaints state their case. Our opinion is then asked for by the chief.

'How do you view this case?' he will say. And that is the time for each one of us who is present to talk. Then the chief bases his judgement of a case on the views of all present and the complaints are redressed with a fine or some strong words from all present.

If there is a case in my village ward, then I will attend my own kgotla and cannot afford to come to the chief's kgotla.

6
Self-Sufficient Skills

Akanyang Malomo

Age: about seventy-one

Occupation: traditional pot-maker

Trade, what we call 'white man's trade', and means of exchange were really established during Khama's rule. Then, fearing that his people might be exploited in some way by the invading traders, he ordered that all trade come under his personal supervision. The result of this personal supervision was that foreign trade became so successfully established that it became a tradition in itself, ousting the traditional skills of the people. Prior to the advent of the white man, being a housewife, for example, was a highly skilled occupation. Women produced most of their household wares, like pots and cups, while the men were skilled in all kinds of leather-work and the production of mats and blankets and clothing. An art that is rapidly dying with the older generation of women is traditional pot-making.

Akanyang Malomo is one of the last traditional pot-makers in Serowe. She learnt her trade from her mother but in turn has no daughter or granddaughter who is willing to carry on the tradition. The younger generation refuse to make pots. They prefer to buy enamel and galvanized-iron water buckets and all their household wares from the shops. Akanyang makes small pots and large pots; the large pots are built up to a height of two feet with a diameter of forty inches. They are fragile and have to be handled with care. Her working tools are simple — a piece of flat wood, a piece of the round part of a calabash and some smooth stones.

*

I was born in Serowe. I have never been to school. My mother used to make these pots for our house and I learnt from her. It was a skill the women had, but not all women had it. Some women came to buy pots from my mother and me. We made our own drinking cups too. A cup was called *sego*. It was made from a gourd we ploughed at the lands. When the squash was dried, we cut it partly open, removed the inside and smoothed it into the shape of a scoop. The *sego* and the water pot always went together and we used the *sego* to draw water from the pot, to drink.

I find the clay for my pots at Moejabane which is twenty-two miles from Serowe. When I start to work, I put the clay into a small dish, wet it and work it with my hands. I keep on like that for an hour; I work it and work it with my hands to make it very soft for shaping. Then I have beside me a dish of water to help me with the shaping. I dip my hand into it all the time as I start to smooth the clay. I roll the clay out in long, thick strips, like a snake. Then I wind these strips round and round in coils and so build up the pot. Then I have beside me this flat piece of wood, a piece of the round part of a squash. I start to shape the pot. These tools, with water, help me to expand the pot into shape. When I come to the mouth of the pot, I take a piece of paper, fold it in half and this helps me turn the mouth outwards and shape it. I remove the pot to a dark place for it to dry, slowly.

When dry, I take some smooth, round stones. I rub the pot over and over for one day to smooth it. This is what makes the pot firm to hold the water or food (watertight). I next put on the decorations. I take a red-coloured stone, crush it to fine powder, and wet the powder and put on my decorations. I also use a black stone (graphite) for decoration. I crush it to powder and into this powder I crush the seeds of the Morotologa tree. I wet the mixture and decorate.

Before the pot can be used for water, or food, it must be burnt. I set the pots on stones so that I may build the fire under the pots. I place wood under the pots and surrounding the pots I make a little shelter of wood to bring all the heat of the fire to the pots. Then I light the fire and burn them. When burnt, they are ready for use. I used to make three pots a day in my young days but now that I am old I make one pot a day. My pots are strong but have to be used carefully. In my mother's days, clay pots were all we used. They served all household needs; they were cooking pots; they were water pots; they were used to store milk. In the days before money was used, the women paid my mother one goat for one pot or one *seroto* of corn for one pot. The *seroto* is not made much these days. It was a basket made to carry corn or anything. If a woman had a pot, she might fill it with a measure of corn, bring it to my mother and so purchase another pot.

Kebotogetse Maseke

Age: eighty

Occupation: traditional tanner

I was born in Serowe. I have never been to school. I tan skins according to the way of our forefathers and the knowledge was passed on to me by my father. When I was young there were no shops like these days. The cow and other animals were our shop. We used their skin to provide us with clothes, shoes, mats and blankets. I learnt the skill of tanning to provide for my family. Many men had this skill in those days and could provide for their families.

The animal skins I use in my work are jackal, sheep, goat and cow. When I get a wet skin, I rub off the remaining pieces of meat with a knife. I use a different method for preparing each skin, according to the article I am making. In all cases, even for shoes, the animal hair is not removed from the skins.

Now, when I make *Tswana blankets* I use mainly jackal skin. I rub off the pieces of meat, then apply the tanning material to the skin. My tanning material is obtained from the roots of four trees — the Monamane, Seswagadi, Mokoba and Mosetha. All these are roots which I have collected and dried. When I want to use them, I stamp the roots in a stamping block with a little water until they are crushed up. That liquid makes the tanning material. Now, the wet leather has to dry in the sun. After drying, I take the skin and bury it in the cattle kraal beneath the manure — not very deep, about three inches. I choose a time when the kraal is unused because if the cows trample on the skins, they will also urinate on them and spoil them. I bury the skin for half a day in the manure. The manure helps to make the skin soft for

44

handling. When I take the skin from the kraal, I pound it and pound it with my hands to make it softer, the same way women rub the washing. Then the skin is ready for use. Now I design my blanket. Ten to eight jackal skins make a blanket. I put them down on the ground to form a design. I take the design from the head to the tail of the jackal and I place four jackal skins in a row. The thread I use for joining them together is cow sinew — you know, along the backbone of the cow are long sinews. These I pull out as long threads, dry and use as sewing thread. When the blanket is complete, I give a finish to the leather by rubbing it with a stone.

When I make *Tswana mats*, I use mainly cow and goat skins. My method of preparing the skin is quite different from the one I use for Tswana blankets. I start again by scraping off the little pieces of meat with a knife. Then I straight away put the skin out in the sun to dry. I stretch the cow or goat skin out on the ground, with the animal hair facing downwards, and knock in pieces of wood on all corners of the skin, like pegs. The skin is left stretched out in the sun for one day. I unpeg the skin in the evening. The next day I treat it to prepare it. I take an animal's brain, either cow or goat and smear it deep on the skin. Then I put the skin in my hut for three days so that the treatment may seep in. I then rub and rub the leather with a stone. As I rub it, I sprinkle water on the skin to make it soft. I also pound the skin with my hands. Then the skin is ready for use. One cow skin makes a mat. Four to ten goat skins make a mat.

When I make *Tswana shoes* I use mainly cow skin. The skin on the face of the cow is used for soles. The treatment of the skin is different from that which I use when making Tswana mats. First I dry the cow skin in the sun. When dry, I put it under manure in the kraal for one day and night. Then I take the skin and beat and beat it with a stick. I return it to the manure for one day to make it soft for handling. Then I begin to shape and cut the shoe. I mostly make simple strap sandals.

No charge was made for Tswana shoes. They were for free. Also the *tshega* worn by men and the *makgabe*, worn by small girls. They were free because they did not need much leather. The *tshega* was a small, round piece of leather to cover the front part of the body and tied round the loins. The *makgabe* was small strips of leather, joined together and tied round the waist. Grown women used to wear a full skirt with a top of goat or sheep skin but they have been wearing European clothes for so long that I have forgotten what we called the skirt of a grown woman. Only my father knew how to make them.

In my young days, money was not used. If someone wanted to purchase a blanket from me — one blanket cost one cow or one blanket cost seven goats. A Tswana mat cost four or six goats.

Mokgojwa Mathware

Age: about ninety-six
Occupation: traditional historian (describing traditional clothes for women)

When I was young, it was possible to see women dressed like this — their dress was a bit complicated and made by persons especially skilled in the task. They first tied in front of them a short, square apron, with a longer apron on top of it, then the real skirt came wrapped around from behind and overlapped the two front skirts. The point of the two front skirts was for seating purposes. Women did not wear pants in those days and were only allowed to sit in two positions: a woman sat either cross-legged and the short, underneath, knee-length skirt fell down in front, covering her, or she sat sideways with her legs folded back, and then the main skirt and the two front skirts provided her with covering. All the skirts had their own separate tie-ups of leather and were made from goat or sheep skin. The two front skirts were called *khiba*, and the main skirt, *mosese*.

Once a woman was married, she acquired a top called a *sekhutlana*, but young girls walked bare-breasted. One could judge a woman's rank and status by the kind of *sekhutlana* she wore. The very rich and important wore *sekhutlana* of jackal and leopard skin; the poor, that of rock rabbit. The *sekhutlana* was a sign of respect for married women and they wore it on all ceremonial occasions like funerals and weddings. There was another *sekhutlana* called a *motati* which was very beautiful and made from the skin of a hartebeest. It had decorations on it and all the hair had been removed from the skin. Women wore the *sekhutlana* very much like they wear shawls today. It was placed around the shoulders and worn like a blanket covering with two leather straps at the top as a tie. The shawl women wear today has the same customary significance as the *sekhutlana*.

Khunong Letsomo

Age: ninety

Occupation: traditional farmer

In the traditional agricultural pattern and land tenure system, we have intact the ancient African way of life, so much so that the very old people like Khunong Letsomo refer to their agricultural techniques as 'our custom'. 'It is our custom to plough in this way and we cannot depart or forget the ways of our forefathers. . . . ' The only dramatic revolution in agriculture for the older people was Khama's introduction of the iron-hand plough, pulled by oxen, which replaced the ancient hoe made by the Bathudi or ancient craftsmen. The hoe was relegated to the position of a weeding implement. The actual design of the ancient hoe, spatulate with a sharp, tapering end, was some time ago patented by a clever white manufacturer and is on sale in the shops, side by side with more modern designs.

The man, who preserved this ancient way of life intact, was Khama. When in 1895 he travelled to England with two other Botswana chiefs to protest against the handing over of Botswana to Rhodes, Khama said at a chapel meeting in Leicester: 'We think that the Chartered Company will take our lands, that they might enslave us to work on their mines. We black people live on the land; we live on the farms. We get our food from the land, and we are afraid that if the British South Africa Company begin in our country we will not get these things and that it will be a great loss to us.'

Little has changed. Today, the lands of the Bamangwato are still not saleable and people still live on the land and get their food from the land. The younger generation either own tractors or hire them to plough their land and purchase new quick-growing varieties of corn and maize developed at research stations; the older generation stick to the hand plough and plant out the traditional, tall, long-maturing Tswana corn.

*

I was born at the time the tribe was moving from Shoshong to Palapye and I was born in Palapye. When I was young there were not the shops that we have today. There wasn't the idea of working for money. All the needs of a person's life had to be obtained from cattle and ploughing. By the time I grew up, the method of ploughing had already changed. We no longer used the hoe which was all our forefathers had. We were using the hand plough given to us by Khama.

I have always been a farmer and ploughed in the old style, with oxen and the hand plough. Whenever there was a good season, we were able to produce crops. Our method was first to broadcast the seed and then plough it in with the ox pulling the plough. I plough mabele, millet, mealies, watermelon, peanuts and beans. I have never changed because I do not know much of the modern ways. The method of first broadcasting the seed and then ploughing it in has always been traditional Tswana custom. With our way we could not turn the soil very deeply; only a few inches down but our way is good, because with shallow ploughing the seeds are not buried deeply. Even when the hoe was used, this was the way we ploughed. This was all we did. It is the custom for both a man and his wife to share the burden of ploughing.

After completing the ploughing, I might be off to the cattle-post to see that all was in order with the cattle and leave my wife to care for the crops. She had to weed the field with a hoe and chase the birds away. She was assisted by her children. Long ago I had many cattle. The herd decreased when they died in droughts. I had some elder sons staying permanently at the cattle-post and caring for the cattle. Their duty was to take the cattle out every day for grazing and watering. My duty was to come to the kraal and judge how many cattle or goats had been lost or killed. If there was loss, I would beat my sons. Cattle were all the wealth that people had. Cattle were all we used to purchase all we needed for the house. Chief Khama had chased out the idea of *bogadi* at the time of marriage but cattle were still needed for many home ceremonies. If all was well at the cattle-post, I then returned to assist my wife with the harvesting. Harvest month is June.

We harvest with our hands, breaking off the head of corn. The women in the meanwhile have made a mud field and the old men like myself have made a *serala*. The *serala* is a raised platform of poles. The harvested corn is placed on top of the *serala* to prevent its damage by the animals. When the harvest is complete, the corn is taken off the *serala* and placed on the mud field. There it is beaten with sticks, then put into baskets to separate the husks from the corn. Then, the seeds for the next season's ploughing have to be separated from household needs. Then we all return to Serowe for the resting time.

Sometimes, if I have a big harvest, I might sell some of my corn to those who have less. In the old days, two bags of corn purchased one cow, and one bag of corn could purchase fourteen goats. If I wanted to sell my cow in those days, one cow could purchase fourteen goats.

Sekgabe Ntshwarisang

Age: seventy
Occupation: traditional hut-builder

The traditional mud hut has contributed much to the serenity and order of village life. A man might be poor and have nothing in his purse but he can always have a home, as beautiful as he and his woman can make it. It costs little or no money to erect a mud hut and the only tools required are a hoe and an axe and some very skilled hand work. The majority of the people in Serowe live in mud huts. They are beautifully tended and kept in repair and the courtyards surrounding the home are kept swept and spotlessly clean. Not every man is a thatcher but every woman knows how to erect the mud wall — the skill is rigidly passed on from mother to daughter for generation unto generation. It may die out though as the younger generation becomes more affluent and the demand for more durable homes arises, and also as the young women turn their attention to acquiring other and new skills. With this in mind, an old woman of the village, Sekgabe Ntshwarisang, was persuaded to impart all the techniques of traditional hut building, for future reference.

A mud hut is called an *nto* in Setswana. The mud wall built by the women is called *polwane*. The wooden rafters of the roof erected by the men are called the *dithomeso* and *lebalelo* and the mud courtyard attached to the home is called the *lelwapa*.

It is only when we get a season of soft, soaking rain that the mud hut shows up as not being a very durable home. The windward side facing the rain slowly crumbles to the ground leaving a huge gaping hole in the wall. And sometimes a fire is set off accidentally and the whole roof goes up in flames in a second.

*

I was born in Serowe and attended primary school up to Standard Two. I have always done housework. I never married so that all the while I lived in my parents' yard until they said: 'Well, you are old enough now to make your own yard.' That is often how a new yard starts; some children have to leave home and they ask the chief for their own yard and build their own *nto*. To make the *nto* was a skill every woman had to have. The skill of home-building was taught to every young girl from about the age of eighteen, because during married life, a woman had to construct all the homes that might be needed by her family. The building of the *nto* is work that is divided between men and women. The women build the *polwane* and *lelwapa*; the men put up the *lebalelo* and do the thatching.

When I was very young — from about the age of twelve to sixteen, I was not allowed by my mother to do the very heavy work of preparing the mud wall; but I had to help in some way. I had to go into the bush with an old water pot and a hoe and collect soil for her. I had to go up and down for water to help mix the mud. I had to fetch wet manure just dropped by the cow. I put it all in a heap near where my mother had to work. It was usual for the woman who was building her home to work alone. An old woman of the family and some children might assist her. But if she liked help and wanted the house quickly, she would say to the other women: 'Come and join me in the work. I'll give you half a bag of corn or one pot of sour milk.'

When I was eighteen, this is what my mother taught me. The first thing I do is scrape out a round, shallow foundation, the shape and size the *nto* will be. I do this with a hoe. The round shape was always the customary shape — the square shape we copied from the way Europeans build their houses.

The next thing I do is layer the foundation with stones. I next make a mixture composed of river-sand, manure and rough soil, in equal parts, mixed with water. I blend it together with a hoe and put it by hand into the spaces between the stones. I let the foundation dry for one day. Then I am ready to start building the *polwane*. I use the same mixture for the *polwane* but now I take a big handful of it, place it on the floor in front of me and knead it and knead it, in the way one prepares bread. This will make the wall strong and smooth. I put it on the foundation and press it into shape with my hands and thumbs. I do this over and over, one layer of mud on top of another. When the wall is half-way complete, I stop and smooth it — it is like putting on plaster. The smoothing on of a layer of rough mud is to prevent the bottom part of the *polwane* from cracking before the whole *polwane* is complete. Then I continue building up the *polwane*. I leave an open space near the top for windows. In my young days we made a very small slit in the wall for light to enter — there were no windows in those days.

Then I complete the rough smoothing of the *polwane* right to the top. I let my work dry for one week.

Now I am ready to do the final smoothing of the *polwane*. For this I find very soft, soft soil. I find this soft soil near the roots of the thorn bush and soft river-sand that water has flowed over. Again, I make a mixture of all three, with wet manure but the final smoothing mixture is much wetter than the mixture for the *polwane*. I take a handful of mud and spread it widely in a big circle. I repeat and repeat until the whole *polwane* is smoothed, inside and out. Now my work is over. I may or may not want to decorate the *polwane* with coloured soil. If I want to decorate it, this is done after thatching. The erection of the *dithomeso* and *lebalelo*, thatching and the door, is a man's work.

The *lelwapa*, which is joined to the *nto*, is built in the same way as the *polwane*. It is a low wall and gives shelter when one would like to sit outdoors with visitors or have a meal. The floor inside the *lelwapa* is smoothed in the same way as the floor inside the hut and decorated with patterns made from wet manure. But I give a special finish to the floor inside the hut. It is rubbed and rubbed with a smooth, round stone to make it very hard and firm.

In the old days we made all our own furniture for our homes. There was never much furniture — we had no tables. By night we spread out Tswana mats and Tswana blankets on the floor for our bed and rolled them up in the morning. We had low chairs made of wood and strips of cow hide across the seat. We had clay water pots and clay cooking pots. We had wooden plates called *mogopo*, for eating meat, porridge and drinking milk — cups and tea-drinking came with the Europeans. Milk was our only drink and it was drunk fresh and sour. To scoop water out of the water pot, we used a *sego*. Other household utensils were a wooden porridge spoon, stamping block with stick, and we also made *totwana* of many shapes as containers for crushed corn and beans which we were just going to cook. A *totwana* isn't exactly a basket, though it is made of the same material, grass or the leaves of trees. I don't know what one would call it in English.

Kefhaletse Tobetsi

Age: about seventy-three
Occupation: traditional basket-maker

I was born in Palapye, the same year the tribe moved from Palapye to Serowe in 1902. All my life I have had only one skill by which I earned my living and fed my family. I make baskets and *totwana*. You can call a *totwana* a grass dish. It is the same shape as the household dishes you buy in the shop and can be made in all different sizes and shapes — large *totwana* and small *totwana*.

My method of working on both a *totwana* or basket is the same except that a basket will take a different shape. I use the same materials for a *totwana* and basket and the same tools. My materials are the leaves of the Mokolwane tree [a kind of palm tree] and a bundle of dried grass. My only tools are a knife and a thick needle. In the old days, before my mother's time, they used sharpened stones as tools. I cut the green leaf of the Mokolwane tree and dry it and I also collect my own bundles of tall grass in the bush. My mother taught me this skill.

The work of making a basket or *totwana* is simple, but the threading or knitting part is fine and this has ruined my eyesight. Now, I have a bucket of cold water beside me in which I soak all my dried materials to make them soft for handling. Next I take the dried leaf of the Mokolwane tree and with my needle split it into long shreds. The base of any basket or *totwana* will be Mokolwane leaf — you can't bend grass easily, and you need a firm, tight base. On to this base I wind a small bundle of grass, which I bind to the base with Mokolwane leaf. This small bundle of grass is wound round and round in a coiled shape, like a sleeping snake. The coil of grass determines the size of the basket or *totwana*. For a small basket or *totwana*, I use a small quantity of grass in the coil; for a large basket or *totwana*, I increase the amount of grass in the coil. The rows of coil before knitting also determine the size of the basket or *totwana*. For a small basket or *totwana*, I make one row of coil. Then I begin to knit. I take the Mokolwane leaf and bind it finely and smoothly over the coil, in a wrapping movement, until the row is smoothly covered. For a large basket or *totwana*, I may make four rows of coil before I knit. It is this work which is a bit fine. The Mokolwane leaf has to be pushed between the rows of coil with a needle and it needs concentration and patience.

If I want to include a decoration on the basket or *totwana*, I take some shreds of the Mokolwane leaf and boil them together with the blue of an indelible pencil. For a black decoration, I boil the leaf with the roots of the Moretwa tree.

In my mother's days when people did not use money, it was a custom for people to purchase a *totwana* or basket from her with corn only; a woman would bring along a pot of corn and take away a basket or *totwana*. They could never cost the price of a goat and are not very expensive. I am paid with money or corn and my baskets or *totwana* are always 60c to 80c each.

The Kgotla Stool (told by Mototegi Kgosi)

The feeling about most traditional items, is their nearness to living nature. The kgotla stool or chair is a one-foot high chunk of the body of what was once a huge tree trunk. It retains its original shape, except that the centre portion has been hollowed out into four stands as leg supports and the two flat bases at either end, serve as reversible seats. What a lot of conversations this 'tree trunk' listens to! The kgotla stool is so light and convenient to carry that whenever the old men go off to kgotla to listen to cases or meetings, they carry their chairs along with them.

An old man, Mototegi Kgosi, gave the following description of its construction: 'Every man made his own kgotla stool. It is just an ordinary block of wood and does not need much skill. I cut a stump of a tree trunk, level it top and bottom, make a hole and hollow out four legs as stands. Before the white man came to Botswana, our forefathers had their own implements for cutting and carving wood. In the big mountains surrounding our country, that's where they used to dig out some iron for implements — they made axes, knives, as well as assegais for war.

'Whenever a man has to go to kgotla, he picks up his stool and takes it along with him. Then when he returns home, he brings it back.'

7
Wagon Transport

Katherine Pretorius or Mma-Seata

Age: sixty-four
Occupation: dressmaker

There are only a few of us left, she says, of the early pioneers. She lives in a large house, surrounded by a big garden crammed with all kinds of plant life and shaded by enormous trees. Her late husband, Hendrick Pretorius, was the village blacksmith. He built his business right behind his big house. In a shed, forty-nine years old, stands the ancient bellows he used for welding, side by side with a modern welding machine used by his son. Some of the old ox wagons are still in use and about seven of them stand around the shed awaiting repair. But in the days of their early settlement in Serowe, they used to do a roaring trade as wagons then were the only means of transport. At the back of the house is an area littered with scrap metal — just like any other engineering junk yard. Apart from making wagons, hand ploughs and other iron work, Katherine Pretorius and her husband, *Seatasamadi*, introduced a unique plant into the village, the 'Green Tree', which was to solve a lot of the old problems of fencing and hedging.

*

I was born in Pretoria, South Africa. My father died when I was twelve years, and my mother re-married Sergeant-Major Brierley, who worked for the Botswana police. My family came to Botswana when I was fifteen.

When I married, my husband and I worked for a South African firm, Mosenthals. They had shops all over the world. We ran a shop for them, first in Maun, then later in Rakops, until they closed down and sold out to R.A. Bailey. When they closed down they offered us the shop in Rakops but it was too far out in the bush. Serowe was the capital then with more services for our children so we refused their offer. On our way to Serowe by wagon — in those days there were no cars, not up in these parts, it was either foot or wagon — we heard that Chief Khama had died. He died in February and we arrived in March 1923.

Those ox wagons — they loaded about three tons! They were sixteen feet long. They had five or six wooden bows over the body, and canvas covers with a flap were stretched over them to make a tent. When we travelled, we used a span of twenty-two oxen. It was just like living in a house. I put all our household goods on the wagon; the beds and furniture. It took us ten days travelling from Rakops to Serowe and now by car it takes half a day. We also had to have a gun as defence against wild animals but those stories about lions jumping on people are just false.

A wagon was slow, but sure. With a car you are never sure. Just think of all the accidents they have with cars these days. We never had accidents like that. The sorts of accidents that used to happen were mostly among the little boys who led the team of oxen. They'd sometimes tire and try to climb on the last ox; their foot would slip and they'd go under the wheel. The more fancy modes of travel were the Cape Cart, a sort of buggy, and the Scotch Cart.

We moved into Serowe when life was still in the old stage and we learnt about the old ways of life. We wanted to start a business of our own and had to approach Chief Sekgoma, who succeeded Khama. There was too much competition for shop-owning and when we thought of the blacksmith trade, Chief Sekgoma himself said: 'That's just the man I want.'

In those days we had to go to the chief for all our requirements; the kgotla was really the main place. Then, no one looked to anyone else — the chief was all. We did have a British administration with the District Commissioner and the police but all our legal arrangements were done at the kgotla with our chief. Things have changed completely.

Chief Sekgoma was like a father to us. He lived next door to my sister-in-law and one morning on my way to visit her I heard someone say, *'Dumela'*. I looked up and saw Chief Sekgoma. He said to me:

'Why does Seatasamadi let you walk like that?'

'People who are poor have no choice,' I replied.

In that year one or two cars had appeared in Serowe, so he said to me: 'What car would you like? Would you like a Dodge? I'll get you a car.'

I believe he would have! We lived like that, sharing everything. Sekgoma died soon after that. He just took ill suddenly and died. About Seatasamadi, I don't know how my husband came to be called that but soon after our arrival here I noticed that everyone called him Seatasamadi. Oh, people here give you a nickname in a second. I am addressed as Mma-Seata.

When we settled down in Serowe, we were very busy. Wagons were our means of transport. Six wagons would come in a day for repair. The busiest times were the winter months; my husband had to prepare the wagons in good order for the ploughing time and the rainy season of October and November. I was then a dressmaker and I sewed for people in Botswana and everywhere. It helped me to bring up the children and build a home. An outbreak of foot-and-mouth disease brought all business to a standstill. I kept the home going with my sewing. Through my sewing I was involved in village life. I taught my helpers how to sew and many women who worked with me left and became dressmakers on their own.

Repairing wagons in those days was much more difficult than what it is today. My husband used a bellows while my son uses an arc welder. The bellows took a much longer time — four steel tyres used to take three to four hours to fit on to the wheels. My husband put the tyres on to a wood fire where they were heated, then joined. Servants had to work the bellows up and down to heat the tyres so that they could be trimmed and fitted for the wheels. My son, instead of all that labour his father had, first cuts the tyres and joins them with the arc welder. The joining of the steel tyres is three times quicker than the way my husband worked, but the joining of the tyre to the wheel is done in the same way his father did and is highly skilled work. We guarantee our wagons for four years, before repairing them again.

I notice you smoke. Before my marriage I also smoked. After three months of marriage I noticed my husband looking at me, quietly. One day I said:

'Don't you like women to smoke?'

And he said: 'Not exactly.'

From that day I never smoked again. I just gave it up. I could not do anything he did not like. I don't think there was anyone to touch him, he was so good. He was a very religious man.

We used to be dead scared of scorpions in the house. One night one of my babies was ill and I took him into bed with us. In the middle of the night I awoke to change the baby's napkin. I intended sticking the napkin-pin into the mattress but accidentally stuck it into my husband's foot. He jumped three feet into the air and screamed: 'What bit me?'

He's been dead eighteen years, this May. He took ill with pneumonia for two months. He left off work. One morning, the bloke that starts the engine for the well had a case and had to go to kgotla. My husband went to crank the engine. Someone who was passing saw him fall and ran to call us. By the time we arrived he was dead of heart failure.

We were not out to make ourselves rich. We were satisfied with a fair income just to get on with life and educate our children. I've been so much a part of village life that when my husband died I was given several head of cattle, just as a gift. If I am ill, people come to see me. Me, myself, at the moment, I am happy in Botswana with self-government because of the way we treat one another. I hope my children will live with the people the way we have.

8
The Breakdown of Family Life

The breakdown of family life is one of the great debating points of the village. Of all the tribes living in Botswana, none has experienced so much change and upheaval as the Bamangwato. It was as though all the old securities people had clung to were stripped away at one blow during Khama's rule. Perhaps the shock waves of his immense reforming energy are only now being experienced by the younger generations. The older people all look like Khama. They move around quietly, Bible in hand. They are absolutely sure of the existence of God. The young live in complete chaos. Nowhere is this more evident than in the breakdown of family life in Serowe. This breakdown affects men and women of the age groups from forty to fifty and all the young people who follow on after them, so much so that most mothers are unmarried mothers with children who will never know who their real father is. Out of every one hundred children born in Serowe, three on the average are legitimate; the rest are illegitimate.

Not one of those I interviewed on the question of the breakdown of family life, failed to acknowledge it as a serious problem. What surprised them considerably was my next question. Was it due to Khama's abolition of such customs as the bride price which had once been securities for women? No one would attribute it to Khama's reforms. They said their grandparents and parents had all managed quite well under Christian custom and they had lived for years and years with these changes.

One could propose a counter-argument to the assertion that 'the old people managed quite well with Khama's reforms' and state that Khama was such a powerful personality that while he was alive, the strength of his rule was security in itself for people. He was followed almost immediately by Tshekedi Khama, another powerful personality, who upheld all the new Christian traditions established by his father. This security seemed to crumble like a pack of cards with the death of the Bamangwato leadership and today there is a gaping hole in the fabric of society. Its main victims are women who now rear large families of children on their own, outside the security of marriage.

All Serowans live with the tail-end of the polygamy story. They all have quantities of relatives, totalling something like six hundred each. They all had grandparents or great-grandparents who had more than one wife and it is a great delight to ask a Serowan to recount his family tree. It reads like the Old Testament and is just as sacred. In the royal line of headmen or chiefs, the family clan stretches way back in time and unites vast numbers of people who are all descendants of the royal line. An old man, Tsogang Sebina, claimed to me that the founding of his Sebina clan stretched back two centuries. We started working out a list like the Bible. ' ... And Mokgopo begat Sebina and Sebina begat Motswaing and Motswaing begat ... '. Halfway through he was flattened by exhaustion because his family tree was so long. He looked up suddenly and, as is the way with old men, uttered a single and profound statement on polygamy:

'In those days a single family often made a nation.'

Polygamy was for nation-building. That was one of its major advantages. Another advantage was that it assured every woman in the society of a husband, and that she was performing her reproductive functions under fairly secure circumstances. A disadvantage was that polygamous households, particularly those of royalty, were a breeding-ground for terrible jealousy and strife. Sekgoma I, the father of Khama, had nine wives and of all his children sixteen were boys. Throughout his rule Khama was afflicted by the ambitions of his brothers, some of whom constantly pushed for power and influence.

Perhaps more central to the security of family life was the tradition of *bogadi*, the bride price or the offering of a gift of cattle by a man to his wife's family at the time of marriage. It was a marriage contract and without it there was no marriage. All children born out of the house of *bogadi* were recognized as legitimate. But its ramifications went deep and stretched out to all the children a woman might bear in her lifetime, irrespective of whether another man other than her husband might have fathered her children. It also had undertones of a sale-bargain, as if women were merely a marketable commodity. Of the five principal tribes in the country only the Bamangwato and Batawana have abandoned the *bogadi* tradition, and there seems to be nothing to bridge the ill-defined gap between one way of life and another. No one seems to know what the right sort of relationship between men and women should be, that would be sacred and of mutual benefit.

Marriage in church certainly struck the final death-blow to polygamy but the immense amount of change and strain people have endured seems unfortunately to have struck a death-blow to the male. He ceased to be the head of a family, and his place has been taken by a gay, dizzy character on a permanent round of drink and women, full of shoddy values and without any sense of responsibility for the children he so haphazardly procreates. His image may have been most effectively captured by a young Botswana writer, C.G. Mararike, in a sad and funny short story entitled very appropriately, *Why Marry?*

The name which everybody in and around town knew was that of Benjamin Baoki, the son of Dintsi Dinko. He called himself 'B.B., the son of D.D.'

There were many reasons why B.B. was popular. One of the reasons was that he was one of the first Africans to obtain a degree in Economics at the London School of Economics. He then was the first African to be an accountant. He was also the first African to buy an automatic Mercedes Benz car.

Perhaps the main reason why he was so popular was that he was very unique in appearance. He had suddenly grown a big stomach which matched his big head and big eyes and ears. Everywhere he went people waved at 'B.B., the son of D.D.', a graduate from London School of Economics. In beer gardens, B.B. was even more popular. When he called for a beer, he did not mention it by name. He only called for 'that thing'. Barmen knew that when the son of D.D. had arrived, he wanted 'that thing'. To B.B., beer was so important that he prohibited people from calling it by name.

'That thing,' B.B. would say when he was drunk, 'is the one which puts me into tune. "That thing" makes men wise and women foolish.'

The son of D.D. could have been married if he wanted to but he saw no point 'in buying a cow if he could get its milk free.'

B.B. was a man about town. It was an honour to a girl to be driven in B.B.'s Benz. It was even an honour to a girl to be spoken to by this graduate son of D.D., the owner of an automatic Benz. Every day B.B. had a girl and he went around looking for 'that thing' which made these girls foolish. . . .

From the Botswana magazine, *Kutlwano*.

*

Mpatelang Kgosi

Age: seventy

Our whole society is falling to pieces and I do not blame the breakdown of family life on Khama's abolition of *bogadi* because we had long lived with the changes Khama made and yet in those days people were afraid to break the law. I blame the evils amongst us on lack of proper leadership. There is no ruler to care for and control the people. Men and women were very self-controlled in the old days because even when customs like *bogadi* had been abolished, men often preferred to marry very young women. Since a man had only a choice of one wife, he would often have to wait until the age of thirty, without any contact with women until his wife was fully grown. There wasn't any question of the girl becoming pregnant or anything like that. Both the men and women of today have very cheap values. To a woman a man means money and there is no peace in her search for money. She moves from one man to another. And no longer do the men care about the position of being a father — they just chase women. What else do they do but encourage the children to do the same?

It looks as though many new evils have come with the laws of Independence. In 1967, the government introduced a new marriage law, whereby once children reach the age of twenty-one they may marry without their parents' consent. The result of this is that we now have a large number of divorces. The new style here is to be married for about two years and then divorce. On top of this, family planning was introduced. We can just give it its proper name, which is birth control. At first I did not mind all the adultery and many bad things that were going on because it was producing children. Now the women have seen that they need not bear children. One day there will be no people at all in this country because the women are reluctant to bear children.

Keitese Lefhoko

Age: forty-nine

Men used to love their wives in the old days and women were tough to get. Their parents made tough bargains too. I really don't know what has caused the breakdown of family life because there are so many factors to consider, but I do know that women no longer regard themselves as a prize that has to be won. They just offer themselves to men, are over-romantic and easily available.

One of the factors that has to be considered is that we may have a shortage of men here. I am the principal of a primary school and I have noted that the enrolment of girls is always higher than that of boys. My present enrolment is 226 girls to 151 boys. And during colonial times, a lot of men left the country to work in the South African mines. Often, they did not return. If there is really a shortage of men, this anxiety must have communicated itself to women and may in part account for their promiscuous behaviour.

Another factor to take into account is that today women have found ways of supporting themselves. Many women make a lot of money brewing and selling traditional beer and since they can purchase all their own needs, they feel no need for a husband. It is always difficult to choose between the old days and the freedom we have now. I did not approve of the old tradition whereby a man had to marry a woman ten years younger than himself. He never married his equal.

Balebe Olebeng

Age: forty-five

I don't know for sure when married life broke down, but by the time I started to notice the world, I could see there was no more marriage here in Serowe. My grandmother had been married and so had my mother but in my time, marriage suddenly went out of fashion. It isn't only for the women of my age group — most of the younger women are unmarried too. In my village ward there are about fifty women. Out of that number, five are married, the rest are unmarried, but we all have children and rear them on our own. I have five children but I have never been married. There isn't so much difference between my life and that of a married woman. All the years, I went like other women to plough my mother's lands, so that I would have food to feed my children. If we had a good year, there was always plenty of corn, pumpkin and mealies. I'd keep some of the harvest for food and some of the seeds for another year, then I would sell some of my crop. I'd then keep this money to pay for the school fees for my children. A woman can also make a good living brewing and selling beer, provided she does not start drinking the beer herself. Once she does that, her whole life falls down — she loses her way between drink and men and you should see the condition of such a woman's yard! Everything is a mess there!

Most of the old people living now grew up outside the customs of polygamy and *bogadi*, so I don't think the break-up of marriage was caused by Khama changing these customs. There were many ways of securing marriage. If a mother had a young son in her yard, she'd have her eye on the yard of a friend who had a suitable young daughter. It was known before they grew up that those two would marry and these arranged marriages between parents, for their children, used to ensure that all children were married. What we began to rebel against was this custom. We wanted to choose our partners for ourselves because as Bamangwato, we suffered from too much freedom. When people are following custom, they cannot do as they like; they have to obey laws. I wonder what laws we Bamangwato obey.

In the old days the most important question was: 'Who was your father?' If you had no proper father you were nothing in the society. The same question is still asked today. Some women are ashamed of having children outside marriage and they have taught the children to say: 'My father was killed by a train.' I have told my children the truth. When they asked me who their father was I said: 'You have none.'

What can we do? You can't force a man to be a father. Sometimes, when you are young, you think you are about to marry, then the man just disappears. But you are expecting his child. The main thing is that every woman wants to have a child. All black people like children, so these days it is not really considered shameful to have children outside marriage. Sometimes a woman is lucky in having grandparents and the children grow up under the care of the grandfather. He is like a father to them and that is all they learn about the ways of a man.

I had two boys and three girls. Both my boys are married — this is usual. All the boys get married. My girls are not yet married. They have children.

For my part, I had my children. I have no worry because having children was the most important thing to me.

Lebang Moremi

Age: eighteen

I don't know anything about the laws of Khama because I live in my own time. I was sixteen when I had my first child. I was still at school and in Standard Six. The reason I had a child was because I grew up in a group of older girls. They were the only playmates I had. They all had lovers secretly, without their parents knowing, but they could not conceal the fact once a baby was on the way. I did not want to be left out from what the older girls were doing, so I began to imitate them and got pregnant without any idea of contraceptives. It was an accident, but I found out what happens to girls who become pregnant — there is no help for them, not even from the law.

My parents are the easy-going sort who hate arguments, so they were never really involved beyond kgotla. When we took the case to kgotla they said they could not listen to it because the boy's parents were not available — they were living in a village in the south. After my baby was born, I took the case on my own to the District Commissioner's office. There were just the two of us, my boyfriend who was twenty-eight, with the District Commissioner and the clerk of court. My boyfriend denied point-blank that he was the father of my child but the District Commissioner accepted my evidence and ordered my boyfriend to pay R10.00 a month as maintenance for the child. My boyfriend agreed to pay, then he just did not pay. I went back to court to report that he was not supporting the child. The law is very casual in cases like this. They said to me: 'Oh, we'll see what we can do.' I waited and waited up till now, but they did nothing.

The morals of the men are very loose. Today, women are eager to grab men and they appear loose too. A woman might have three or four boyfriends — always in the hope of marriage. One or two of them will father children, but very rarely do they offer marriage. I wish I knew what goes on in the minds of these men. I blame the law for this state of affairs, nothing in the law, either at kgotla or the police camp, protects a woman. In the case of kgotla, from Chief Tshekedi's time, a ruling was made whereby a woman could claim damages in the form of cattle for the first child only. There is no pressure for damages for the second, third, and so on. So a man knows that if he makes a baby with a woman who already has a child, the kgotla won't trouble him to pay damages, and from then onwards we women get taken advantage of. We have a second appeal for help — to the District Commissioner's office. This involves money for maintenance, not cattle. There was a new maintenance law passed two years ago whereby the men are required to pay R5.00 a week maintenance now. This frightens the men a little. My friends have told me that their boyfriends agree to pay in court, then they suddenly disappear from the village. If they don't, they'll keep turning up at the house with a small packet of soap now and then, or some sugar or tea so that the women don't make trouble. Very, very few pay maintenance.

Many, many women are now rearing children on their own and it is not a good life. Children see one man after another calling on their mother and they lose all respect for her. Our children run wild, are very cheeky and have become thieves. Most of the thefts which now take place in Serowe are done by small boys. They raid houses for money, cigarettes or food. Theft was never a part of our life. I had a father and I know what a beating meant for bad behaviour.

9
The End of an Era

⟨ひひひひひひひひひひひひひひひひひひ⟩

Ramosamo Kebonang

Age: about one-hundred-and-four
Occupation: jack-of-all-trades

During research for this book, I was fortunate in that I was thrown into
the company of the old village men for lengthy periods — Serowans
proudly refer to them as 'our traditional historians'. It is impossible to
translate in straightforward interviews the haunting magic that
surrounds these ancient men. The era of colonial domination seems
quite irrelevant to them as they patiently sit and recreate their
complicated piece of past history. It was often bits and bits of what they
could recollect, and it often came out in short statements rather than
coherent stories: They had kings in the old days, long ago, they said.
Then, a single family often made a nation. They also had a tangled story
to tell of clan disputes and abrupt migrations ...

The basic pattern of tribal movement and migration is not as
complicated as the profusion of new names and identities that sprang
up around it. The drama was always the same: in a large clan, hostilities
of an intolerable nature would develop. One of the clan leaders would
pack up house and home and a whole section of the people would move
off with him. Their destinies, culture and mother-tongue, were
completely altered by new surroundings, new customs, strange

associations. Each old man was concerned with picking up his little piece of the gigantic puzzle, but what had long been lost was the stormy heart of the drama and the ancient dislike of hate, jealousy, rivalry and bloodshed which had shaped those lines of extreme quiet and humility on their faces:

'Whenever trouble broke out,' they said, 'people would rather move away than fight. Once far away, they could discuss the trouble and so could the enemy. . . . '

All that was left were intangible certainties in my mind that in their own way, these old men and their forefathers had played out all the universal human dramas, and had fought against all forms of oppression and corruption for all kinds of freedoms. They had kept no written records of their searches, enquiries and philosophical anguish. All that was written of this period by white historians trod rough-shod over their history dismissing it as 'petty, tribal wars', denying for a long time that black men were a dignified part of the human race. Almost overnight they invented a new name for a black man, that of 'boy'. It had seemed more important that a black man should be known as a 'good boy' or a 'bad boy' and hurry up and down with the suitcases of his master, who was creating 'real' history. My own work concentrated more on the everyday world, so that I never seemed to find the time to linger on the past or to sort out what it was that made these old men so infinitely attractive to me. They still imagined themselves as the caretakers of their whole environment and during a conversation, they would suddenly break off and take another track, explaining in great detail the basic functions of men and women — that they were there to produce children and quite a lot of them — and the simple belief that they had a whole body of holy customs and beliefs locked away in their subconscious minds.

One interview I had with the old man, Ramosamo Kebonang, seemed at first the most frustrating task I had ever undertaken. He was very old and ill. He wheezed and whined his way through the interview. He couldn't concentrate and he said all sorts of irrelevant things. Yet later when I came home I laughed to myself and thought: 'I've had a lovely day today with Ramosamo Kebonang!' I decided to record the irrelevant.

It wasn't as though Serowe people had not warned me off old Ramosamo Kebonang. Ever since the wind blew news of my book around the village, people began to take a keen interest in my activities, guiding me here and there to all their good story-tellers.

'What are you doing today, Mrs Head?' they asked.

'Oh, I want to see old Ramosamo Kebonang today,' I replied. 'I hear that he is the oldest man in the village and he may have something to say.'

'Don't go and see Ramosamo!' they said, alarmed. 'He's very stupid and he has the history of the tribes mixed up in his head. You mustn't trust all these old men. Some of them are born stupid. Ramosamo is like that.'

In spite of this advice I kept my appointment with Ramosamo Kebonang. I had an interpreter who led the way into his yard.

'*Dumela Phuti*,' my interpreter said. (*Phuti* indicated Ramosamo's connections with Bamangwato royalty.) Then the interpreter added:

'I have brought you a Mongwato. She would like some information from you.' (Mongwato was meant to indicate that I was a member of the Bamangwato tribe.)

'*Dumela* Mongwato,' old Ramosamo said to me, absent-mindedly.

As soon as I returned his greeting, he started slightly, blinked to clear the mist from his ancient eyes, and said in high astonishment: 'Yo! she isn't even a proper Motswana!' Then he said to me loudly:

'*O tswa kae kae*?' ('Where's your original home?')

'South Africa,' I said.

'Well, that's all right,' Ramosamo said kindly. 'What we like is for all foreigners to accept themselves as Mongwato and stay peacefully with us. This custom started from the time of our King Khama. King Khama used to be the lover of foreigners, both black and white. In the case of black people we have very large village wards in Serowe now of foreign tribes. It came about that we cannot easily trace who is a foreigner these days. They have added to the Bamangwato tribe and all talk Setswana.'

I had learned from experience that tossing around the name of the beloved King Khama was one way to get the old people talking, so I said: 'How did all these foreign tribes come to Khama?' And Ramosamo Kebonang straight away started to show how the history of the tribes was mixed up in his head: 'The Barotse ... er ... they came from Zambia. It's only today that they have that independence name, Zambia, and you should hear how they are boasting of it! Before that they were just Barotse but now they like to say that Zambia was once their country ... the Barotse ... er ... I think they were seeking work at one time ... '

He got completely stuck there and lost his concentration. I had time to take note of my surroundings. Three old men of the neighbourhood rushed into the yard; their rapid walk and the eager looks they threw in our direction, showed that they were devoured by curiosity. Without fuss, they put down their kgotla stools near us and for the next three hours sat completely immobile. Their eyes were round and still and filled with wonder. I thought: It's not only little children who like stories. Old men too. The white-haired Ramosamo must have been a real V.I.P. in his heyday. He had a full, long face with a burnt-copper complexion and arched, arrogant eyebrows. A number of servants moved quietly around the yard, busy with chores. They looked like Basarwa people.

I had a number of leads to get him to talk and the first lead I chose ran me straight into a dead-end.

'I was told,' I said, 'your family were involved in the dispute between Khama and his son, Sekgoma II, and you packed up your house and followed Sekgoma.'

'Not me,' he said. 'My father went away with Sekgoma. I stayed with Khama. It was family disturbances which I refuse to explain.'

I was dismayed. I had had dreams of recording the endless moves from one village to another from an eye-witness. All the old men are guarded about controversies involving their chiefs and cover up the past with a thick blanket of silence as soon as one probes in the wrong direction. On seeing my dismay old Ramosamo attempted to placate me by throwing out the usual trivia about Khama — all the old men have it pat like a record they repeat: 'I was pleased by everything Khama did,' he said. 'You know, in his time, every single person in Bamangwato country had cattle and quite a lot too. . . . '

All this while, he had been a very busy old man. He could hardly walk but while he sat in his chair, his hands worked away at softening a piece of semi-sun-dried animal skin with the skill of a craftsman who knew his job.

'What work did you do in your lifetime?' I asked.

'I lived on my ploughing and cattle, like most other people,' he said. 'But if you ask about making things for the house, I made everything — mats, karosses, porridge spoons, the porridge bowl which we call *mogopo* and the *kika*, which is the stamping block for corn. The only thing I couldn't do was thatch — thatching is not every man's skill — otherwise I put up my own *dithomeso* and *lebalelo*.'

In a twinkling the servants set his whole workshop before me. Everything had, just a movement away, been a tree trunk. The wood had been only slightly worked to serve man, otherwise one might have been eating out of trees or touching them all the time.

He was a rather scornful old man. I asked him how he made a

porridge spoon and he shook his head to indicate that I was very stupid: 'Take a branch of any tree,' he said. 'Begin shaping it and you have a porridge spoon. Now, the *mogopo* and the *kika*, I've only made from two kinds of trees — the Morule and Motswrewe. When I make the *mogopo* bowl, I have a block of tree trunk, one foot high. Out of that block I am going to get two bowls. I split it straight down the centre with an axe, then I take a knife and scoop out the centre to shape the bowls. Then I use a sharper knife for the final shaping and smoothing.'

The *kika* or wooden stamping block retained the whole shape of the tree trunk and stood two feet high. It had a hollowed-out hole into which corn was poured. A heavy wooden pestle was pounded into the hollow to crush the corn.

'Before the white man came,' he went on, 'we had our own implements for carving. The iron was dug out from the hills by our grandfathers. None of the people of my age could make the iron implements. It was done by my elders. My age group became used to buying implements from the white traders. I had one of the old implements which we made ourselves but it was taken from me by Chief Tshekedi. I like some of the things the white man brought, like iron bolts which keep the cross-beams of the roof secure. In the old days we could not secure the roof with cross-beams. When I was young we had in the centre of the floor of the hut a tall trunk of a tree which stretched upwards and the rafters were secured to it with the bark of a tree.'

Old Ramosamo then announced that it was time for lunch. One of the old men who had listened with wide eyes to everything, suddenly leaned forward and made a solemn speech: 'I want to say that this kind of talk is very good,' he said. 'Also, everything that has been said here, is the truth.'

All those present, and we were a lot of unexpected guests, were served bowls of porridge, with a piece of meat and a little of the soup the meat had cooked in. Something about that day was lovely — it was like stepping back into an ancient world where everything had been balanced and sane; a daily repetitive rhythm of work and kindly, humorous chatter. I thought: Serowe may be the only village in southern Africa where a black man can say with immense dignity: 'I like some of the things the white man brought, like iron bolts . . . ' The white man hasn't trampled here on human dignity possibly because the Bamangwato produced a king like Khama who fought battles of principle on all sides against both white and black.

70

10
Sekgoma II, the Son of Khama the Great
(told by Grant Kgosi)

People might think that Sekgoma II, the son of Khama, ruled for one year, during 1924, but no. He parted from his father in 1904 and while in exile, he ruled a large number of Bamangwato people. He was driven into several places of exile by his father and lived one year at Ekotwe, near Palapye, then was moved by Khama to Mogonono near Palla Road, then again to Lephepe for about two years. In 1907 he was removed by force with his people and cattle to Tsebanana, then to Nyekati. He remained at Nyekati until 1916.

In 1916 his father was kicked on the knee by a horse and he came home by himself, without his people. He was asked by Khama to stay in Serowe and attend kgotla to make himself known to the people. So Sekgoma II actually ruled for about nineteen years and for nine years he ruled legally in Serowe. Sekgoma had been marrying all the time during his exiles but this time Khama said that he should marry a woman given to him by the Bamangwato people and himself. Khama chose Tebogo Kebailele, the daughter of his younger brother — we used to marry cousins here. She was to bear the future heir, Seretse, the first President of Botswana.

The reason Sekgoma II is never mentioned, except for the one year he ruled in Serowe as chief, is because he was living all the time under the shadow of his father, King Khama.

PART TWO

The Era of Tshekedi Khama (1926—59)

'All my work has been helping my people.'

Tshekedi Khama: from the biography by Mary Benson

11
Tshekedi Khama

Tshekedi Khama was the son of Khama the Great. It was one of those rare occasions when the greatness of the father was passed on to the son. At the age of sixty, Khama married a young wife, Semane, who was the mother of Tshekedi. But on the death of Khama in 1923, a first-born son by his first wife, Mma-Bessie, ruled the tribe. He was Sekgoma II and he died suddenly in 1925 after a long period of ill health, leaving a small son, Seretse Khama, aged four, as heir to the Bamangwato chieftaincy. Tshekedi Khama was installed as regent to rule the tribe, in place of the real heir who was a minor. This simple and convenient arrangement seemed to spark off a number of catastrophes, still lamented to this day by the older members of the tribe. Controversy and dispute came to be Tshekedi's second name. But did he ever accept blame? A framed mute, humorous legacy he left in his office at the tribal administration headquarters in Serowe, is an eloquent summary of how he must have pictured himself to himself — Rudyard Kipling's *If*: 'If you can keep your head when all about you /Are losing theirs and blaming it on you ... '

Unlike his father, Khama, a comprehensive and sensitive biography has been written about him — *Tshekedi Khama* by Mary Benson, which deals with all aspects of his life and rule. And unlike his father Khama, who was naturally gifted with a form of poetic–visionary expression, all Tshekedi Khama's utterances and writings are so downright, pragmatic, commonsensical and geared to the real world, that today in Serowe, this is the strongest theme we inherit from his era.

His time was famed for educational progress, and the ideal of self-help was introduced into Serowe life long before it became an international byword or necessity. I worked on self-help projects in a much later period and was amazed at the old men who would come and peer at the work and join in the pick-digging. When I commented on it, people replied: 'They used to work like that with Tshekedi. My father who passed away helped to build Masokola School, you know.'

In Khama's time, primary school education started in elementary form under the trees. During Tshekedi's time most of the primary school buildings were erected with the use of 'voluntary' regiment labour. People today query the voluntary side. They say the labour was forced and unpopular because during the time an age regiment or *mephato* worked on some construction project, they worked for no pay and had to feed themselves. Khama had abolished the initiation ceremony, *bogwera*, which was attached to the age regiment system but the age regiments continued to be called (the last age regiment called in Serowe was for Tshekedi's eldest son and the system seems to have been abandoned). Tshekedi changed the name 'age regiments' to 'work regiments' and all people in regiments could be called on, if not fully employed, to work on self-help projects. The number of self-help projects people worked on stretched from schools to one college to grain silos and the water reticulation system. People seem anxious to bury this period of severe, Spartan work and yet it is one of the most glorious aspects of Serowe's history.

On the other hand, relationships between Botswana and British were not at all the happy family affair the independence speeches would have us believe. The black man here was as despised by the colonial ruler as he was everywhere else. The peculiar twists matters took in Bamangwato country was that here British colonialism chose to persecute a single black man and so relentlessly that a psychological explanation is more fitting than a rational explanation of many unhappy events. Almost anything Tshekedi did was opposed by colonial authority and they twice exiled him from Bamangwato country without a proper trial. The first case of exile shows clearly what riled the British — they were putting down a native who was too proud. They had to backtrack three weeks later when the story sped around the world as a sensational news story. Simply, a young white man had stepped over the dividing line between black and white in Serowe. He liked Batswana girls and one day assaulted a Motswana man over a girl. That was why he turned up at the kgotla in the first place; most tribesmen traditionally appealed to the chief. The young man's behaviour caused such indignation that at one point during the trial he was flogged by several tribesmen. The navy was called in and Tshekedi was deposed. The address of the acting High Commissioner, Admiral Evans, took the tone of: 'I'm telling you, boy, we are not going to stand this sort of thing from you.' Psychologically it was so out of place with other developments in Serowe, that one is forced to take the story back to Khama's time and propose tentatively that in this conflict with the British, Tshekedi was made to suffer from a backwash of suppressed British resentment against his father's rule. Khama is on record as having said to the white man: ... 'Well, I am black, but if I am black, I am chief in my own country at present. When you white men rule in the country, then you can do as you like; at present I rule ... ' and no other black man in southern Africa had dared say that. Khama had also made the white man's tenure in Bamangwato country very insecure; if they riled him they had to leave, in spite of their brick houses and shops. About Tshekedi one continually gets the impression of a struggle for psychological advantage on the part of the British, and it is this hidden undertone of the unspoken and possibly real source of the resentment, which was Khama whom they had raised to the pinnacle of a God, that makes their behaviour towards Tshekedi so inexplicable.

The next exile and dispute which involved Tshekedi was a more serious affair than that first paltry show of power by the British. It involved the death of the Bamangwato chieftaincy which had been for a long time the most powerful in the country. Tshekedi's nephew, Seretse, went off and married an Englishwoman. Tshekedi opposed the marriage on the grounds that a king or chief could not do as he pleased as he was the servant of the people and an heir to the chieftaincy was at stake. His nephew insisted on his right to marry whom he wished. The story of the actual dispute between the two men is nobly unfolded by Mary Benson; neither seems at fault in his conduct and Serowans have told me that they were still arguing about the matter when the British took matters into their own hands and exiled both Tshekedi and Seretse, with painful results — rioting broke out and a number of people were killed. All self-help projects came to an abrupt halt but by then four primary schools had been built in Serowe and one college. It is the underlying achievement of community service which I have attempted to re-invoke from some Serowans' testimony. It tends to get overshadowed by the controversies of the time, but it isn't controversy the younger generation have inherited. People never consciously count their gains. Serowe has continued to offer all kinds of educational stimulus to its people and its past has created its present.

12
The Building of Moeng College

Lenyeletse Seretse

Age: fifty-three

Occupation: Central District Council secretary

Someone once remarked to me: 'I like Lenyeletse for his humanity, but he's difficult to get along with because he's so conservative.' That man was an idealist, with the natural irritation of his kind for the type of person who likes the slow, proper channels to initiate new schemes. Surprisingly, Lenyeletse Seretse has moved from the big-minded planning of Tshekedi's era to what some might say is the small, petty, rubber-stamp bureaucracy of independence. Today, the building of a new school creates no hazards and sacrifices — its place is neatly allocated in a five year plan for district rural development and no doubt, after all the committees and councillors have hummed over it, the school will materialize. It wasn't like that in Tshekedi Khama's time. Then, everything people gained, they gained by their own efforts and sacrifices. Lenyeletse was involved in this great drama as he was more or less adopted by Tshekedi, after the death of his father. He tells a valuable story of the building of Moeng College on regimental labour and of Tshekedi's efforts to create the Bamangwato Tribal Administration.

Lenyeletse is a little complicated — a soft, friendly, amiable personality makes him one of the most popular men in the village. Side by side with that, he has the closed, reserved face of a man who knows too much, and isn't telling. On being approached for a story, he made some alarmed mutterings about the need for official clearance before he could say anything, with the result that his story is thoroughly weeded of any 'dangerous' controversy. I had to be content with that.

*

I was born on the 25 June, 1920. My father died just before I was born, and *Lenyeletse* means 'relations have passed away'. My family had lost a lot of relatives at that time so my uncle, Gasebalwe, named me Lenyeletse. My grandfather, Seretse, was the brother of Khama the Great. Here, in our custom, we used to take the first name of a grandparent or parent as a surname so that no family had fixed surnames, but compulsory registration of births may change this and give people more fixed surnames.

It was a tradition for boys to spend their childhood at the cattle-post and that is where I lived, at the family cattle-post, till the age of ten. Masarwa people, who were the slaves of my family, ran the cattle-post and we whiled away the time doing clay modelling, mostly models of the cows we looked after. I started school at the age of ten. I have only a brother, years older than I. He had been to college and when he came to the cattle-post he taught me to read and write a little so that by the time I started school I could read. For a year I attended primary school in Serowe and my uncle, Gasebalwe, paid for my education. After that, all my education was paid for by Tshekedi. The way he took note of me was due to my friendship with Seretse.* We were playmates in the village and in the old days it wasn't allowed that anyone should eat out of the same plate with royalty. One day Tshekedi passed by and found me eating out of the same plate with my friend. He stopped and asked: 'Who are you?' and Seretse said we were friends. I only had on a *tshega* like all the other children but you never knew how Tshekedi was thinking things out. He had a group of boys he was about to send off to Tiger Kloof College in South Africa and suddenly included me in the group.

I completed my primary education at Tiger Kloof and Tshekedi sent me on to Lovedale College for a commercial course, which I did not complete. I was at Lovedale for two years when I was suddenly expelled

*Seretse Khama, the first President of Botswana.

for insubordination to my teachers. The trouble was I was inattentive in lessons and used to just sit and stare up at the ceiling if a lesson did not interest me. I remember one of my teachers saying: 'Lenyeletse, you don't make a noise but you just annoy me!' All I had in my favour was that I was one of the best athletes in the school, but I had to come home and face Tshekedi. I was nineteen then. Of course he said he didn't want to see the sight of me as he'd spent his own money on my education. An appeal to the college failed so Tshekedi employed me in his office as a clerk for a year. A year later Tshekedi sent me to the Jan Hofmeyer School of social work, where two years later I obtained a diploma. I returned to Serowe and worked under Tshekedi's tribal administration as a social worker. It was the first job of its kind in Serowe. It was mostly youth recreation work, organizing sports and we had organized soccer for the first time. I also taught physical training in the schools. My salary was very low — I was getting R16.00 a month.

We had an age regiment called at that time for Seretse who was to be future chief and it involved all the people of Seretse's age group, to which I belonged. All that happened was that early one morning the group had to assemble at the dam. The old men and Tshekedi then delivered speeches about how we ought to conduct ourselves as men; we were told we were now men and had to pay our taxes. I was twenty-three then.

Tshekedi never got over my expulsion from Lovedale College. He had been brooding about it, thinking perhaps I was a failure. He said nothing about his actual thoughts. What he said to me was: 'I am sending you with the Malekantwa regiment to build Moeng College. What do you think about it?'

I was too afraid of Tshekedi to say what I actually thought; that he must have made a mistake; that only the unemployed were forced to join work regiments; that I was a fully employed person. I quietly said I'd go. I was afraid of him in the sense that he was like my father. He then observed that I didn't seem to care much for the tribal way of life with its social responsibilities and that as one of the most senior members of the Malekantwa regiment, next to Seretse who was in England, I would have to take charge of the work at Moeng.

In Tshekedi's time, work regiments were a part of everyday village life and he had a terrific amount of projects going on all at the same time. It's so different today where no single man is an initiator of projects, but then, he was the sole initiator of all the work projects. He concentrated mainly on schools and the water supply, and the use of regiment labour was the only means of self-help. His method of mobilizing people into work regiments spread from Serowe to all the outlying villages in Bamangwato country. And unlike today, there was no aid money to build schools — the regiment labour people offered was free, and apart from that he asked for donations of cattle — Moeng College was entirely built on cattle donations from the tribe and regiment labour. He also levied new taxes such as cattle sales commission and site rents; this mostly affected the white traders. It was just done by the word of Tshekedi, even though it was discussed in a most democratic manner at the kgotla. Today, when we levy new taxes in the council, we have to get legal authority to do so.

I knew of all these activities but you had to work in regiment labour to understand what it meant! This is how work regiments were called up: someone would go to the top of Serowe Hill and shout as loud as he could the name of the regiment, say for instance: 'Malekantwa! Malekantwa!' All people of that age regiment knew they had to go to kgotla. There Tshekedi would tell us of his proposed project and the work we were expected to do. In the case of going to Moeng, we straight away planned our movements and work; when we had to leave, how we had to leave, and when we started work.

The suffering we went through! It was 1948. It was a year of drought. It was hot, as only drought years can be and we worked all day outdoors. Each man had to bring along his own rations, paid for out of his own pocket, but it didn't really work out. Those of us who had more means were forced to share with those who had less. Soon, we were all starving. Some members of the regiment had brought their horses. They died. We ate them. We ate wild rabbits or anything we could catch in the bush. So many men wanted to back out under such conditions but there wasn't any means to do so. Men who left a work regiment were put on trial and punished. I think what kept everything together is the fact that I always stay even-tempered, no matter what happens. Tshekedi had a contractor for the college; we provided the free labour. We pushed wheelbarrows up and down, mixed cement, moulded bricks and by the end of it some of us had learnt how to lay bricks. We were on the construction site for ten months and had put up most of the buildings when we were called back, with the intention of another regiment taking our place. We assembled at the kgotla to give our report; we had survived starvation and hardship with no casualties — we had a regiment before us, clearing the bush and some of its members had died. I was about to walk away, relieved it was all over, when to my surprise Tshekedi called my uncle and me to one side. He simply said: 'I punished him. In my eyes he has earned respect again.'

I resumed work, this time as principal clerk for Tshekedi. It was like a promotion. Not long after this an event occurred which seemed to set the clock back all round. Word arrived of Seretse's marriage to an Englishwoman. At first it was kept quiet in an attempt to sort out the situation, fearing the impact of the news on the people. That seemed to be an initial blunder. People got hold of the story on their own and split into camps. There is a section of the community that powerfully believes in magic — they were absolutely convinced that Tshekedi wanted the chieftainship for himself and had stumbled upon a particularly potent potion which had made Seretse marry the foreign woman so that he would remain chief. There were so many desperate issues at that time — independence was not in sight; there was South Africa; there was the role of the British Government in Botswana which people looked on with distrust. Tension was inevitable. Riots broke out in many parts of Bamangwato country in 1951 and 1952, the most serious being in 1952 when some lives were lost.

My own interpretation of the situation was that Tshekedi was only fighting to maintain the Bamangwato chieftainship. So many other people's personal reasons and ambitions taint the whole story but this aspect of it is the most touching. It wasn't ever a question of Tshekedi wanting the chieftainship for himself. But the way in which he tried to secure the chieftainship, which was already lost, for future generations, is what caused all the hostilities.

13
The Principles of Moeng College

Thato Matome

Age: forty-six

Occupation: school-teacher

There is something beautiful about her — and most Serowe women have her expression –– serious, intent, kind, genial, accommodating, reserved, with now and then a flicker of humour. I think it comes from all the listening they do and from the unwritten 'law' which governs all aspects of the traditional way of life. So many peoples of the earth have their traditional ways of life, by which they really mean their means of survival — the white man in South Africa often refers to his traditional way of life and it creates an ugly expression on his face. Traditional African life has its mean individuals and its good individuals — the mean are often embarrassed into a display of generosity; the good, and Thato Matome is one of them, are simply a direct expression of all that is to be most treasured in the 'law' or traditional custom. This law or custom which people often refer to is so sacred, personal and immediate that it is written in the heart. It dictates how man should care for man. All that was naturally beautiful in the society was sharpened and given direction by such men as Tshekedi Khama, and Thato Matome grew up during the Tshekedi era.

She is a personal friend. Always when we meet and part I say to myself: 'What a wonderful woman!' But I can never tell why I say so. It's a vague impression of having encountered someone who is entirely, and utterly good.

*

We Bamangwato have had a colourful history. I have it mostly from hearsay, from the stories the old people have handed down to us about our chiefs but my generation can still feel its inspiration and it is something that we should build on.

I grew up when Chief Tshekedi was ruling the tribe. What distinguished those days was that we were encouraged to learn and education often went beyond book learning — there was a great stress on character building. I attended primary school in Serowe and I was born into an atmosphere where there wasn't any time for mischief. All children were kept fully occupied. We started the day with school, then in the afternoons we had family chores; lighting the fire, cooking meals, then in the evenings we were sent off to *Dikaelo*. *Dikaelo* was Bible study classes and it had been started by Chief Tshekedi's mother, Semane. We were given simple Bible stories, the singing of psalms and hymns and yearly there'd be a competition for all the *Dikaelo* groups in the village. This way of life affected us all — it created a people who were keen to learn, responsible, and that's where the leadership of the country comes from today.

I was in it all because my grandfather was a minister of the church. I joined the Girls' Life Brigade and attended Sunday school. Oh, but all that marching business we did on Sunday — that's why I don't want to march anywhere these days! Actually, I can't tell you anything about the Girls' Life Brigade; I can't tell you what its aims were or its constitution; it was just that marching part that was so exciting to me as a child. On a Sunday, once a year, we were all on parade. We assembled at a certain spot and marched through the village in khaki uniforms to church.

It wasn't all work and study. We had so many games typically belonging to us and moonlit evenings were always set aside as playtime for children. A very local game for girls was *Khurutshe* — it was a game of passing a wild fruit from one girl to another. The point of the game was to keep up a rhythmic clapping while the fruit was passed round in an endless circle. We were also, as girls, very imitative of our mothers. We built small mud houses, had children, played at weddings and getting married, but we were never as children allowed to play with fire for fear we would burn down the grass roofs of the huts. We always brought cooked food from home and then pretended hard to be cooking it again!

At that time, schooling ended with primary education in Serowe. For further education most of us had to take the train to South Africa. It was always a big do! We all had to assemble at the kgotla and Chief Tshekedi provided free transport for us to Palapye station and on our return, free transport back to Serowe. The older students, who had completed their education, jumped on the trucks to cheer us on. It was never consciously in our minds and yet, being given free transport did create in us a sense of indebtedness to come back and help our people. I don't even think we thought of it then as children and it is only on looking back as adults that we value those little gestures of Chief Tshekedi. Then, for us, it was only the excitement of jumping on the back of a truck and going far away for an education. There was so much controversy during Chief Tshekedi's rule that he is branded by all kinds of names — a cruel man, an exploiter of the people and so on, but no other man cared for us as much as he did.

I was one of the pioneer teachers at Moeng College, which was built by Chief Tshekedi. I arrived at Moeng a week or two after the opening — that was in 1949 and I was twenty-one years old. It was a challenge to work in this school which was an experiment in education, an experiment in social relationships. Chief Tshekedi himself drew up the policy by which the school was run. He wanted Moeng College to be his ideal of what a Bamangwato College should be.

As an experiment in education, side by side with their academic instruction, the children were taught not to despise the traditional tasks of their parents — they stamped corn, worked in the gardens, baked their own bread, milked their own cows — all the food they ate, except sugar and tea, was grown on the school farm. And all the students, boys and girls, had to take a compulsory course in agriculture and domestic science. I was teaching domestic science. I was young and inexperienced and often teaching people much older than I. It was no joke teaching boys domestic science! There was a terrible boy, twice my size in height and he'd stand in the middle of the classroom, arms akimbo, and demand: 'What is the point of teaching boys domestic science?' He'd never want to co-operate and I'd have to discipline him under pressure and threat.

As an experiment in social relationships, houses that were built for the teaching staff were the equivalent of houses built for white government officials. It was the only college at that time in southern Africa, where housing conditions for white and black teachers were equal. The institutions I attended in South Africa had always provided inferior living quarters for black teachers, and Moeng College was also the only college where black and white teachers could live together in the same hostel. I think it was a contrast to the houses provided in Botswana itself for the civil servants. In the civil service, different types of housing were provided for white and black civil servants and the housing for black civil servants was always inferior. It was Chief Tshekedi's special wish that the housing for all teachers at Moeng College be of an equal standard. He wasn't one of those public, breast-beating anti-racialists but he'd quietly achieve great things like this. It created a totally new relationship between black and white teachers, which was an unfamiliar situation at that time.

During the time I taught at Moeng, Chief Tshekedi frequently visited the school. We knew by then that he had become an international figure and was considered a great man but he never carried his fame around with him. All teachers would meet him at a dinner. I think I had feeble ideas about education then and I used to be very uplifted that such a great man would quietly sit and listen to the problems I had teaching boys domestic science. I know, no government official, then or now, would have the time or interest to listen to the ideas of a young and inexperienced teacher. Chief Tshekedi's manner was always quiet and fatherly but there was something else indescribable about him that was very magnetic, like a force. I'd say one felt towards him what one felt about God. Perhaps I felt that way because I was young. Once he knew you, he treated you as a personal friend and always kept in touch through letters. The last letter I received from him was an invitation to visit his new home at Pilikwe but before I could pay him a visit, he died. His letter shows you how friendly he was — what is that phrase? He could live with kings and commoners with equal ease.

You will forgive me for having failed to reply to your several letters and I feel now you will not regard my seeming negligence to my friends to mean 'out of sight, out of mind'. I am back in my own country after very much difficulty and severe trials. . . . I suppose you do not know that I have established my new home between Palapye and Moeng. It takes me only an hour and thirty minutes to drive to the college. Thus you have a home close to your work where you can spend some of your week-ends.
           Yours very sincerely,
           Tshekedi Khama

My life has always been uneventful and quiet. It looks like I have repeated one day, many times over. The only time I ever departed from my routine was when I took a trip to America to attend a three-month summer school. The Association of University Women in America, in conjunction with the State Department, invited me over. My name was nominated by the Botswana Government.

I was surprised by what I learnt in America — how little they know of Africans. They expect us to be creatures of the past, in pre-historic dress. They don't really expect us to be educated or know English at all. A professor looked very surprised when I started talking English. I was only in the company of white people during my stay there and they continually passed remarks like this: 'Did you buy this dress only when you got on the plane?' And in my presence they'd say to each other: 'Did you hear? She can *actually* talk English.' They didn't seem to know that their behaviour was insulting.

I liked the trip to America, while it lasted — but I wouldn't like to live there. It isn't the kind of life I'd like. It's too rushed and competitive. I like Africa and its leisure.

What I like about independence in Botswana is that it has given Botswana people a dignity and respect they didn't have in colonial days and the times are especially good for the young. Today, the young can rise to the highest levels in education and employment, and the range of careers for them has widened.

14
Regiment Labour over the Years

Makatse Modikwa

Age: eighty

Occupation: farmer and headman

I am a Mokwena by birth and that is a state higher than a Mongwato, but all this really makes no difference because when the question is asked here: 'Who is a Mongwato?' we all say we are Mongwato — even the foreign tribes do this.

My father was headman of Malokatsela ward and I am second headman of the same ward. The reason I am second headman is because my father had two houses and was married under the old custom of polygamy; that meant that he had two wives; that meant that he had a first-born son of the first house who would always be senior to me born of the second house. I am a Christian and my first marriage took place in the London Missionary Society church. There's nothing really wrong with Christian marriages if the woman is good but I divorced that wife after four years — she did not obey my rules; she did not care for me and she did not prepare food on time. When I married the second time, I thought I'd better marry under Setswana custom as I did not understand the ways of that first wife. This proved to be a good decision because I am still living with the second wife. When we marry under Setswana custom, the rules for marriage are similar to the

Christian rites, except that the marriage ceremony is really conducted by the parents — both my parents and my wife's parents offer us rules for a good life. There was only a slight difference between my marriage and that of my father's which was also held under Setswana custom. He had paid *bogadi* for his wives but I could not because by that time Khama had abolished *bogadi*.

Bogadi was not really the purchase of women as is thought today. It was like an appreciation to the parents for rearing their daughter well over the years and when we offered *bogadi* cattle it meant that we were paying back the parents for the care of this child. The difficulty with *bogadi* was that it secured a man's rights over his children — when a woman was married with a dowry, the children belonged to the husband; if he failed to pay the dowry, the children would not be his. That often meant that only rich people could have their children and poor people often had difficulties finding the *bogadi* cattle. This was what worried Khama and he abolished *bogadi*.

As a young boy I looked after my father's cattle and while at the cattle-post I was taught how to make Tswana mats and blankets by an old man. I had two teachers in fact and this skill of preparing the skins was to be my one major source of income throughout my life because the way things went with me, I was to offer most of my services for free to help develop the community. People pay me either with money or a cow for my work.

I was fifteen when I started attending primary school in Serowe. We had a book where we learnt ABC. I learnt English though I cannot understand it now. I only attended school for four years, then I hurried off to get married. My father was quite rich and important with chiefs like Khama and Tshekedi so I never worried about higher education. The rest of my education came from working under Chief Khama and Chief Tshekedi. When we work with chiefs and the old people, we take the rules of our custom from them. These rules tell us how to work with people so that they are never treated harshly, so that one should not quarrel or react roughly in a dispute and to see that if a person does not understand something, it must be patiently explained to him. So I became involved in tribal affairs and to me it was nothing but work, work, work.

I joined my age regiment in 1911 and at that time Chief Khama wanted a little job done for himself. He took us to the Shashane River to make wells for his cattle. We dug these wells in the soft river-sand with spades. In Setswana the name for this sort of work is *go sokola* and that is how we got the name of our regiment, Masokola. Most of the community services Serowe now has, were given to it by our Masokola regiment. It was one of the largest regiments ever called and I worked on all the jobs assigned to our regiment.

The next job Khama asked us to do was build the big brick house near the kgotla. This house belonged to the tribe and was to be used by a chief who was working for the tribe. This house we built was burnt down in 1952 during the riots. Chief Tshekedi was the occupant at that time.

Just before Khama's death we started to have trucks in Serowe and Khama called the Masokola regiment to build the thirty-six mile road between Palapye and Serowe. The whole regiment of one thousand men was on the job and we divided into groups — one group chopped down bushes, the second group moved behind, digging the deep roots of the trees out of the soil, and the third group filled in the dongas. We then levelled the road with soil, poured water on it and stamped it down with our feet. It was completed in one month. It may seem surprising but the regiments then were like a war machine — if the chief had given an order to demolish the whole village of Serowe, we would have done it in four hours!

During the rule of Sekgoma II, the tribe needed a dam for watering their cattle and a site was chosen at the bottom of Swaneng Hill. The Masokola regiment was called forth to build it. We closed the stream running beneath the hill, dug a foundation and filled it with sacks of manure and river-sand. We built up the wall with sacks of sand and then covered it all with soil. Thirty-nine years later Patrick van Rensburg came to build Swaneng Hill School near the same spot. He announced that he wanted to make repairs on our dam. People had not taken care of it and it was damaged. His announcement travelled round the village and reached me. I straightaway hurried out of my house and joined van Rensburg and the students in the repair work. I was pleased because the ideas of van Rensburg were the same we had heard from our chiefs — to develop the community.

When Chief Tshekedi started ruling the tribe, regiment work was to grow like a fever on the people. I remember that as soon as we heard work was in progress, even if we were not involved, we would loan our wagons and drums to carry equipment and water to the building sites. The first job we did under Chief Tshekedi was really for the British Government. There had been a number of outbreaks of foot-and-mouth disease between the Botswana and Rhodesian border and we were asked to build a quarantine fence near Palapye as a disease-control measure for cattle. When we returned to Serowe and reported at kgotla, we were told by Chief Tshekedi that the government had paid a certain sum of money for the work done. It was the only sum of money we were ever to receive for work and a few members of the Masokola regiment immediately said that it should be equally shared among us all. Others thought it should go to the community. We voted and the majority were in favour of building a primary school for the children and that was how the building of Masokola Primary School started. That was the one school I am sure was all our own and built with our own labour and everything. Chief Tshekedi only chose the site, but we collected the concrete, the water we brought with our own drums, and we moulded and baked our own bricks from earth and sand. Four other primary schools were built in various ways, partly with contract labour and partly with regiment labour but the tribe always paid for their construction with their cattle.

It wasn't only good things that we did. Sometimes a chief would send a regiment to do something so bad that you did not know your own mind any more and this was the case in 1946 when the Masokola regiment was sent to crush the Bakalanga rebellion. A quarrel had been brewing between the Bamangwato and the Bakalanga since 1943. All foreign tribes, although welcomed, had to follow some of the rules of the Bamangwato. The quarrel first developed about ploughing. In those days the chief gave people permission to plough, but permission was first granted in Serowe, then to the outside villages. The Bakalanga, who lived in Mswazi village under their chief, John Mswazi, used to start ploughing as soon as the rainy season started. The reason for this was that they were never big cattle-owners like the Bamangwato and always lived off ploughing. They were warned three times not to break the custom and their reply was that they were chiefs in their own right, that they did not want to be ruled by the Bamangwato, nor did they want to pay tax directly to Chief Tshekedi — in future they'd pay tax directly to the British Government. Due to this attitude there was at first little sympathy felt for the Bakalanga. The order Chief Tshekedi gave our regiment was to arrest all the men and bring them back to Serowe for trial, failing which we were to confiscate their cattle and possessions.

On our arrival at Mswazi village, everything was turned upside down. The women and little children were frightened and ran off into the forest. As we pursued them to tell them that our mission was a peaceful one and we meant them no harm, we saw some pregnant women giving birth under the bushes in the hot sun. I saw this with my own eyes. Everything was messed up! This is against our custom.

It is shameful for a man to see a woman giving birth. We killed no one and the men resisted arrest. They said we could take all the things they had acquired in our country and they and their families left Bamangwato country for Rhodesia. We brought back their cattle and possessions and a sale was made of all the goods. This money was retained by Tshekedi and later it was all returned to the Bakalanga people by Seretse.

All my life I have worked for the tribe. That meant that my own home and cattle had no one to care for them and many of my cattle died. I became poor. Everybody made sacrifices for the community and we were all caught up in the same idea. Regiment work was regarded by the people as the custom of Chiefs Khama, Sekgoma II and Tshekedi and all the old people like myself liked it very much. I grew up under Chief Tshekedi and understood his ways. I am happy and yet not so happy with independence. New rules have been introduced which I don't understand. We built our own dams and our own boreholes — the central borehole in Serowe was paid for with our cattle and the water was free for a long time. Now we pay. Today, after all this hard work no rewards come to the people of Serowe. It costs us 5c a day to give one cow a drink of water. If a man has one hundred cows he pays R5.00 a day and that comes to R150.00 a month. How is he going to pay?

15
Regiment Labour for the Serowe Primary Schools

╔═══════════════════════════════════════╗

Lekoto Digate

Age: eighty-six
Occupation: retired cattleman

The funny thing about me is that I had a hand in building a number of the primary schools in Serowe but I never attended school myself. All my life I have herded cattle or stayed at home. When there was work to be done, I helped anywhere.

The first thing to understand about our *mephato* (age regiment system) was that it had always been the most organized part of our life. Long ago the regiments were our armies to defend the tribe and during times of war the chief would call forth the regiments. They could also be called forth to collect stray cattle in the bush, to plough the lands of the chief or to kill wild animals which threatened the village. From Khama's time the work of regiments began to change — more and more we started to build schools and roads and dams for watering cattle. But it was during Chief Tshekedi's time that the idea came to people. They began to see that the life of a regiment belonged to the tribe. At that time regiment work for the tribe was so well organized, something was going on nearly every day.

My age regiment is Matsapa and during Khama's time we were called forth to build what is now called Khama Memorial School. We moulded and baked our own bricks then and worked beside two white men who were bricklayers. A portion of the building which was incomplete when King Khama died was later completed by Chief Tshekedi. During Tshekedi's time, I was one who with another were especially appointed and ordered by the chief to climb to the top of Serowe Hill and blow a bugle to call the regiments to work. The order could be given at any time. Due to my work of blowing the bugle, I used to join in all the work that was being done. I helped in the building of three schools — Masokola, Simon Rathsosa and Central School. Central School had only to be enlarged by Chief Tshekedi's regiment, Maletamotse. A part of the building had been erected during King Khama's time.

I remember the men used to say: 'Our jobs are heavy, but the work is a pleasure. It is for the progress of the people.'

Under Chief Tshekedi, regiment work was always a free gift to the tribe.

16
The Establishment of Pilikwe Village by Tshekedi Khama

Today, Pilikwe village is almost a ruin. A few old men sit under the shady trees near the kgotla. The children who attend the Pilikwe Primary School play games among the deserted homesteads. It is a village of the very young and the very old, and it lacks that feeling of other villages where life is lived at full tilt and there is a day-long bustle and business. Pilikwe was founded in 1953, about six years before the death of Tshekedi. One can still see signs of the vigour of its beginnings — each homestead has a neat pit toilet in the yard (which is something Serowe lacks; there are excreta all around the pathways and dongas in Serowe) and each Pilikwe hut or rondavel is just that much smarter and more distinguished-looking.

The families who made the big move with Tshekedi all belonged to the upper crust of Serowe society and this detail alone is an indication of the quality of African society. When men, who are rich, secure and in key positions in a society, break up their homes and jobs overnight to face the unknown, homeless — their motivations bear examining. This historical story was the last of the migrations in the old African tradition — a tradition established over the centuries to avert bloodshed in a crisis and underlying the basic non-violent nature of African society as it was then. This gives the lie to white historians who, for their own ends, damned African people as savages. The story has many twists and turns. When hostilities broke out in the Bamangwato clan over the marriage of their future chief, Seretse, to an Englishwoman, the source was Tshekedi's opposition to the marriage. Men like Gabolebye Dinti

Marobele had little to gain when they moved away with Tshekedi. They did it for a man they valued.

It is perhaps worth remembering in this context that it was during the last years of his life, at Pilikwe, that Tshekedi, with the help of Guy Clutton-Brock, made a first attempt, far ahead of its time, at a communal farm in the shape of the Bamangwato Development Association. The project came to an end after Tshekedi's death, but it is an astonishing pointer to a modern development of the traditional concept of communal land under the chief.

*

Gabolebye Dinti Marobele

Age: sixty-nine

Occupation: retired teacher

I was born in Serowe in 1905 and I started my education in a primary school here, run by the London Missionary Society. At that time there were only two primary schools in Serowe and the other one was called the Serowe Public School and run by Chief Khama. Usually wealthy men sent their sons out of Serowe to continue their education in South Africa, and as my father was wealthy and could afford to pay for my education, I left after Standard Four and continued my education at Lovedale.

Tshekedi was at Lovedale at the same time and we used to take the train down together. I grew up with Tshekedi and we did everything together because my father was a headman, and the headmen were chief's councillors; so the sons of headmen were regarded with esteem and that was how I became acquainted with Tshekedi. We were only at Lovedale for one-and-a-half years. There was a strike about food in 1920 and we were expelled. We returned home and Chief Khama asked a Mr and Mrs Johnston to teach our group who had been expelled. That was for about three years, then just before Chief Khama died in 1923, most of us returned to Lovedale, but I went on to Healdtown College, while Tshekedi went on to Fort Hare College. A few years later I came back to Serowe as a teacher and found that Tshekedi had been appointed chief of the Bamangwato.

At that time there were few educated people to assist Tshekedi in tribal affairs. Of the number of young and educated men in the village, it was his habit to use our services as advisers, so he would often call me to assist him when important tribal issues had to be dealt with. I would leave school for certain periods and go down with Tshekedi to Mafeking and Cape Town. But when it concerned purely traditional affairs, he chose old men who had worked with Chief Khama as his advisers.

Then I resigned from teaching and was away for five years, until 1945, in the war. On my return to Serowe, I found a lot of work going on. The project to build Moeng College was in the offing and Tshekedi called his own age regiment, Maletamotse, to which I belong, to do the initial work of clearing the bush and moulding the bricks for the building. As soon as someone went to the top of the hill and called out the name of our regiment, I volunteered for this work. On my return from the bush, I took up the job of grain organizer. This scheme had been in existence for about ten years. It was a scheme whereby people ploughed, harvested and handed over the grain freely for storage in the tribal granaries. There were lands especially set aside and ploughed for this work. I used to travel all over Bamangwato country and collect the grain for storage. During drought years, the grain was resold to people at a price cheaper than the stores could sell. Today, when they talk about self-help and credit it only to independence, we older people really know that Tshekedi was the father of self-help.

Tshekedi was flushed with the success and response of the people to regiment labour. He had succeeded in constructing a number of primary schools in Serowe and just at this time was about to embark on a larger project of extending primary school construction in Bamangwato country as a whole. Certain areas in the northern part of the country had no school facilities at all. Just at this time too, news came through of Seretse's marriage in England, which we regarded as a traditionally illegal marriage. It was so unexpected that it had the effect of going off like a bomb. I can tell you how unexpected it was because a few days before the news came through I had heard Tshekedi giving a man some instructions about taming a horse which he intended to be a gift to Seretse. He explained that Seretse was a little nervous of such animals, therefore the horse should be tamed and the man should hurry as 'the chief will be coming home soon'. The news of the marriage almost made Tshekedi mad. It was the heirs and the Bamangwato chieftainship that he wanted to protect. He remarked to someone at that time, in great distress, that the children of such a marriage would marry away from the tribe, which is just what is happening today. I thought at first the young man was joking. I certainly did not believe it. I met Seretse at the Victory Day parade in London and he did not seem taken up with the English. He said to me: 'The English like to show you their nice side but they hide their poverty and slums.'

The first public mood of the people was to press for Seretse not to marry the Englishwoman. Since he was certain he wanted his wife, the mood of the people swayed towards securing their chief, in spite of the illegal marriage. It was then that Tshekedi's stand set the pot boiling. He would not accept the marriage under any circumstances. And that was the whole story. The people became just as adamant that Tshekedi was trying to steal the chieftainship from Seretse and I remember standing up in kgotla one day and trying to set the facts straight on this point, but I was shouted at from all sides. Seretse was married in 1948 and by June 1949 life became impossible for Tshekedi or anyone who supported him in Serowe. Tshekedi simply said then that he would go into voluntary exile. If we had stayed, there would have been bloodshed. So his first move was to the Bakwena Reserve and about two hundred of us removed ourselves with him. This had always been an African tradition. Whenever it was felt that tensions had built up, either an uncle or son would remove himself from the main body of the tribe and this has recurred so frequently and is so much a part of our history, that the stories are really endless. The point about Tshekedi was that it was the last time it could happen, so it was the last time we lived out our traditional history.

I was among those two hundred and what at first seemed a joke, turned our whole life upside down. My father had died, so I packed up with my wife, mother and family. Tshekedi bought four red trucks and the women and children were transported on them, while the men took wagons and their cattle on foot. Those of us who left had all been at the head of the tribal administration — senior treasurers, tax collectors, heads of tribal police and so forth — and we'd all been in a position to judge the quality of Tshekedi's character. It was not a question of loving power or position, which we all had. It was a question of moving off with a man we could not do without. It takes a man years to build his home, so you can see what it cost us. That is our history and that is the way our history always turned out. It broke our lives.

The Chief of Bakwena gave us a very remote area in which to live, Rametsana. No Bakwena would live there because it was infested with lions. The lions used to come right inside the village and kill our cattle — I was the first man to shoot a lion there! Rametsana hadn't a school

98

so the first thing we did was put up a school for our children. We were at Rametsana for three years. It wasn't really a permanent settlement; it was a temporary solution to hostilities and a way of resolving a dispute peacefully. We actually have a saying about a violent person: 'He is a Matebele!', indicating that a way of resolving a dispute by bloodshed is really only practised by the Matebele.

Finally, Tshekedi moved back to Bamangwato country and about forty-eight miles from Serowe established Pilikwe village. That is where I have my home now.

Our traditional system was not autocratic. It was very much like the British system. We too had our 'House of Lords' and 'House of Commons'. Our *Dikgosana*, the uncles or royal relatives of the chief, were our House of Lords and the House of Commons was the headmen or *Bakgosi*, all of whom were advisers to the chief. And this is what the older people regret losing. I prefer the older system. Independence is called democracy, but it is not as I know it. Before the chief could pass any law, it was first discussed with the above two parties, and then with the people. The government has now been removed too far away from the people.

17
The Zeerust Refugees

🌀🌀🌀🌀🌀🌀🌀🌀🌀🌀🌀🌀🌀🌀🌀🌀🌀🌀🌀🌀🌀🌀🌀

Galeboe Motswabangwe

Age: seventy-two

Occupation: housewife and farmer

Gopane village, eighteen miles outside the town of Zeerust in the Transvaal, South Africa, was up until the year 1957 a quiet, ordinary typical African village. A pattern of life had built up over the years — the older people clung to the traditional ways of living off their ploughing and sent their children to Johannesburg either for work or to acquire an education. In 1957, the South African Government introduced influx control or the compulsory carrying of the 'pass book' by African women. Influx control had long existed for African men and was the source of excruciating suffering. If a man walked out of his home without his 'pass', he simply disappeared for a stretch of six months or so. When he reappeared he would say that he had served a sentence on a prison farm for being without his 'pass' or reference book.

African women were later to tell a similar tale but then, in 1957, people still thought they could protest about laws imposed on them against their will. Once the bill enforcing influx control on African women had become law, the South African authorities chose Gopane village as the first area in the country where those hated 'pass books' were issued to women. A number of things happened at the same time.

The chief of the area, Abraham Moilwa, notified the government that the 'pass book' was not going to be accepted by the women. The children who had been sent to acquire an education in Johannesburg, abruptly returned, collected all the 'pass books' and burnt them. In retaliation, a large police force surrounded Gopane village and started shooting people.

Old Galeboe Motswabangwe led a column of women in a protest demonstration that day and saw three village men shot dead before her eyes; the wounded and dying were being carried away on stretchers. That broke the people and the protest against the 'pass'. She fled with her family and a group of her villagers to Botswana. Ahead of them raced Chief Abraham Moilwa straight to Tshekedi Khama at his village in Pilikwe to request protection for his people. In the shock of the moment he wanted to arrange the transfer of his whole tribe, the Bafurutshe, to Pilikwe, as he feared their extermination. Negotiations were still under way when Tshekedi died. Giving help and shelter to homeless refugees had been a pattern of Botswana life going back at least to the period of *Mfecane*, or destructive tribal wars, in the early nineteenth century when the Bamangwato began to emerge not as a small clan-based tribe but as a stable nation, absorbing the wandering refugees who had lost their homelands in the wars.

*

My tribe is the Bafurutshe. Bafurutshe and Batswana are both Setswana-speaking tribes and we are relatives in a way. Zeerust which is near my home village, Gopane, is only twelve miles from the Botswana border. I was born in Gopane village in 1902 and all my life I have been a housewife and helped my husband with the ploughing. I had four children, three of whom lived with me at Gopane and the eldest son went away to Johannesburg.

Gopane village is eighteen miles outside the town of Zeerust and it was always a quiet life we had. We used to grow big cabbages and watermelon and pumpkin and we lived off our ploughing. Trouble came to us in 1957 and the whole trouble was inspired by our children who had been educated in Johannesburg. That year the women were handed reference books by the Boers and our children came and collected the reference books. They said they didn't want their mothers to carry the 'pass' and they burnt them.

After this, we found Gopane village surrounded by the Boer police, with one Van Rooyen, at the head of them. We wanted to show the police that we did not like the 'pass' and I was one of those who led a group of women to where we could be seen by the police. We were not prepared to fight. Van Rooyen talked to us. He said we had given our reference books to our children and they had burnt them. We replied that our sons were not against men carrying 'the pass' but they were against their mothers carrying passes. Suddenly the police began shooting everybody. People were caught by bullets. They were dying. I saw three men dead in front of me. Others were being taken to hospital. Others were arrested and taken directly to jail.

When I saw all this with my own eyes, I became frightened and ran away. There was a small group of us, about twelve and we came directly to Bechuanaland. There was no immigration at that time and we went straight through to Lobatse. Our chief, Abraham Moilwa, was a few days ahead of us and he went directly to Chief Tshekedi. I don't know what negotiations Abraham had with Tshekedi but later he told me that he had wanted to recruit all his people to stay with Tshekedi. I did not know that Tshekedi had been helping everybody who was in trouble but I suspect he was a friendly chief.

When we ran away, we left everything behind us, our home and furniture. We had nothing. I put my youngest child on my back and we walked through the bush, hiding away from the police who were looking for us. Only when we arrived in Lobatse did we feel free. In Lobatse we were approached by the British High Commissioner and told that we would be given food, clothing and blankets. This help continued for eight months during the year 1958 and then we were told to settle in the villages.

There was a big desertion from Zeerust at that time. The Bafurutshe tribe was temporarily dispersed and all the people were waiting to come to Chief Tshekedi who had promised us protection. On the death of Tshekedi they lost hope and scattered themselves. Word came to us that after our desertion of Zeerust, a bad drought took hold of the area and the Boers could not plough. They had irrigation schemes there and planted wheat and oranges. They were no longer able to do so, so I don't see what the Boers gained.

My family and I came to Pilikwe village where our Chief Moilwa had been staying with Chief Tshekedi. We were allocated a piece of land for our house and a piece of land where we could plough. We then built our own house, got our own corn and started to plough.

18
The Traders

C C C C C C C C C C C C C C C C C C C C C C C C

Billy Woodford

Age: thirty-nine
Occupation: trader

> Commerce in the form of white traders under the 'protection' of the State, was an integral part of the national economy of the Bamangwato Reserve ... the white traders owed their presence in the reserve initially to the chief, a right for which Khama had struggled in his early reign, though eroded in principle by the colonial administration taking over the renewal of trading licences. White traders were still 'tribesmen' in many respects, with their futures and their families (increasingly with local-born wives, white or black) tied up with the fortunes of the Ngwato State.

Quentin Neil Parsons: 'Khama III, the Bamangwato and the British, with Special Reference to 1895-1923' (Ph.D. thesis)

My grandfather came out from England and was the architect of the British South Africa Railways. He helped to design the railway from Kimberley to Palapye. That was as far as he worked for the company, then he came to Serowe and opened a boarding-house and butchery.

Everyone wanted to come to Serowe in those days. It was like a paradise with running water. The Sepane River ran right through the village and there was a trickle left of it when I was a child. Our old house still stands in the central part of the village. I've never heard of grandmother and all the family, so I presume my grandfather had left her in England, but in about 1909 my dad joined grandfather and he worked for a Mr Johnson out at Moijabane and then later for Parr Brothers in Serowe. In 1914, when the war broke out, my dad joined the Rhodesian Army and he served in the forces till 1918 — he only got back to Serowe in 1919. During that period he had saved £300, with which he opened his own business. In the meantime my grandfather had also opened a shop in Serowe — so both had moved into the trading business. Dad married a Miss Vialls in 1921 and settled here.

Serowe was quite 'dry' until recently. Hard liquor was out! I'm afraid we Woodfords were always heavy drinkers — we used to drink ourselves to death! But if you gave the locals even a tot of liquor, you were right out of the country the next day, so all our drinking was private. It was Khama's law that all traders had to erect their buildings of corrugated iron and wood, so that in case — to put it vulgarly — you were 'kicked out', you could pick up your building and move. That's why you see so many old corrugated iron buildings around the village. But an actual expulsion of a trader only happened once here, in the case of an employee of the Bechuanaland Trading Association.

The kgotla was always the big place here and whatever you wanted had to come from there. In bygone days, trading rights were granted by Chief Khama, but in my time, it was granted by Tshekedi Khama. Traders have always been accused of exploiting the local people but this is not entirely true. However, people believe what they want to believe. There have been years and years of drought here and famine conditions. There have been years and years when foot-and-mouth disease was endemic and the dread of the country. It has almost been stamped out now, but during outbreaks, a quarantine would be declared and no cattle could be sold outside the country. It was during these times that traders gave credit and we had to wait years for people to pay. Often we lost a lot of money because people did not pay at all, so I don't see where exploitation comes in. I don't think anyone has made a million on trading, but you can make a fairly good living. I've never touched cattle myself or accepted them in exchange for goods, but some have made a lot of money with a combination of trading and cattle and it was particularly popular in the old days.

I only came into business in 1957. I was young then and under a fallacy that if I became a trader I'd make a million in no time. I'd been away from Serowe for a number of years for schooling in Johannesburg, after which I worked for the Anglo-American Company for five years. I had a lust to travel and needed money so I returned to Serowe and opened up my own business. Instead, I became completely tied down in the business and have hardly moved away. Trading has changed a lot over the years but for a long time, going back to the old days, we had a kind of an affiliation of all traders called the Chamber of Commerce. It was quite a large affiliation from a number of areas and each village had its own Chamber of Commerce, but when we had our annual and general meetings the chairman and secretary would always be Serowe people, because Serowe was the capital of the Bamangwato Reserve.

The purpose of this affiliation was to discuss business problems and complaints in the north of the country, which problems and complaints were then referred to the British Government or its representatives. Actual government price control on basic foodstuffs like mealie meal, flour, corn and tea only came in after the Second World War, but prior to that I've no idea what was going on. Serowe traders have always been a tightly-knit group. We are in direct competition with each other but there have been 'mutual understandings'. For instance, one trader alone would stock and sell all building materials and I would not touch it. I would refer all my customers to him. And we also had basic agreements about certain commodities, like tea. At some stage the price of tea kept on fluctuating, so we all agreed to sell it at R1.00 a pound.

You'd tend to hang together as a group, even though, as an individual, you had no particular feelings of hostility towards a new event. When Pat van Rensburg opened up the Swaneng Co-operative Store, it was an unknown quantity at that stage. We did not know what kind of effect it would have. His application had to go before the licensing board and all Serowe traders, as a group, opposed it. We were overruled by the licensing board.

I belong to Serowe because I was born here. I participate in all the funerals and weddings because we are a closely-knit community but otherwise I like my own company. After work hours I like the solitude of my own room.

Sonny Pretorius

Age: forty-four
Occupation: blacksmith

Sonny Pretorius belongs to that tradition of traders and settlers who first made their way into the country during Khama's time, and he gives a brilliant outline of the position of white traders in the society, weaving the thread from his father's time to his own time. They were storekeepers, hunters, makers and repairers of wagons and in their way, they deeply absorbed the attitudes of their adopted environment. Sonny Pretorius is more than most white traders — he is a member of the Bamangwato tribe and proudly showed me a certificate defining his status: I, Hendrick Carel Pretorius hereby submit that I am a tribesman, under Headman Topo Sebena of Sebena Ward, and shall uphold all obligations pertaining to this status. The Tribal Authority, M.M. Sekgoma has accepted my application.

*

Ah, I'm not a good Pretorius. Some people have said to me: 'You're an Afrikaner. Go and live in South Africa. You'll get whatever you like with a name like Pretorius.' It would kill me quickly there. I sometimes go down to Johannesburg for shopping. I get muddled by this people-can't-go-in-there. I sometimes leave before schedule. When I drive the car back over the border into Botswana, I stop, open the flask of tea and then just sit and see a dove fly by. Botswana is the only place that's normal, to my way of thinking.

I was born in Serowe, 3 February 1929. I am a tribesman. I belong to Sebena Ward. My age regiment is Mahetsakgang, same as Tshekedi's son, Leapeetswe. I first had citizenship, but I wanted more, to have responsibility, so I became a member of the tribe.

They call me Sani, a kind of Setswana pronunciation of my name. I was never away from Serowe for long, except for schooling. I went to Christian Brothers College, Kimberley but it was far removed from myself. I hated it. My dad was born in Botswana and my grandfather came here as a young man.

When my dad was fourteen, his father gave him a gun, a Scotch Cart and a horse and set him off to find his fortune. In those days if you had a gun, a cart and a horse, you were a man. That's all you required. My dad went up to Ngamiland and found a job in Maun. He ran a trading store. These trading stores became a tradition. Cattle were sold through the store and people bought goods through the store. When there were bad outbreaks of foot-and-mouth disease, there were about four or five, it would kill the cattle. The store-keeper would then keep people alive and in good years they would keep him alive. So they carried him and he carried them. He lived in deep bush then for months and months without tea, sugar or coffee. We were big coffee drinkers. Milk from cattle was the equivalent of a cup of tea, or drinks from wild fruits in season like Morule wine. Excellent stuff! Here is our recipe:

> Peel the skin of the Morule fruit. Put water on. Stand overnight. Strain it. Add sugar or honey to help ferment it. Allow to stand for three or four days and it starts knocking you.

Sometimes my dad had to close the store at midday and go out with a gun because a lion had killed his cattle. There wasn't anyone to say: 'You musn't close now.' Other men made a livelihood transporting goods across country by wagon. 'Transport riding' it was called and it became a big sideline, just after the death of Khama. And if you made it from here to Maun and back you were considered a good transport rider. What a trip! Only the hardiest, toughest spans of oxen could make this trip and back. It's even difficult these days by truck, there's too much sand. The traders then used gold coins for trading but by the time I was born we had already changed to paper money. We were using pounds, shillings and pence. Transport riding began to die out in the 1930s. That was when they began to get their first trucks. Change just seems to slip in. You never notice it happening.

For instance, in my dad's days cattle were about 50c a head. These days a beast is R80.00 a head and to set up in the cattle business you have to have at least R10,000 for sinking boreholes, buying and selling cattle and keeping modern licks and feed. In my grandfather's time people paid for blacksmith services with cattle. In bad years my father was paid with cattle. I, too, am paid with cattle when I repair wagons. This bartering was a tradition for us in the blacksmith business. It keeps the wheels going for everyone, so you accept it.

I started my apprenticeship as a blacksmith with my father about 1947. It's exactly the same as garage work. I do mostly repair work on wagons, three a week, shortening rims, mending spokes. It's just like a bearing falling off a car, except that we work with both iron and wood.

I think in every way like a Mongwato and like everyone else I have three homes; my home in Serowe, my lands and my cattle-post. My land is fifty acres and I usually plough mealies and beans. I use the crop for myself as rations for my cattle herders. Corn is out because of the birds. They come in millions and after two months your crop is finished. Oh, yes, you see nice green leaves, but no corn. I just gave up. I don't think Botswana, due to the climate, could ever be self-sufficient in food. It's a hard country. We depend on dry-land farming and you've got to trust to the weather. This year we didn't plough. We had *Mata-Ka-Debi* . . . He-Who-Comes-With-Bad-Things. He came in from the west — bad winds, storms, lightning and hail, then after that, no rain. We don't plough. The signs of a good year — we may get a storm but there's usually no violent winds and storms. After that we get steady rain. It comes in from the east, soft gentle rains that soak in — often for a month. That's how we've lived for years and years — hard times, good times.

Serowe hasn't changed much, except over the last thirteen years. I don't think there is any part of Africa where people make thatched huts like the Bamangwato. This is why Serowe appears to have stayed the same. Our thatch-making is a hundred per cent leak-proof and smooth like the thatch in England. It lasts for twenty years. It will not blow off. I have a hut at my cattle-post and I keep my bed and all my tools in there. I've seen some bad huts elsewhere. Going north, like Bulawayo, they build the thatch in steps. The storms rip the thatch off. Going south — those Barolong homes are made of mud, with zinc on the roof and huge boulders on top of the zinc — in the summer it's like a baked oven. Our thatch is cool in summer, warm in winter. We only get hell from lightning. If lightning strikes it, it's gone in minutes. Lots of homes are struck and people killed every year.

I hear some fellows died in the bush from eating poisoned fruit. I know all the fruits of the desert. I wouldn't die. A fellow also died just outside Serowe, from thirst. It's semi-desert just outside Serowe, but you still die of thirst. It's not the actual Kalahari. Like my dad I am a hunter. I've taken a couple of parties out into the bush and some professors after photographs about the Bushmen. I was about seventeen when the Bushmen taught me how to find water in the desert. I was out hunting with my gun-bearer. Suddenly it got cloudy and we couldn't get our bearings by the sun anymore. I lost the spoor of my truck and we began to walk round and round in circles and were lost. By the following day we were dying of thirst. Suddenly we encountered

a group of Bushmen. I knew a bit of their language so I said: *'Tsaa.'*
Tsaa is water in their language. I said: *'Gagone Tsaa.'*

In sign language one of the men told me to shoot a hartebeest. Next, he took the top of the Tswang grass to make a pile of it like a filter. Next, he cut open the gut. It was filled with rumen, a yellow-green liquid. Then he showed me how to extract water from the rumen by using the Tswang grass as a filter. It makes the clearest water and tastes good. We got a half a gallon of water from the rumen of that hartebeest. Of course it doesn't do to filter the rumen of pigs and goats. They eat all sorts of things. But the hartebeest and buck live on leaves. You find whole bits of leaves floating about in the rumen.

That's how I've lived. I am far removed from politics. It's an argument that has no ending. I steer clear of it.

19
Modern and Traditional Medical Services

The Hospital

Rosemary Pretorius

Age: forty-four
Occupation: retired midwife

Serowe has only one hospital. There is a little story attached to its founding. The Duke of Windsor, who was then the Prince of Wales, arrived in Serowe in 1925 to unveil a tombstone above the grave of Khama the Great. He was then offered the sum of £700 by Khama's son, Chief Sekgoma II, as food for his journey home. The prince declined the money and asked that the money be used towards the cost of erecting a hospital. He added a gift of £300 out of his own purse. The hospital was opened in 1929 by a British High Commissioner, the Earl of Athlone, and it was named the Sekgoma Memorial Hospital, after Chief Sekgoma II, who had died in 1925.

Before the hospital opened, very limited medical facilities were provided by the London Missionary Society, but illness is an ever-present reality in any society and for ages people in Serowe relied chiefly on their traditional 'Tswana doctor' for medical treatment. The Tswana doctor is basically a herbalist, but he is a dubious sort of person.

He tends to split the village in two; the older people firmly believe in his treatment, while the younger people prefer modern medicine, and for a long time a minor war has been waged between the hospital and the patients of the Tswana doctor. Rosemary Pretorius who was a midwife at the Sekgoma Memorial Hospital evokes this war with big-hearted generosity, giving a balanced account of the many calamities which threaten childbirth in Serowe.

*

I came to Serowe in July 1959 from Wiltshire, England. I had come over with a friend, Miss Bradley, who was to do general nursing. I did not know Botswana. It was rather interesting, the way we came. We arrived at Palapye and thought we'd arrived in Serowe, only to discover that we had another thirty-two miles to go. We were very thrilled on the way because we saw steenbuck and duiker — in those days there were a lot more wild animals on the road. The drive up through Serowe to the hospital didn't give us any idea of the size of the village — there were just these few huts on the side of the road. It wasn't until we bought a scooter and began exploring that we realized how big Serowe was.

I did not know Setswana, but the Batswana nurses at the hospital knew English, otherwise it might have been very difficult, working here. It never failed to amaze me, the way we were immediately welcomed — it shows the character of the Batswana people — they are very friendly.

In England, I'd done a lot of post-graduate training but after completing my training, I specialized in midwifery as I liked it best. I'd been taught all the complications of childbirth, but in England you very rarely encounter them. It was only when I worked here that I experienced the whole range of my learning, as a daily occurrence.

Our biggest problem was toxaemia pregnancies, which result in still-births. We can only watch for the symptoms if mothers regularly attend antenatal clinics. There is rising blood pressure, the kidneys become affected and this results in fits which endanger the life of both mother and baby.

Unfortunately, pregnant mothers lived at the lands and did not attend antenatal clinics. There is that tradition — everyone is told, right, you must go and plough — and in October, there is a great exodus from the village. With that exodus, it meant that it was too far for the mother to get into the antenatal clinic. Very often labour would start and mothers suffering from toxaemia pregnancies would be brought in in a serious condition. This was the cause of most still-births. We had an average of one a week caused by toxaemia pregnancies, which is far too high.

The next major problem was that we had a lot of women with deformed pelvises. We presumed it was caused by women carrying water and heavy weights on their heads. There is a marked curvature of the spine which throws the pelvis forward and this results in a long labour and difficult delivery. I usually had to pull the baby out with a forceps delivery. Fortunately, most women had very small babies; the average weight would be about six pounds, which is quite a bit smaller than the average for a European. Normally, that would be the weight of a premature baby but there was no need for us to treat them as such because they were very vigorous. We usually kept them in hospital for two weeks to make sure they were getting on satisfactorily. The length of stay in hospital for most mothers was three days.

Another complication we got a lot of was club feet due to deformity of the mother's pelvis. These we treated immediately by putting on little plasters to correct the deformity, but it was difficult to get the mothers to keep coming back for treatment. There was lack of confidence between the hospital and the patients. It was aggravated by the continual change of medical and nursing staff; by the long distances patients had to travel — there were no clinics in the outlying villages — and unfortunately, there were a large number of women who consulted their Tswana doctor. He is a herbalist cum witch-doctor. There are many herbs, I know, that the Tswana doctor uses which are most effective, but his treatment goes hand-in-hand with superstitions and these are most difficult to deal with.

For instance, we would have many women who would refuse antibiotics and injections needed after delivery, because their Tswana doctor had told them they must not have a needle put into their flesh or they would die. And we had, after operations, what appeared to be psychological deaths. There was no reason for the death apart from the fear the patient expressed before the operation that they wouldn't wake up again. This happened on quite a number of occasions. I couldn't sort out what this terrible fear was.

On several occasions I was accused of being the cause of still-births. Apparently, the custom was, after a first still-birth, for a witch-doctor to be called to cleanse the mother before she was touched by anyone. Immediately after the birth and afterbirth had been expelled, she had to be left and a witch-doctor called. In one particular case, I delivered

112

from a woman two still-born babies. On the second occasion, the girl's mother approached me. She was very angry.

'It's your fault my daughter has a second still-born baby,' she said. 'You did not allow the Tswana doctor to come into the hospital the last time, to do the cleansing.'

My first reaction was: 'Oh dear, what is this?'

I'd been completely unaware of this custom but the other nursing staff had already dealt with cases like this and told me not to worry. At first, I was continually astounded but this sort of conflict between the old ways and the new ways was very noticeable when I first arrived. We had a section, the antenatal clinic attached to the maternity hospital, where these things were explained to mothers. They very humorously nicknamed the antenatal clinic, 'Hygiene'. 'I'm going to "Hygiene" now,' they would say. Our first lesson for all pregnant mothers was hygiene. There we attempted to build up confidence in the hospital.

One thing we had no difficulty with was breast-feeding babies, which was something I'd always had a big battle with in England. In England, I think it was the kind of life people lived; the stress of modern life reduced the milk supply and then there would be fads that came in — that breast-feeding babies wasn't necessary — but we seldom had breast abscess or breast inflammation here, which was a common occurrence in England.

Despite the reluctance of many women to come to the hospital, we were kept extremely busy and the reason for this is the size of Serowe. We lacked beds and many facilities but we did good work. I am very pleased at the progress over the last few years; health centres and clinics have been established in many of the outlying districts. In retirement, I have directed my energies into the activities of the Botswana Red Cross Society, and I am its director in Serowe.

I had never enjoyed nursing as much as I have in Serowe because here all my learning was brought into use. It would never have happened in England.

Well, our contract was up at that time, after two years and my friend, Miss Bradley, and I were about to leave. So she said: 'Oh, let's have a holiday in the bush first.' So someone said: 'You want to see the bush? Then Sonny Pretorius is just the man to take you there.'

Well, after that holiday I married him. Serowe has become my home because my husband was born here and he has taught me all its ways.

The Establishment of Antenatal Clinics

Since Botswana obtained independence in 1966, medical services have expanded in Bamangwato country, or the Central District, as it has been known since independence. This expansion has mainly taken the form of establishing clinics in the outlying areas and it has helped to offset the high maternal and infant mortality experienced by Rosemary Pretorius in 1959.

Marit Kromberg

Age: thirty-four

Occupation: administrator of maternal and child health services and family planning services

' . . . ideas that have immense results are always simple.'

Leo Tolstoy: *War and Peace*

That Tolstoyan simplicity is always present in the work of Dr Marit Kromberg, and anyone with some experience of rural poverty cannot but appreciate some of the proposals she has made with regard to child nutrition. When village babies are weaned from the mother's breast, they are moved onto what often amounts to a 'death diet', a thin gruel-like porridge, cooked only with salt and water, which provides no nutrients for a growing body. When planning improvements in nutrition for children, Dr Kromberg worked on what was within reach of all mothers — basic mealie meal porridge — then taught that it was of great value if eaten in combination with something else, like spinach or milk or eggs. As she sees it, everything in society is potentially useful and from that point, people can be helped along by combining an understanding of their traditional customs and wisdom, with modern medical practices.

*

I come from Norway and I've been working in Botswana for seven years. I am in love with Botswana — the whole situation is right for me here; the climate, this stark, semi-desert vegetation, and my work.

I started off as a general practitioner at the Sekgoma Memorial Hospital. There were only two of us working as G.P.s and we were always very rushed. It was also frustrating work because it was only curative and there wasn't enough time to work on the preventive side. We had casualty after casualty come in and that filled up twenty-four hours of our time. So many of our emergencies should not have occurred at all. For example, I'd be woken up at midnight to save the life of a baby, almost dead from diarrhoea — that was the biggest problem we had at that time. I'd give intravenous drips, save its life and feel very heroic. Then, a month later I'd be woken up again — same baby, same condition, same treatment. The second and third time round, you begin to feel like a fool. You don't feel you are saving a human life any more. Every time the baby's brain has been deprived of oxygen there is some brain damage, and the baby's chances of living until the age of five are very slim. A terrible conflict arises within you about the pointlessness of what you are doing, and a sense of standing still. The real work of developing the health of the people should be done outside the hospital and here my whole time was taken up with emergencies. We were trapped in a vicious circle from which there was no release. What I wanted to do was get in on some health planning with the District Council and the central government.

By a series of very fortunate events, I was able to break out of this vicious circle. First, there was a demand by my women patients for family planning; and secondly, in 1968, a delegation came from the International Planned Parenthood Federation to see whether family planning was wanted in Botswana. We were able to show them that some of the women wanted it and also to demonstrate that some women feared to plan, due to the high death rate among babies — perhaps a third of any woman's babies, at that time, did not live to the age of five and this made it very difficult for a mother to plan. So the government entered into agreement with the I.P.P.F. to receive assistance to improve maternal and child health and then we could introduce family planning.

A form of traditional family planning was in existence. There is this belief that *serathane*, a condition of bewitchment, will afflict the child if the parents do not observe the customs which cause child spacing; either by physical separation or abstinence. In the old days polygamy also helped family planning because then a husband had an alternative wife. *Serathane* proves that people had an understanding of the effect of child spacing on the health of their children. In modern medical terms, we talk about the deprived child, the child suddenly taken off the breast or deprived of the mother's personal care and love through the advent of a new baby. Long ago, some ancient wise man must have noted the same thing and ordained that child spacing was the correct thing to do. A sound decision has, along the line, become mixed up with other traditional beliefs, so that our conclusions are the same, but not the way we explain things. The older people also lacked a convenient method to practise their customs. In this period, where one man has one wife and should be faithful to her, it imposes much greater discipline on him to space his children. But *serathane* provides the key and by referring mothers to this belief, which they all know about, we can build on it for motivation and now provide mothers with modern methods of family spacing.

The outcome of this visit by the I.P.P.F. was that they wanted a doctor to start a pilot project and as the women had already made me interested, I applied and got the job. I joined the Serowe Central District Clinic. The fight to reduce the high death rate in babies from diarrhoea was one of our major projects. Diarrhoea has three causes: it is a symptom of another disease like pneumonia, it is caused by malnutrition, it is caused by germs. Of the three possible causes, we concentrated on nutrition because if a baby is well fed, his ability to resist disease and all the hazards of life, is that much greater. The basic sort of diet of children is plain soft porridge, cooked in water. Mealie meal has eight amino-acids but they cannot be made to work unless they are in combination with something like spinach, beans, meat, milk or eggs. We told mothers that they had to give something extra with that plain porridge. We took from mothers a history of what foodstuffs they had available, and in the case of very poor mothers we would give them powdered milk to add to the diet. When mothers attended the clinic, they were given demonstrations in cooking beans, etc., which were fed to the children to give them a taste for porridge in combination with something else.

We also taught mothers home nursing — the moment a baby's stools are loose, she should give him water, water, water — boiled water with a little sugar. He will never develop the kind of shock the babies get by losing water until the blood almost stops because there is so little water in it. This home nursing improved the health of the children so dramatically that it made a profound impact on the parents. We called a meeting of the grandmothers and mothers, and an old grandmother stood up and said: 'We used to laugh at you and your boiled water but we have seen the babies live and are now convinced.' The hospital reported that babies no longer came in with severe diarrhoea.

A further bonus we earned was that the Central District Council ruled that all preventive child care services would be free — if the mother brought the child for weighing and immunization and followed our advice, it was the responsibility of the clinic if the child got ill. If she had not been attending clinic regularly and following our advice, she had to pay. We also immunized children against all the childhood diseases that we could get vaccinations for. With vaccinations we eradicated whooping cough from Serowe. Word spread about our work and now people demand to have such clinics in their areas.

I am interested in politics, but not at the power level or the party political level. My interest in African freedom and independence is concerned with removing the burden of ill-health, and sharing my knowledge about the causes of disease and death so that people may enjoy their freedom and strength, without having to suffer preventable disease or ill-timed pregnancy.

Traditional Medicine

Death and its Causes — Village Style

It was only in the year 1972 that the following government proclamation appeared on the Serowe Post Office notice-board:

> Government Notice No. 279 of 1972 which appears in Vol. X No. 50 of *Botswana Gazette* dated 6 October 1972 announces that Serowe has been appointed, gazetted and added to the first Schedule of the Births and Deaths Registration Act No. 48 of 1968 as an area where compulsory Registration of Births and Deaths should be effected as from the 25 September 1972 . . .

Prior to this date, dead bodies were not issued with a respectable death certificate, and Serowans tended to die extraordinary and somewhat disrespectful deaths in the arms of 'bad women'. Traditionally, sexual relationships are the major cause of death among men and

117

women, while children have either been bewitched or poisoned. Traditionally too, some other living being must take the blame, as people get their sicknesses and death from each other. The way everything gets mixed up in life, there's always some unfortunate accused around at the time of the victim's death, as will be seen in the case of the young wife who caused her husband to die from 'Malwetse sickness'. The situation is often complicated through the divinations of the Tswana doctor or the 'Faith Healing' priest, whom ordinary, illiterate villagers are in the habit of consulting.

Things change so slowly here that for ages people only had their own wealth of traditional wisdom to refer to, without official help or modern medicine, and the following stories bear testimony to this. They are also village secrets, so my informants are covered by pseudonyms.

*

'Before death certificates were issued in 1972, how were·people considered dead by the authorities?' I asked.

'Bontle.' Before 1972, people who died were taken and buried straight away by relatives. Small babies and children up to the age of two years were buried in a hut in the yard of their parents. People who died while ploughing at the lands or taking care of cattle at the cattle-posts, were buried there. If it was a man who had died, a report had to be made to kgotla because he was a tax-payer. It was noted against his name that he was dead and would no longer pay tax. There was no enquiry into the cause of death by the authorities but people knew in Tswana custom the causes of death. In Tswana custom, someone might be the cause of the death but no revenge was taken against them.

I have noticed the change because recently two children fell into a deep well at the lands and died. Their parents handed their bodies over to the police who took them to hospital for examination. This was never done before. Before, when children or grown people died in accidents a report was made to the chief, but the relatives alone were responsible for the burial of the body; the police were not involved. The chief never said we should take the body to the hospital for a certificate or examination. In cases of murder, a report was made to the chief first; the chief had then to decide what was to be done with the murderer. We were not allowed to bury the dead body of the murdered person until the chief had looked at it.

*

Boswagadi sickness

'Patricia': My brother died of *Boswagadi* sickness. In our custom, *Boswagadi* is a sickness which men and women take from each other. If a woman has a husband who passed away, she must not take a boyfriend or lover till after one year, because she can give her boyfriend *Boswagadi* sickness, which is very dangerous. During the one year a husband or wife has to stay alone they are given medicine by the Tswana doctor to clean their insides. This medicine is eaten with porridge.

Now, we all know that my brother went to work in a village where there are a lot of bad women and slept with a *Boswagadi*. When they brought him home, his whole body was swollen up, the skin was soft like water, then he died — you could press your thumb on the skin and it would go deep inside. That is what we call *Boswagadi* sickness. You see how dangerous it is!

Malwetse sickness

'Rose': We had a big case in our yard. My cousin was accused by the old people of killing her husband. They say she gave him *Malwetse* sickness. This sickness and death is caused by a woman who is two or three months pregnant by one man and who sleeps with another.

My cousin's husband was working in another village, away from the wife. While he was away, she took two boyfriends who made her pregnant. Then the husband returned to Serowe. He slept with the wife that night. The next morning he was very sick. The old people took him to the Tswana doctor. The Tswana doctor said:

'Causes of the sickness *Malwetse* is the wife. He cannot pass water. He cannot pass underneath altogether, all the passages are blocked up. She is pregnant by another man and this has blocked up the passages. She is the one who gives him this sickness.'

The old people looked at the wife. She was very afraid so she said: 'I am not pregnant.'

The Tswana doctor became angry and said: 'All right, this woman makes me a liar. Better take him to hospital. I can't help him.'

The old people took the husband and wife to the Water Church where they heal people with Blessed Water. There the priest said the same thing as the Tswana doctor:

'Causes of the sickness is the wife. She is pregnant.'

At this the wife became very afraid. She could not be a liar any more and said: 'It's true.'

The priest then thought he could help the man. He gave him Blessed Water. As he took one sip, the husband started to pass blood, through the nose, through the mouth and underneath too. His stomach was swollen up. They took him to hospital. The same day, he died. The old people say it was caused by *Malwetse*. They called all the relatives to have a case with the wife. She was crying like hell.

They all asked: 'Is it true you are pregnant?'

She said: 'Yes.'

They all asked: 'Is it your husband?'

She said: 'No.'

They said: 'You are crying like that, hey? You are the one who killed him.'

I was there to see it all but I doubt these stories. They are only for Batswana people. All Batswana people know them but I keep on wondering what white people do about these things. The old people say that *Malwetse* sickness is also caused by a man sleeping with a woman who has her monthly bleeding. We have a saying: *'Fa motho a bonye kdwedi ga robale le monna,'* which means: 'If you see the moon don't take a man to bed.' If a woman takes a man at that time, he may not die immediately but the matter will trouble him with pains and block all his passages up. The Tswana doctor understands this *Malwetse* sickness better than the hospital. Often when we take people to hospital suffering from *Malwetse*, they pass away. The Tswana doctor knows how to open all the passages that are blocked up.

Tshenyegelo sickness

'Lorato': *Tshenyegelo* sickness and death come from sleeping with a woman who has had a miscarriage, but a lot of men die from sleeping with bad women who sell their bodies. It is the habit of these women to take out babies with pills or wire or medicine. They don't worry about going to the Tswana doctor for cleansing and when they sell the body to men, those men die. I noticed this custom of cleansing after abortion when my cousin got married. His wife was three months pregnant and miscarried. The Tswana doctor gave her medicine and told her to stay for three months, not sleeping with the husband. They followed this rule and all was well. A person with *Tshenyegelo* sickness gets a pain in the back, the stomach swells up and they die.

The old people also say that *Thebamo*, which is tuberculosis, is caused by sleeping with a woman who has miscarried.

Sejeso — (*death through poisoning*)

'Violet': A lot of people have *Sejeso*. It is caused by someone who is jealous of you or your family and puts poison in your food. I have *Sejeso* in my stomach. There is something in my stomach which moves around and it has been doing this for many years. The *Sejeso* was put in my stomach when I was eight years old. My uncle gave a party at that time to name their first-born child and my cousin and I were invited. Someone with jealousy for the family gave us poisoned food. We both became ill. I vomited. My cousin who did not vomit, passed away. I was lucky I lived but the *Sejeso* still troubles me.

*

Death and its Causes — Village Style: A Doctor Comments

Mostly as a gesture to the young wife who was so painfully accused of causing the death of her husband through 'Malwetse sickness', I asked Dr Marit Kromberg to comment on the interviews I had had with village women:

Boswagadi sickness: The man had oedema, that is, retention of water in the tissues of the body. Some people have wondered whether it might be diabetes, but it could not, since diabetes tends to dry out the body. The oedema could have been caused by heart failure or kidney failure. A number of diseases, such as tuberculosis, rheumatic fever or syphilis could have caused the heart or kidneys to fail. My interpretation of the *Boswagadi* sickness in this case would not be valid for all cases of this sickness. I am sure *Boswagadi* is the name for the offence and not for the symptoms. The custom of observing *Boswagadi*, whereby the husband or the wife of the deceased abstain from sexual relationships with others for a year, would not only be respectful to the deceased but also a sensible precaution. The husband or wife of the surviving spouse could have died of an infectious disease. Before the time of scientific medicine, quarantine was often used to prevent the spread of disease.

Malwetse sickness: The history is decorated with details probably added for effect, not from observation, and this makes it difficult to analyse. Certainly promiscuity assists the spread of venereal diseases, and the custom would promote health. But in this story, if the man was 'blocked up' he must have been ill for quite some time, that is, before

121

he returned to his faithless wife. He probably collected his own diseases through his own unfaithfulness OR by living in poor socio-economic surroundings while he was away. The story doesn't say where *he'd* been! The dramatic death by bleeding from all passages is possibly sudden haemorrhage from ruptured varicose veins around the oesophagus, passed through the bowels and also vomited, or bleeding from a stomach ulcer, but it is seldom so dramatic or violent. If he bled from the lungs it would be tuberculosis, but he would hardly have passed blood underneath. If the person suffering from Malwetse sickness had been taken to hospital *in time*! he could probably have been cured. Again, I do not think *Malwetse* sickness describes a particular set of symptoms, but it is probably the name for the offence. It could even be the name for psychosomatic symptoms arising from guilt in a person who knew that taboos had been broken. In such cases I'm sure only the Tswana doctor could give absolution and restore health.

Tshenyegelo sickness: The prescribed abstinence is a useful custom to protect the woman who needs to recover after an abortion. European medicine prescribes six weeks' abstinence and six months without getting pregnant after an abortion. Our customs aim at protecting the woman. It is interesting to note how these Tswana concepts of sickness always assume that the male victim is completely innocent. The woman was blamed for breaking the custom and causing the sickness. One wonders whether this was due to male chauvinism or to a high incidence of infectious diseases.

The Tswana Doctor

Gabaipone Khunong

Age: thirty-six
Occupation: Tswana doctor

Traditional medicine is as old as the history of the tribe with an extensive range of treatments and a large and complicated medical vocabulary that is perfectly comprehended by all the poor and illiterate people of the village. I had some background understanding of daily village dramas, so I was both sympathetic and antagonistic to the work of the Tswana doctor and his rival, the 'Faith Healing' priest. I compiled the traditional medical section on my own and was greatly relieved, at a later stage, to have my work commented on by Dr Marit Kromberg who also expressed a sympathy for traditional medicine. The observations of the Tswana doctor are acute and accurate, but something goes wrong along the line — his treatments are almost entirely psychological.

'Our conclusions are the same, but not the way we explain things,' said Dr Kromberg.

For example, both Dr Kromberg and the Tswana doctor, Gabaipone Khunong, were presented with a high death rate in babies from diarrhoea. Severe forms of diarrhoea which killed babies were so built into the way of life people lived that Gabaipone Khunong looked very surprised when I asked him to explain in detail what he meant by the following:

'My treatment for the *pogwana* and *khujwana* is the same because the *pogwana* and *khujwana* are joined together in sickness. If something is wrong with the *pogwana*, something is wrong with *khujwana*. The *pogwana* is the top part of the baby's head (the fontanelle) and the *khujwana* is the navel. Sometimes the *pogwana* falls down ... '

With considerable alarm, I asked him how a baby's fontanelle could 'fall down'.

'But your baby's *pogwana* fell down too,' Gabaipone replied calmly. 'It happens to every child.'

I insisted that I had never seen this on my baby and we argued so much that in the end I was forced to refer to the baby book I had used for my son. About the baby's fontanelle, the book said, very mildly: 'The fontanelle is a good guide as to whether or not the baby needs water. If it forms a slight depression in the baby's scalp, offer the baby water as he may be thirsty ... ' It said nothing at all about severe forms of diarrhoea whereby the baby is so dehydrated due to loss of fluids from the body that his circulation stops and his fontanelle collapses. Gabaipone's treatment for this form of diarrhoea is to ' ... use herbs called *bohita* and *mamata*. I burn these herbs in a clay pot, mix them with oil from sour milk and rub it on the head and navel of the child.' His fee is high, 50c plus one goat, for a kind of treatment that may result in the death of the baby. The hospital fee for treatment is 40c.

Like any other medical practitioner, Gabaipone Khunong has a busy round. The day I met him, he was treating a patient for snake bite. He opened a tin and showed me the snake-bite ointment — a black, oily mixture like tar, with a pleasant smell of herbs. Then he had just nipped into the bush and dug up a bulb; *Maitsatsaula*, he called it. It looked exactly like an onion, except that it was absolutely tasteless. Around his neck he wore a necklace of porcupine quills, interspersed with small rings of grass bound with beads. It is the mark of his trade, the Tswana doctor, a source of power to him in his work, and it was made for him by an old doctor, Segola Sebonego, to whom he is apprenticed.

*

The way in which I became a Tswana doctor was like this: One day in 1958 I went to the village of Shoshong for a visit. Shoshong is far away from Serowe and on my way there I stopped off at a village and drank beer. I became dead drunk and during this time I took a girl to bed. This girl had just aborted a child and was suffering from *Tshenyegelo* sickness but she wanted my money and did not tell me about it. From this girl I became very sick. When I arrived at Shoshong, I was seriously ill. In the yard where I was visiting there was an old woman who was a Tswana doctor for small children and all the sicknesses men get from bad women. She looked at me, saw this *Tshenyegelo* sickness and straight away went into the bush for the right medicine to cure me. After three days' treatment, I was better. I began to think: 'This sort of knowledge can help people. I would like to be a Tswana doctor too.'

I asked the woman to teach me everything. She said: 'All right but pay me R3.00 for lessons.'

That is how I became a Tswana doctor. She taught me all her work. I cure the ailments of small children and the sicknesses obtained from bad women. I also learnt to cure snake bite and bring people good luck.

Small children have four main ailments — *mototwane*, *pogwana*, *lenyokwane* and *khujwana*. Before I begin any treatment, I charge 50c as down payment. At the end of the treatment I charge one goat. That's all I charge for children.

My other duties are to bring people good luck and ease their troubles. A very big trouble is caused by a husband or wife taking another lover. A man may have left his house for some time to work in another town. During this time he has taken another woman. When he returns to Serowe, he does not go near his home but straight to the home of relatives. If he goes near his home all the people in his household can die or his children become abnormal. He therefore tells everything to the relatives and they bring the man straight to me. Now, I take my medicine and go with the man to his home. This medicine is called *ntshu* and is made from the intestines of a porcupine and *serepe* herbs.

I rub *ntshu* on the underfeet of both the husband and wife and if they have children, the children as well — if I don't do this, they will all die. Then I crush some *serepe* herbs. Each day, three times a day, they put a pinch of herbs in their tea until the herbs are finished. The last treatment I give them is with *bohita* herbs which I burn in an old clay pot. As the smoke arises, I cover both husband and wife with a blanket so that they may breathe in the smoke. This cleansing ceremony is called *lerotse* and is very expensive. My payment is one cow.

The ceremony for good luck is called *lesego* and for this I use herbs called *leswalo* which I find in dongas where the rain-water collects. I dry it and crush it. Next I kill a pure white goat, take the dry fat inside its body and mix with the herbs, and into this I put the crushed pips of the red watermelon and mix all together. Then I give it to my customer. The mixture is dry. He takes a pinch of it and burns it; then he inhales the smoke; then he takes the ash and rubs it on his face; then he leaves home to find work or a girlfriend or anything he needs. *Lesego* is very expensive — a small tin costs R5.00.

Sometimes I do not charge people at all. Sometimes, at night, I dream that the *Badimo*, who are our ancestors, are talking to me. They say: 'Khunong, someone who is sick is coming to see you tomorrow. Treat him with this medicine which you will find in the bush.' This is a free gift from God and I cannot charge people at all that day.

I am not yet a big Tswana doctor because I haven't the bones which help the big Tswana doctor to see many things. When I have the bones, I will be able to see and understand many things. I only use herbs. The bones are with my old teacher, Segola Sebonego, who is passing on all his knowledge to me before he dies. One day he has promised to give me the bones too.

*

That's more or less the endless round of ordinary village life, accusation and counter-accusation and psychological fears. Men like Gabaipone Khunong and Segola Sebonego trade on these fears and earn large salaries — sometimes, so Gabaipone told me, as much as R15.00 a day. Both the Tswana doctors and the people they treat are absolutely convinced of the rightness of their ways. Both operate on knowledge of some other fearsome factor in the background — the *baloi* or witch-doctors. Apparently, they are almost a myth. They are said to concoct their medicines from human parts and at some dim time, they operated openly as terrible realities in the society. They are always

125

present — any unpleasant person is said to have dealings with the *baloi* and has the power to kill people or make them ill. Gabaipone and Segola act as endless antidotes to the troubles caused by the *baloi*. All I can say about the two men is that they have an innocent and absolute belief in their own worth in the society, but I cannot help wondering how many people they kill rather than cure.

20
The End of an Era

Grant Kgosi

Age: about sixty-seven
Occupation: tribal kgotla voluntary assessor and special observer

Grant Kgosi is really the end of a long era of tradition. For the young, who are a generation or two behind him, there is so much more to do other than sit under the shady trees of the village kgotla and split hairs for an endless length of time about human justice. Tribal administration may never be officially abolished in Botswana; it may just die a quiet and silent death as the kgotla becomes more and more deserted. It cannot be officially abolished as it was once a deeply sacred part of village life — it was government for the people, of the people, by the people — in its way. It provided an opportunity for every single member of the community to participate in the laws and government of the day. Since the administration of the past was one of verbal dialogue, reasoning and consultation, it meant that a man need not have school learning but just the normal quota of human intelligence he was born with, in order to feel that he was a power and influence in his society and that he could have his say.

In every way, Grant Kgosi, is a supreme example of the grandeur and charm of this old world on which the sun is setting. It was grand because it represented a vague, vast and indefinable law, yet every living man knew its rules. It had charm because it was infinitely kind and no matter what the issue, its rules ran close to the heart of the matter — men always left the kgotla at the end of the day with a clear understanding of the truth, even if justice had miscarried. Grant Kgosi is all this, with a little touch of originality all his own. He has a primary education and a passion for writing official letters to government departments. All his correspondence is about the affairs of people who are in trouble — from the need for compulsory branding of cattle to prevent stock theft, to the salaries of cooks in the primary school. To alarm them into doing something about it and to show them that he can be just as important as they, each letter is stamped with his own rubber stamp. It says simply: 'THE GOLDEN MERCY: A Happy Example.'

I queried the stamp, delighted.

'My stamp means just what it says,' he said. 'My mercy is golden. You will never find a man as kind as me. Also, I have been born with some faculties and I must use them. If I think a job needs doing, I do it.'

Whether anything is done about all his pleas on behalf of others, to higher authority, I do not know, but he certainly gets replies and showed me a number of letters with important letter-heads stating that they had taken due note of his correspondence of such and such a date. He learnt about the effectiveness of letters with a rubber stamp when he was involved in a workers' movement in Kimberley, South Africa — the Kimberley General Workers' Union — and their struggle for higher wages.

His letters are so memorable that I would like to include two of them in this chapter. One he addressed to me; the other to the chairman of the Botswana Commission of Enquiry into the Salaries of Local Government workers. They only need slight translation into another kind of version of English to make them coherent:

Head, Esq.,
    re: Collection of stories, past and present of the Bamangwato.
Dear Friend,
Greetings.
I, Grant Kgosi, have the honour to offer you myself for quite a length of time, as long as you may desire, no matter how many days, weeks and/or even months. I believe you want a collection based on the late King Khama the Great, as well as on the late statesman, Tshekedi Khama, who is the only founder of Moeng College, the

128

existing ministerial 'parliament' and who was the shelter and sword of all the other chiefs in the country, with their portions of land and their wealth as well.

Your affectionate servant,
G.M. Kgosi.

The Chairman & Members,
Botswana Commission of Enquiry into
Salaries & Conditions of Local Govt. Workers.
Sirs,
I, Grant Kgosi, have the honour to voice my views on the following:
There are some unprotected persons. They are the women cookers in the primary schools. I beg to plea on their behalf in order to detail their poor povertyness. They should be paid better wages than the present R3.00 or R4.00. They have also got children attending school, the same as any other person. But they slave for next to nothing at all.

Yours faithfully,
G.M. Kgosi (Special Observer)

*

I was born in Serowe. I am not sure when. With old people like me, we are never sure of our age. I attended the mission school at Serowe for about five years, then when I was about fifteen I left Serowe to work in Mafeking. I worked in the scullery of a hotel. From there I went to Cape Town where I had several jobs, in the scullery of the Queen's Hotel, then as a labourer in the Plaza Cinema, then as an orderly in the Langa Township Hospital. While I lived in Langa Township I attended night school for two years and completed my Standard Six. I left Serowe in 1930 and returned in 1952. I returned because I was unemployed. But in South Africa I learnt about the condition of African people. I worked for a time in Kimberley and we had a movement there — the Kimberley General Workers' Union. It was not really politics. It was about the wages paid to labourers. We were struggling to get better wages. There I came upon the idea that people should have correspondence with those in authority to mention their grievances.

I was an old man when I returned to Serowe, so I took up kgotla work. I contribute voluntary service to the kgotla for which I am not paid. Bamangwato people are used to this: we may serve freely, but we see how to manage for our daily life through the sale of goats and cattle. At kgotla I am one of the assessors who helps the chief to try a case which is brought before us.

This is the way the affairs of Serowe are run at kgotla: The chief's kgotla has always been the central part of our people's lives. It can only be abolished by government. Today, I see that the young people are leaving the village and going to the town to look for work, so the kgotla is mainly for old men. We old people don't want to overlook the customs of our forefathers, but the young, who are after money, will only attend kgotla if there is a great attraction, like the visit of the President of Botswana or very important meetings. The older people are concerned with sacrificing their lives — we stay at kgotla, assist without pay, intending not to let the motto of our chiefs totally disappear. The kgotla is the place where those who have brains, may learn much wisdom. Every day some problem of life is brought to kgotla and there we learn to look deeply into the heart of a bad man and the heart of a good man. We can always see what is good and what is bad.

I will tell you about a case that was never settled, then you will see how bad a man can be. This case was brought in from a small village outside Serowe. A man happened to take another man's wife, while the husband was away in South Africa. And all the years while the husband was away, the lover avoided pregnating the woman. There came the day when someone brought a message to the wife that the husband was arriving. The lover straight away made the woman pregnant because any child that arrived would be thought to be the child of the husband. Then something went wrong and the husband was delayed in South Africa for two months, then arrived home. The wife at that time was already two months pregnant and in a worried state of mind, she went secretly to the lover and reported that she had conceived. He told her to keep silent and have proper sexual connection with the husband. Now this is a very bitter thing in our custom! People knows that if a husband has connection with a wife who is pregnant by another man, he may die. We in kgotla therefore asked the husband:

'Did you connect properly with the wife?' And he said yes, but that he did not become ill or anything.

Trouble came when the woman gave birth. According to the time of the husband's arrival, the child was not a full nine months. The child arrived in seven months' time. But the baby was not premature, so the hospital said.

Now it was time for the lover to speak. He denied everything. He did not know the woman. The child was not his. The woman was a liar.

Witnesses were called forth who said they knew this was the woman's man-friend while the husband was away. He denied this too. Then the woman asked for special permission to mention something. She said she could prove that she knew the lover: the size of the man's organ was not the normal size. It was small. It was special. It was all of its own kind.

This kept everyone surprised for a time because the lover was very big built and here we are told that he had nothing there! The court straightaway called for a medical examination of the lover. This the chief refused to agree to out of delicate feeling for the man's sake. He wanted to settle the case. He said:

'The guilty party is the *nyatsi* (lover). I order him to pay the husband four head of cattle as damages.'

Can you believe it? The lover refused to pay and to this day the case has not been settled. It was sent on to the magistrate's court. A woman is never as bad as a man. I think the same Form that made woman, made me because I am so kind.

The chief's kgotla favours the important man. It is not easy in the chief's kgotla to get judgement against an important man. An ordinary man lost twenty goats and these goats were brought before the kgotla of a small village outside Serowe. When the owner came to claim the goats he was told that indeed, goats by his earmark had been entered into the books of the tribal kgotla police, but that the goats had now been removed to the tribal kgotla's cattle-post where the stray stock are kept. So he was ordered to go and have a look at them. So he went. But on arrival at the cattle-post, there were no goats there by his earmark. He sent a note to the chief of that village who replied: 'Oh, I have given those goats to an important man in Serowe.'

The owner was very surprised. He started to make a case to reclaim his goats and this case was heard in Serowe. When the case came up, the goats were also brought to kgotla. They were no longer twenty. They were nineteen. The important man stated that the twentieth one was lost. The court could see by the earmarks that the goats belonged to the ordinary man. The important man refused to hand the goats over. Both men had billy-goats in their kraal and they had to prove, so he said, whose billy-goats had fathered the present herd of goats. He knew what he was saying. He was the chief's relative. When the chief came to give judgement on the case, he said:

'According to the earmarks, the goats belong to the complainant. But no one should take the goats. Their blood has to be analysed by a specialist to see whose billy-goats fathered this herd.'

This dodge made the case long and complicated. Both parties had to employ solicitors. The case started in 1971. While it was in progress, the important man died. Up till this day, the goats wait for their case to be solved. They are at present at the home of the dead man and we hear that they have offspring that number one hundred. That is what kgotla does for the important man. He favours him.

My age regiment is Maletamotse, the regiment of Chief Tshekedi. During the dispute between Tshekedi and Seretse people were split apart. Some had to support Seretse. Some were Tshekedi's followers. It isn't in my heart to do that. I wanted both to live in peace. But in 1953 Tshekedi left Serowe with his followers and established a new village at Pilikwe and became headman of that village. I think Chief Tshekedi was not rewarded for his deeds. He gave us Moeng College and so many other things. It is the motto of the tribe that they should have a chief but it happened that the whole of Botswana fell under the protection of the Bamangwato chiefs like Khama and Tshekedi because they were so great.

We have no monuments in Serowe. At the top of Serowe Hill are the ruins left by one of our chiefs, [Kgari ruled possibly 1817-26]. Our grandfathers told us that Chief Kgari lived there a long time ago. The ruins are stone walls — the same stone walls can be seen on Swaneng Hill, but no one is sure who lived on Swaneng Hill. I would like to have a monument built on Serowe Hill to commemorate the ruins of Kgari. I would like a big clock up there with a loud bell.

I like independence. There's no use hating the changes we see. What is needed is arguments to see that the government is following the right line.

PART THREE

The Swaneng Project (1963 —)
Patrick van Rensburg

'What happiness it is to work from dawn to dusk for your family and yourself, to build a roof over their heads, to till the soil to feed them, to create your own world like Robinson Crusoe, in imitation of the creator of the universe.'

Boris Pasternak: *Dr Zhivago*

21
Patrick van Rensburg

He has an air of impersonal abstraction, the legend and the fame. The legend was his diplomatic position in South Africa and his abdication from that position on moral grounds. In later years the fame of his educational theories for developing countries spread far and wide. Part of the legend is almost inaccessible as it is personal; in his writings he seems to lack the gift of self-revelation, or perhaps the personal is relegated to some unimportant backroom of his life. Had he been a Tolstoy we might have had *My Confession* and *What I Believe*, in relation to that tortuous country, South Africa. What we do have is an obscurely written semi-autobiography, *Guilty Land*, which deals with and dismisses his life in South Africa, while his major writing talents (and they are prolific) have been deflected into the production of new educational theories, project work and rural development.

Writing of the earlier part of his life in *Guilty Land* he said: 'In February 1956 I was sent to Leopoldville as the South African Vice-Consul. I was twenty-four years old, and it was the first time I had been outside South·Africa. . . . I began to enjoy myself in Leopoldville. I had many friends now. I was young. . . . ' It was in the Belgian Congo that he began to examine his own background. In March 1957, too much happened all at once: the independence of Ghana and, at the same time, more oppressive legislation in South Africa like the Bantu Education Act. In May 1957 he quietly resigned his post. With that gesture, went the loss of his home country and the withdrawal of his passport in 1960. He fled as a refugee to England. A year in England convinced him that there were enough offers of financial help to enable him to initiate new ideas and projects.

In May 1962, he returned to Africa, to what was then the Bechuanaland Protectorate, and asked permission to build and start a secondary school, wherever it might be needed most. While awaiting the decision and a grant of land, he and his British wife taught in a primary school in Serowe. In September 1962, the Bamangwato Tribal Administration gave him a large plot of land and permission to go ahead with the school, and the Swaneng Project was born. Initially, it was a secondary school catering for students up to G.C.E. 'O' level (at that time there were only six secondary schools in Botswana with a total enrolment of six hundred students). Later the school became much more — a village development workshop embracing the whole community and its needs. The school is situated near Swaneng Hill, five miles outside Serowe, and its first teaching staff were volunteers from abroad.

Perhaps he already knew of the older generation who had helped build the primary schools of Serowe with voluntary labour in Tshekedi's time, and that their offspring would understand a call to service. In one of his early papers on the construction of Swaneng Hill School, we find the following:

Although it was late in the year, I wanted very much to open in February, 1963. It meant a desperate rush, but there were many things that made the effort seem not only worthwhile, but vital. I had become acutely aware of the crying need for more schools. I had been teaching boys and girls in a Standard Six class; in the keen competition for the insufficient places in secondary schools, some of them would have to go without a secondary education. I asked the boys to come and help clear the newly-granted site of thorn trees. It was the incredible response of sometimes twenty schoolboys walking miles to help, that drove me to do all in my power to get the school going in time to take such boys as these. . . .

And that was how the school was built, bit by bit over the years. Initially teachers would teach with only one wall of a classroom constructed, and at weekends both teachers and students would join forces to continue the building of the school. Finance came from aid money and further building was done through organized work camps. From the outset, van Rensburg knew that he didn't want to educate people merely in order to provide a new elite for white collar jobs:

The minimum that is required of us is that we should make each of our pupils an agent of progress. To do that, it might be enough simply to awaken in each a desire to better himself. But in fact, we would like to go further. We hope that when our pupils leave us, they will consciously recognize their role as agents for progress. Most of all, we would like them to feel under some compulsion to fight hunger, poverty and ignorance in their country. At Swaneng Hill School, we will certainly discourage any notion that education is just a ladder on which ambition climbs to privilege.

This early paper goes on to outline plans for the whole community: the intention of building the first co-operative store, worries about soil erosion and water shortages and how these may be combated, and hints that community development will be on the school's curriculum.

The project started at a time of change from Colonial rule to independence when there was a gap of uncertainty about the future. Often at such times one gets the impression that many minds suddenly come together to think out what that future should be. This period is often temporary and intense, with a sudden explosion of life and creative activity. A short while later, Swaneng Hill School became a joint enterprise of academic and technical training, known as 'the Brigades'. The Brigades took in primary school leavers. Any technical skill that could be taught became a Brigade, such as farming, building, carpentry, engineering, weaving and tanning. It is a system of earning while you learn. In a paper on the Brigades, Patrick van Rensburg wrote:

Most developing countries are familiar with the 'school-leaver problem'. Primary education can be provided more cheaply than secondary education and has expanded more quickly. The shortage of resources — for which both primary and secondary education compete — also explains the lack of job opportunities. Hence large numbers of young primary school graduates in search of work or further education or training. My own encounter with the problem came a year or two after I had founded Swaneng Hill School, in Serowe. We were trying to run this school with such limited funds as we had been able to raise; we had large numbers of people pressing us to admit them to our school. I had always been dimly aware that there was such a thing as the 'drop-out'. Now I was meeting some of the people characterized as a 'problem'. The experience of running a secondary school with limited resources gave me an insight into the problem and suggested a solution. We didn't have the resources to expand secondary education; nor did the country and its government. Perhaps we could provide vocational training if it could pay for itself. We called a meeting of young men and told them we could train them as builders if they were willing to work while training. About forty accepted and the Builders' Brigade was born.

In 1969, Pat van Rensburg once again came to a cross-roads. The school was becoming too elite. The buildings were complete, and it had lost that first rush of eager idealism. He resigned as principal of Swaneng Hill School in favour of more involvement with rural development and the poor and the ordinary 'have-nots'. Though I have written this short introduction to the Swaneng project around its founder, his actual personality has long been lost in its massive development. It engages many local people and foreign volunteers; the volunteers have tended to make Serowe one of the most international villages in Africa, and local people have tended to own the projects they work on. The Swaneng project means all sorts of things to all sorts of people but to me it means respect for man, no matter who he is.

22
The Volunteer Staff of Swaneng Hill School

The ideas and ideals of the volunteer staff I interviewed are representative of the ideals of young people from many nations and countries, who have taught for a time on a voluntary basis at Swaneng Hill Secondary School.

*

Jacklyn Cock

Age: thirty-one
Private volunteer

I was born in the Cape Province. My family have lived in the same part of South Africa for six generations, and at a standard of living I now can see as most analogous to that of a nineteenth-century Russian land-owning family. Our settlement in South Africa stretches back to the Honourable William Cock who, in 1820, brought out a group of British settlers, and remained. South Africans who live near the top of a caste society have perhaps an arrogance and pride they are unaware of, and when I first came to Serowe I suppose I had that kind of pride. Swaneng has been the making of me in many ways.

As a child, I had never been allowed into the kitchen. The closest my mother then came to domestic chores, was her once-a-week discussion with the cook on the household menus. At Swaneng Hill School I was expected to take my turn cooking large meals for about twenty people in the communal kitchen. We ate on bare tables, out of enamel plates and, new to me, food like goat meat and mealie meal. For the first few weeks, Swaneng was a traumatic experience for me. I suppose my main feeling was one of shame — for my domestic ineptitude, lack of physical skills and low stamina. The academic accolades behind me seemed totally meaningless in this new environment — I have two degrees from Rhodes University, and obtained double distinctions in both. I could have had an academic career in South Africa but decided against it because academic values seemed at best a luxury in the face of so much physical need. What were most needed here were practical skills in things like bricklaying and trench gardening. On Saturday mornings, after voluntary work, I used to come home blistered and weepy from tiredness.

Pat van Rensburg was always enormously gentle and encouraging. Like Pat, I wanted to stay somewhere in southern Africa which is, after all, an economic, cultural and social unit. During my stay in South Africa, I had felt myself becoming choked with anger, both against myself and the greed and indifference of those around me. Here I learned more gentleness and humility as volunteers from twelve nationalities united in the struggle against want and racism.

When I first came here in September 1969, Swaneng, under Pat's leadership, was a close, warm community. One of the key ideas at Swaneng at that time was that a privileged education brought responsibility. Pat was very anxious to discourage the idea that education is simply a ladder to affluence and status. He felt that the educated minority in a developing country like Botswana should be committed to rural development and social justice. They should not themselves form an alienated selfish elite, as has happened in so many countries which have followed the Colonial pattern. He drew up for secondary schools a new course which came to be termed 'Development Studies'. The aim of this course was to equip the students, not only with commitment, but also with the confidence, understanding and skill to tackle for themselves the development problems facing their country. I teach mainly Development Studies.

We start Development Studies in Form One by trying to give the students some of the skills to handle their own environment. We study local production and economic institutions like banks, how advertising manipulates us all, how our local Consumers' Co-operative Society Stores works, how prices in the local supermarket vary with supply and demand, and so on. In academic terms, the aim is to give students an understanding of the meaning and purpose of economic development, the situation and problems of the developing countries today, and the processes involved in economic growth and social change.

The Form Three students study the economy of Great Britain as the first country to industrialize; the U.S.S.R., Tanzania and Botswana — here especially we try to create a greater awareness of their own privileged position in society and to instil sympathy for the less privileged. Always we try to use active, question-centred teaching methods; the aim is to avoid getting the students simply to repeat what the teacher or some book has told them, and instead to think for themselves. This is helped by the fact that much of the course material is controversial — we cover topics such as planned or market economies, the workings of a one-party state, and so on. At all times we emphasize debate and encourage students to formulate their own opinions.

Pat has founded, so far, three secondary schools in Botswana. At all three of the schools, Development Studies is not treated as simply another academic subject. It is linked to a programme of manual work — unpopular with staff and students and not altogether successful — whereby the students make some contribution to the upkeep and development of their school and the local community. For example, I took a group of students down to the village development project, *Boiteko*, to dig trench beds for the garden.

On the wall of my classroom there is a quotation by Julius Nyerere:

> Some of our citizens will have large amounts of money spent on their education. . . . They are like the man who has been given all the food available in a starving village in order that he might have the strength to bring back supplies from a distant place. If he takes the food and does not bring help to his brothers he is a traitor. . . . Similarly if any of the young men and women who are given education by the people of this republic adopt attitudes of superiority or fail to use their knowledge to help the development of this country then they are betraying us.

How much gets home to the students? One of my Form Two students has this to say, in an essay he wrote for me:

> I think that 'Development Studies' should be taught in all secondary

schools in Botswana. This subject helps people to understand their society. Many students who have studied this subject do not think only of themselves. They do not think they are superior to other people who have less money. They can develop their country slowly and well. They do not want to improve only their own standard of living, but also that of others as well.

Peter Fewster

Age: forty-five
Private volunteer

It is only in the last thirteen years that people in England have become aware of the rest of the world and the condition of world poverty. Prior to that they did not care much about the colonies. Oxfam was only started in 1942 and for a long time people were more concerned with building up England after the Second World War. It was in 1671 that George Fox spoke against slavery and it was in 1807 that Britain officially abolished it. If it took one hundred and thirty years to make people aware of a social evil like slavery, then we shouldn't despair that it may take more than thirteen years to remove world poverty.

I was not a Christian until the age of thirty; I'd been an agnostic most of my life. A change just came over me at the age of thirty and I joined the Congregational Church. Three other men and I in the church formed a fellowship and desperately wanted to start something. We allocated responsibilities for ourselves — one would work on youth problems, another on world poverty, another on church unity and another on the problems of the aged. I concentrated on world poverty and started a local group of War on Want in my small town in north Wales.

Most of my initial work was for villages in India. We raised funds and worked out how much would be needed to set a small village on its feet but a lot of my work at that time was teaching people, making them aware of the many people who died of starvation. Once I became more familiar with poverty I suggested to War on Want that we'd like a project on another continent that was good but had no support. War on Want suggested Swaneng Hill School. We were sent a film of the school — that was in the year 1964 — and I made up a commentary and showed it about forty times to different groups. My wife, Diane, in turn showed it to about fifty women's groups. That was how we became involved. We both stepped right into that film — Swaneng became more real and Wales, more and more unreal. When we finally came here, we knew our way around just through that film — we recognized the drive up to the school, the common room and the turn-off to the wash houses. I felt I was called here by Christ. Diane did not feel this way, but still she came along with me. I think she's a braver personality than I. We fitted in nicely too. At that time Pat van Rensburg needed someone to teach science and lay bricks, which I could do, and he needed a secretary and someone to start a nursery school, which Diane could do.

We sold our house and furniture to pay for our passages to Africa. I was a formal, respectable man with a good job in industry. I was a deacon of the Church and secretary of the Council of Churches. When people heard that I was going to Africa, they thought I was mad.

It was those years of bad drought, 1965-66, when we arrived and half a million cattle died. It was October and it was very hot. My first job was dam building. I was pushing soil in a wheel-barrow up a hill all day and I honestly thought I would die. Staff and students were working to get the school dam finished; someone kept on saying it would rain at the end of October. It didn't. We worked right through January on the dam and got a little rain in February, oh, just a little puddle at the bottom of the dam.

I taught science and tried to plant trees. It was a hope that if we could plant trees, it would help to draw the rainfall. My work was mostly experimental. I kept a small seedling nursery of trees around my house. A lot of people bought trees off me and started growing them and I've tried most things. I am sure we could cover Botswana with mulberry trees — they would provide shade, fruit and they grow easily. I planted them from cuttings and I only watered them to start them off. Once they were big enough I didn't bother about them any more. If they are planted out in an open place, they have to be protected by thorn bushes until they are six feet high and can't be knocked over by the goats. Most of my work was damaged by goats. I planted out the whole of Swaneng with fruit trees, mostly the kind that would grow easily in a dry climate like this — figs, mulberries and pomegranates. I also planted shade trees, the Syringa, Erythrina and Eucalyptus Citriodora.

If we could shade the ground, it would stop the sun burning up the humus on the ground. In England, in the woods, you get a thick mat of leaves on the ground which holds the rain like a sponge and grass springs up between it. In an area of the school where I planted a lot

143

of figs and mulberries, we are beginning to get the same effect — it looks just like an English wood.

We have been happy here.

23
The Brigades

The Brigades are a broadly based, creative, educational programme, functioning under the slogan: Earn While You Learn; the basic principle behind the slogan being that all Brigades, while imparting a technical skill to their trainees, should cover their own educational costs. The founder and general co-ordinator of all Brigade activities is Pat van Rensburg. The first Brigade in Serowe, the Builders' Brigade, was launched in early 1965 in the grounds of Swaneng Hill Secondary School. The list of Brigades has grown and grown since then and reads something like this: printing, stonemasonry, carpentry, silk-screen printing, textile work, wool-spinning, dyeing and weaving, electrical work, farming and tanning . . . with more to come. As long as a skill can be taught and a few instructors found, a Brigade is formed almost overnight. Prior to 1965, the great majority of young people leaving primary school had little future. Young boys were recruited as labour for the South African mines; young girls were often domestic servants, and if employed locally, worked for abysmal wages of R2.00 or one pound a month.

The Brigades are possibly the most interesting aspect of all the work done so far on the Swaneng project. They are small factory units and slowly they build up a labour force, for as yet unrealized industrial development. They are both a delight and a pain. Brigade work is at present a delight; its character is creative, haphazard and as yet unconfined in any formal, technical institution. Brigade work is done anywhere — in rough tin sheds, under trees and in roughly made low-cost buildings. It is an endless delight to eat an egg or a chicken, or purchase a woollen blanket that silently bears the stamp: Made in Serowe.

A Farmers' Brigade trainee has a humorous cliché to explain the dark side of Brigade life: 'There's no gains, without pains' he likes to say. The farmers' unit was one of those Brigades whose training scheme came to an end due to a number of hurdles and problems too difficult to overcome. Most training courses in Brigades last for two to three years, and trainees on completion of their courses are forced to find employment in keeping with the skills they have acquired. This employment may be non-existent in the country — for example, a wool-weaver trying to find employment when there is no business sector to absorb his skill.

The other painful question surrounding Brigades is whether it is wise to create a skilled labour force that will eventually be exploited by the rich manufacturers, starting the cycle of poverty all over again at another level. The long-term goal, a buffer against this outcome, is that all future Brigade trainees will set themselves up in powerful, co-operative-type, producer units. It is then argued that the present instruction of Brigade trainees should be altered to orientate them towards that goal. This would suggest a need for government commitment to such a vast programme which is not yet forthcoming, and so the situation remains unresolved. A few of the Brigades, like the engineering workshop and the Printers' Brigade, rose quite rapidly to the position of business establishments and directly employed their trainees, but for many Brigade trainees the future is very uncertain. Each year more and more of the young who are unable to attend secondary school turn to a Brigade as an automatic alternative.

At first, most Brigades had their workshops in the grounds of Swaneng Hill Secondary School, and were administered by the Swaneng Hill School Board. Later it was found that the integration of the school and the Brigades was impractical. The latter needed a body which was able to deal effectively with business and technical matters. In 1972, the Serowe Brigades Development Trust was established. The trustees were people working in professions more related to Brigade activities.

All Brigade trainees are given eight hours of classroom instruction in their respective trades, four hours of which are devoted to academic subjects such as English, Mathematics and Development Studies. Practical work occupies forty hours a week outside the classroom. On joining a Brigade all trainees are handed a list of rules and regulations which govern their stay in a Brigade. The following is a sample:

1. *Self-Help.* Brigades are self-help organisations which provide technical training. 'Self-help' means that the Brigades must cover their costs through production.

2. *Fees.* Each trainee is required to pay a fee of R12.00 per year to help pay for his or her instruction.

3. *Benefits.* Trainees will receive technical training according to the Brigade to which they are attached. This training will be based on technical instruction and productive work, and the income thereby generated will be used in the first instance to cover the following costs: cost of materials, manager's salary, cost of replacing machinery, instructor's salary, cost of food. If and when the above costs have been covered by productivity, then further benefits may become available to trainees in the form of bonus, new overalls, better food ...

The Farmers' Brigade

Vernon Gibberd

Age: thirty-four
Occupation: manager of Serowe Farmers' Brigade

Each day, early in the morning, the milk cart of the Serowe Farmers' Brigade wends its way through the dusty tracks and pathways of Serowe. At a shout from the young lads and the clank of the milk cans, housewives on the route hurry outdoors with their jugs to collect their daily supply of fresh milk, eggs, cheese and vegetables. Although today, the milk cart is a familiar part of the Serowe scene, such farming produce was an undreamed-of wonder a few years ago. Apart from cattle-ranching and goat rearing, agriculture is almost the farmers' despair in this arid, drought-stricken land. Serowans will tell you that they have some kind of 'cradle know-how' to raise a few cattle and goats; it was their means of subsistence. It is almost impossible to raise crops, vegetables and milk in a succession of drought years, and drought is what one has to expect more than any other climatic condition.

Against this background, the Serowe Farmers' Brigade appears one of the wonders of the world for its achievements so far, and no other Brigade was presented with so many insurmountable problems. It started in 1967 as a very expensive training scheme financed by the Danish Government's External Aid Programme, but it could not solve the problems of settlement and employment of its first graduates. At present, the original scheme has benefited a few of the early graduates who are now employed on the farm, while a new experiment in farm training is being evolved. Vernon Gibberd, who has been its manager for some years and who also specializes in research into drought conditions, describes the successes and difficulties of this Brigade.

*

I have lived in Botswana for over ten years now. I arrived on a Friday, 13 September, 1963 and with all the droughts I've lived through, I should be superstitious of that date, but I'm not. The value of being here in farming for a long time is that you begin to see the changes in the veld, which the average foreign expert never notices because he's here so short a time. And the veld or natural grazing of Botswana is still surely one of its greatest natural resources. The copper and diamond mines do not really belong to the people. They belong to the mining companies and, to a certain extent, the government, but every Motswana citizen has the right to graze freely his livestock, and the recent introduction of beef price protections shows an even brighter future for beef than copper and diamonds.

I only joined the Serowe Farmers' Brigade in 1969 but prior to that I had done most of my research work at the Bamangwato Development Association farm started by Tshekedi Khama and Guy Clutton-Brock. It was eight years ago that I accidentally stumbled upon 'flood-spreading' as a means of intensive water conservation. We had two dieseline tanks at the farm and frequently a heavy duty lorry would turn up to fill the tanks. Its heavy tyres made four deep ruts near the tank and one winter morning I noticed a thick growth of green grass in all the ruts. I stopped and thought: 'Now why would grass be growing *and green* in winter?' I stood for a time studying the area and later worked out the 'flood-spreading' method of cultivation. With this method, you have a narrow strip of cultivated land, on the contour, with a bare strip of land above it. The bare, or uncultivated, strip acts as a watershed for collecting all the rain-water into the cultivated strip.

My research has mainly been on water and irrigation. When I first arrived at the Bamangwato Development Association farm, I spent the first year using water out of drums. This water was brought three miles by ox wagon, from a well, and ever since then I have never been able to use water freely. I introduced the *hafir*— research on it had originally been done in the Sudan. A *hafir* is simply a hole in the ground collecting run-off rain-water. You store water in it by lining the *hafir* with polythene plastic. I was able to grow vegetables at the farm with water drawn from the *hafirs* by *shadouf* or hand-pump. Building a *hafir* is hard work, therefore the water must be used very carefully. I devised a system of trickle irrigation, using cheap polythene with holes in it, fed from a low-pressure supply — an upturned drum on a heap of earth. This allows a fixed and known amount of water to run gently on to a fixed and known area, at a fixed and known frequency. Therefore you use *exactly* what the crop needs, without buying any expensive technology. The *hafir* attracted attention. A few were built at primary schools and two by community development courses, but people's initial enthusiasm was killed by sheer lack of government support for a *hafir*-construction programme.

There isn't much government support for our work. I was once asked to present a paper on *hafirs* at a meeting of the government's prestigious 'Natural Resources Technical Committee'. The only other agenda item came first and I was put into the remaining ten minutes of the meeting. My paper received no support — only ill- or un-informed criticism. After a while, light dawned on me. Every single person in the room lived in a grand, type one, government house, with an unlimited supply of subsidized pure water. And I thought: 'Put them all at the lands and let them walk three miles for every drop and they might be ready to support a *hafir* programme.'

There are many other innovations we have introduced which the trainees will tell you about. Our Farmers' Brigade Training scheme has not really come to an end. Brigade-type training has already become a tradition in Serowe — large numbers of trainees are selected from primary school leavers throughout the country and form the bulk of the labour force. The Farmers' Brigade is in a transitional stage. We are experimenting with a new training–settlement programme in a village a few miles outside Serowe. What we do now is take the training and farm development programme to a village and help that village start and run its own farmers' Brigade. This programme is loosely tied up with other training groups so that it forms a whole village development project. The reasons for our change from the traditional Brigade training programme, were that we could not provide employment for our graduates and all Farmers' Brigade graduates wanted employment. The Farmers' Brigade course was originally designed to lead to a co-operative, productive settlement farm but no government help was forthcoming to establish the scheme. The original training scheme was very complex and nearly impossible to manage.

Today, the Serowe Farmers' Brigade has mainly become an employment concern, with a paid staff. We have employed our former trainees. Their work is of a high standard. I'd like to think that the whole thing has been worthwhile, even if it just proves to those highly paid civil servants in Gaborone that our primary school leavers can produce stuff that is as good or better than what they like to buy from South Africa and Rhodesia in their jazzy supermarkets.

Phenyo Nthobatsang

Age: twenty-five
Occupation: gardener

I was among the first group of trainees who joined the Serowe Farmers' Brigade, and our training period then was three years. The training scheme looked very successful in the beginning. There were forty of us. Just as we were about to complete the course, most of the trainees resigned and fourteen of us completed the course. There were always very mixed feelings about the course. When we first started, we were given a bonus of R1.00 a month out of the profit of the total farm sales. The trainees felt this bonus was very little. That was one complaint. We felt that the farm work was quite hard. The second complaint was employment. Would we have employment once we completed the course? It was proposed by the management that we settle into a farming co-operative to solve the employment problem. Most of the trainees were not in favour of a co-operative because trainees knew that farming is very difficult here and they feared it would be a long time before they reaped financial rewards from this experiment.

But a group of eight of us, of which I was one, were prepared to try out co-operative farming. Six trainees remained at the farm as instructors of the second intake of trainees. Our group went to Selebi-Phikwe to start our co-operative settlement. We intended catering for the new copper-mining town. We did land clearing, built our own mud huts and made a *hafir*. We were also given waste water from the mines and poured it into our *hafir*. It turned out to be insufficient for our vegetable garden. After two months, we also had chickens. We tried to sell both vegetables and eggs to the township but our production was very low. After ten months, the co-operative project broke down and we were forced to abandon it. The Serowe Farmers' Brigade had been keeping us going with funds and we had a basic salary of R20.00, R10.00 of which we invested in the co-operative farm. This was a sore point for the settlers — they did not like to invest that R10.00 and kept on complaining, but what really made the experiment collapse was lack of water.

The group of eight returned to Serowe. Five of us were employed on the farm and the others dispersed in various directions. Some of us had financial and other problems at home — the brigades attracted a lot of trainees who were very poor, that's why there was always a complaint about money. In my own case there were too many children at home and my parents couldn't afford to give us all a secondary education, so I decided to make a sacrifice for my younger brothers and took up Brigade work. It wasn't a hard sacrifice for me because I'd always wanted to be a farmer.

In the original training course, I used to rotate from one project to another. I spent six months each in the chicken house, with the dairy and dairy cows, the cattle ranch and gardens. I did not do much tractor work on the lands. I sorted out my training and decided to specialize in gardening. The whole idea of having a vegetable garden in Serowe is a completely new thing and the main reason we succeed in growing vegetables here is because of the new methods we use like the deep-trench bed, which helps us to get control of the soil because we continually manure it and have a depth of two feet of loose, cultivated soil with which to work. Another thing that aids our vegetable production is that we sow our seed in plastic bags which contain a six-inch mixture of soil, manure and river-sand for drainage. Most people usually put their seed down in seed beds and, on transplanting, the roots are always damaged. They can't recover because the rate of evaporation is too high in our dry climate. This discourages people very much. But with our method of transplanting from plastic bags — a plastic bag is easy to tear or cut — we do not disturb the roots. We have three large vegetable gardens here and supply Serowe each day with fresh vegetables. It's like a miracle. All our people ever had before was wild spinach from the bush, and from their ploughing, young bean leaves, and in very good rainy seasons, pumpkin and green mealies.

I'd like to be a vegetable farmer on my own one day. I've learnt how to calculate how much you will earn by how much you put into the soil. I also know how to care for the land and how to overcome some of the difficulties of growing things here.

I like independence which has come to my country, but it does not immediately help the very poor people. At present it helps the rich.

Tlhagiso Mpusang

Age: twenty-nine

Occupation: assistant manager of Serowe Farmers' Brigade

In our custom, all young boys herd cattle and help their parents plough the land during the rainy season. We herded cattle and ploughed the land in the traditional way. I have been on the Serowe Farmers' Brigade farm for seven years now and there is such a big difference between the experience of my childhood and all the work I have done here — here the work is more profitable and lighter.

I like cattle because I've cared for them all my life and at the farm I've mainly specialized in the care of livestock at our cattle ranch and at the dairy house, but I've also done a lot of tractor work on the lands.

It is easy now, once I have so much knowledge, to look back on our traditional way of rearing cattle and ploughing the land and be critical of all the errors we made. At that time I was only aware that our suffering was great and the work very difficult. My day at my father's cattle-post began at sunrise. We would let the cattle out of the kraal and go with them into the bush. They would graze and be brought back to the kraal at midday to be milked. The calves had in the meanwhile been kraaled until midday but we competed with them for milk from their mothers. Our parents forced us, while at the cattle-post, to live almost entirely on a diet of milk — they would never send us rations like mealie meal — so it meant that the young calves did not get enough milk from their mothers. Even when the calves were older, we still kraaled them until midday, then let them out for grazing. They never had a long enough grazing period during the day and all this wrong treatment affected their growth. After the midday milking, the cows would be driven out to graze again, then brought back at evening, milked and kraaled. Watering the cattle was a whole day's work. The distance between a cattle-post like ours and the water points was so great that we could only water our cattle every second day. So, we were either grazing them full-time or watering them full-time but never both on the same day. The result was that on grazing days, the cattle would just lie under the trees and not graze because they were too thirsty. When you know all this, you appreciate methods that lighten the burden of cattle rearing.

At the farm's cattle ranch, we are the pioneers of a new system of cattle grazing — short rotation grazing. Not even the government agricultural departments use short rotation grazing. We have 700 cattle on our ranch and they are enclosed within fenced grazing camps and water is reticulated to all the camps. The camps are divided into small paddocks and about 30 cows are kept in one paddock, the size of an acre of land, for three days only. Then they are moved on to the next paddock. The cattle have supplementary feed of bonemeal and salt licks. Short rotation grazing is very effective and even during drought years, we always have grass within the paddocks and we never have to feed the ranch cattle on concentrates or anything as we do with the dairy cows. The ranch cattle are for beef production only.

The dairy herd at the farm here also graze within paddocks on the short rotation grazing system, but during the dry season their diet is of a higher quality than the ranch cattle. They are fed a high protein food concentrate and mineral salts to maintain their health and improve the quality of the milk. They are also fed silage and molasses to stimulate milk production. When we have rains, the cows are taken off concentrate and mostly graze on fresh grass because then they get enough protein from green grass and milk production is higher. There is a very important point I'd like to make about the young calves which we were not aware of when I was young. When cows gave birth to calves, we did not know about the *colostrum* or first milk of the cow. We used to milk it out of the cows, but here we've learnt that the *colostrum* is absolutely necessary for the young calf. It is full of antibodies which will protect the young calf from various diseases — that's why we allow the calf to suckle from its mother for four days; after which it is taken away and bucket-fed on whole cow's milk for three months; then skimmed milk for two months.

Each rainy season, when I was young, I would take six oxen from my parent's cattle-post to their lands for the ploughing time. We harnessed the six oxen on to a single-furrow hand plough. The seed was first broadcast on the land and then ploughed in. It sounds as though we got things going right away, but actually the oxen were always in a poor condition after the dry season and we could never make use of the early rains. We always had to wait for one to two months for the oxen to graze on fresh greens and gain weight, before they were fit enough to pull the plough. Also, over the last few years, winter ploughing has been widely advertised by the Department of Agriculture as being absolutely necessary for our dry conditions — for ploughing in crop residues for soil humus, for retaining the moisture of the rainy season in the soil, for the destruction of the larvae of insects which have been breeding over the summer — but most of our parents who use the hand plough and oxen cannot do winter ploughing because there is never any water at the lands at that time for the oxen to drink. Only tractor ploughing can solve all these problems.

We are so well equipped here with a tractor and seed planter that it seems easy enough to think along the lines of our own learning and to say that the hand plough ought to be done away with, as that five-inch scratching of the surface of the soil each year is a source of soil erosion. But how many people can afford a tractor which turns the soil deeply one foot down, so that the rain sinks in deeply instead of rushing over the land?

I have always had a love of farming and when the Serowe Farmers' Brigade came into existence I joined because it promised to teach us improved methods of farming.

The Tannery Brigade

Gaboutlwelwe Kgasa

Age: sixty-eight
Occupation: tanner, organizer of Serowe Tannery Brigade

The tannery has a terrible stench, so terrible it nauseates one. I remarked on this to Gaboutlwelwe Kgasa and he sniffed appreciatively and said: 'Ah, that is a good smell we have today. It shows that the leather is going to turn out the right way. When it's right, I can smell. When it's wrong, I can smell.'

Animal skins, mostly goat skins, hang from a rafter and about ten trainees busy themselves at different chores. The older trainees do leather work with lacquer applications and live among nice smells; the junior trainees work with stench; they handle the wet skins, and process them into leather. There are ten concrete troughs in the tannery and two marked *Soaking* and *Lime*, and it is from these troughs that the appalling smells emanate as the leather goes through various phases of fermentation.

I like my name, Gaboutlwelwe. It was given to me by my father who was a priest and it means: If someone is hurt you can't feel his pain.

Tanning is my profession and Pat van Rensburg was looking for someone to teach people tanning and leatherwork in Serowe. I started the tannery brigade in 1970. I had my education at Tiger Kloof College, the missionary college of W.C. Willoughby. It taught technical skills as well as academic training. By day we did technical training — I did tannery for four years — and in the evenings, we attended classes. I passed my tanning and won a certificate but failed my academic studies. On the recommendation of the principal of Tiger Kloof College, I went for further training in modern tanning methods at Rhodes University in Grahamstown, South Africa — one could do that in those days; Bantu education had not yet been thought of. Then I started work in my home village, Kanye, as an instructor in tanning for a school programme for nine years.

The Second World War broke out and I went to the war. My company were the gunners and I was a Sergeant-Major. We were fighting in the central Mediterranean with Montgomery's Eighth Army. I enjoyed fighting in the war — I don't know why the memory of it gives me so much pleasure — I think there were so many challenges — fear of this and fear of that. It made me very military-minded. I know my rights and am not afraid to talk of them.

All my life, I've either been working with animals or their skins. The abattoir opened in Lobatse in 1956 and I found work as a cattle agent, recruiting cattle for sale to the abattoir. My employers were the Kanye tribal administration. I handled 700 cattle per day with a flow of tremendous amounts of money. My salary was R30.00 a month. It was a lot of money in those days when the cost of living was low. I resigned from this work in 1969 due to an accident — I was driving 416 head of cattle to the abattoir, one died and I was taking it back to the village when my truck collided with a car. I had to appear before my employers, the tribal committee, who ordered that as I had had the accident while on duty, they as my employers, should pay the fine. They paid and their books were sent on to the District Commissioner, who

155

was a white man, for auditing. He noted this payment of a fine and made a new ruling — he called me to his office and ordered that I should pay the fine. I refused to do so and referred him back to my employers, the tribal committee. Silently, the District Commissioner arranged for my arrest and I was thrown in jail for three days. He really did that, I think, because I was involved in politics which did not please him. I wonder what kind of independence we have. The independence of Botswana makes me feel uneasy. I cannot see the future clearly and fear that a muddle will soon take place. When I came out of jail I thought I ought to resign from that job. I was out of work for a year in 1969, then joined the Tannery Brigade.

Initially, to start off the work, we borrowed R200 from Swaneng Hill School which we paid back when Oxfam sent a grant of R5,000. This grant was used for our building and equipment. It has to be paid back, with interest. We received an additional donation from the Danish Government of R4,000. On the average I take in ten to fifteen new trainees every year. We concentrate mainly on tanning for the production of leather. We buy our skins from local people and this supplies us with the bulk of our raw materials so that we don't need to order leather for our work from South Africa. Each new trainee works a year and a half in the tannery — we do this for future job creation — cattle are Botswana's major industry and the government is keen on the production of hides and skins locally and with their background in tanning some of my trainees have already found employment with government. The total training period is three years. A further year and a half is spent on leathercraft and a year on acquiring technique.

We are a part of rural development and the principle is that our resources should be taken from our environment — that's why we buy our raw materials, mostly goat skins, locally. In tanning, instead of wattle bark, we use a local root called *Mosetsane*. Instead of bran and boric acid, we use beer waste to de-lime or draw the excess of lime from the skin. Instead of a glazing machine, we glaze the leather with an ordinary cold drink bottle. And some of our natural resources, like soda ash, which we need for fur production, have just been discovered at the Makarikari pan — the uses of soda ash are very wide in the tanning industry. All seems to be going well like that, you get everything worked out within your means, you strain to cover costs, to pay back grants, when something happens to turn everything upside down. A white consultant was appointed to aid all the brigades in marketing problems. He did not think he had to consult me. He went straight to Johannesburg and bought a whole lot of expensive machinery which we don't need at present. He only sent the bills and material to me. I have been most unhappy about this.

The range of goods we produce are handbags, sandals, surgical shoes, mocassins and veld boots. Our main market is among the local people who like our sandals. And we have a co-operative marketing shop, Botswanacraft, which absorbs a lot of our goods. We cover our costs all right.

Gabaipone Khunong

Age: thirty-six

Occupation: trainee tanner

I was born in Serowe and only attended primary school up to Standard Two. Then, for many years I lived at the cattle-post with my father and while there, my father taught me to tan skins in the traditional way. I know all the old methods of tanning and used to produce blankets, mats and trousers for men from steenbuck. I earned my living this way before I joined the Tannery Brigade. The reason I joined the Brigade was that I was curious about the work they were doing and I wanted to improve my skill as a tanner. There is a big difference between the traditional way of tanning skins and the modern way I am learning now.

I think the modern way of tanning skins is much quicker than the traditional way. If I prepare a wet goat skin in the tannery, it is ready almost immediately for use; the traditional way takes about one month. Also the quantity of skins I can prepare in one day is much greater; if I could prepare ten skins a day, when I am self-employed, I would be free to get on with other work. I also notice that the hair on the animal skins is removed with lime. In the traditional way, it is very difficult to remove the hair. We only had a tool, a *petwane* — it looks like a hoe; it was a piece of iron we used to scrape the hairs off if we wanted a smooth skin, but it wasn't possible to remove all the hairs, that is why all Tswana mats and blankets retain the animal hair just as it looked when the animal was alive.

I am still working in the tanning section of the Brigade and have not yet moved on to leatherwork. I am very impressed with all the new things I have learnt here. I am interested to learn but unsure just now if I will be able to purchase all the new materials to set up my own business as a tanner because it is too costly. The traditional way of

157

tanning is our custom; that I cannot forget. But I do not mind learning new things too.

The Builders' Brigade

Elija Makgoeng

Age: twenty-eight

Occupation: manager of Serowe Builders' Brigade

The Brigade movement is slowly becoming a national institution; Brigades of all kinds have been established in villages throughout the country. But in 1965, for about a year, forty trainees of the Serowe Builders' Brigade had to pioneer the new concept of all that Brigades were to mean, alone. Of the forty young men who stepped forward for the experiment, twenty dropped out mid-way during the course; twenty completed the course and at the end of it took a government trade test which equipped them with a new profession.

Brigades as a whole have enormous problems, the most difficult one being job creation. It seemed a happy accident then that building was chosen for the first demonstration Brigade. It automatically created jobs for its graduates who were quickly absorbed into public and private business sectors; it established a new form of education in the country and made Brigade life an alternative choice for many young people without careers.

Elija Makgoeng was among the original twenty graduates of the Serowe Builders' Brigade. In 1974, he was appointed its first local manager. I asked him to recall his pioneer days.

*

I wasn't in Serowe that day in 1965 when Pat van Rensburg called a kgotla meeting, inviting all young men wanting to become builders to come forward for enrolment. I was at my father's cattle-post. I'd just completed primary school then and had no career before me, other than to look after cattle. It was my elder brother who came hurrying to the cattle-post to tell me about this kgotla meeting.

'Here is something new,' he said. 'What do you think about it? Would you like to join?'

I thank God that I decided to join there and then because today I am a builder of no mean reputation. The community frowned on the project at that time. It was not so long ago that they had lived through Chief Tshekedi's times when almost the whole village had contributed free, voluntary labour for his projects. They worked then because it was the order of the chief but regimental labour had always been a debatable matter. The Builder's Brigade had the same overtones. We had to work for no pay but everyone chose to overlook the fact that we were being given training and academic instruction without paying school fees. Then they heard about the free breakfast and lunch provided during work hours and people would pass remarks to us like this: 'You are really destitutes begging for that free breakfast and free lunch!' Or they'd say: 'You are the sons of rich men, aren't you? You can afford to work for no pay!' The community is always like that. Serowe people are very suspicious of a new idea. Later, when they see that it makes sense and succeeds, they accept it completely.

We were also despised by the students of Swaneng Hill Secondary School who thought they were superior to us — our Brigade started as an off-shoot of Swaneng Hill School and our training programme started with experiments on small buildings in the Swaneng School grounds. I know the students of that time would like the public to believe in the good image they projected of themselves but they tortured us in many subtle ways. They came from the families of the rich who could afford the high fees for secondary education. We were all primary school leavers and our parents were poor. They had a school truck which brought them in to school every day. They would not let us get on to the truck because our poverty made us inferior to them. And they despised us because our course of instruction differed from theirs — we did have academic studies and theory but we worked at the same time. They resented it, when during our theory time, we were taught by their teachers of the secondary school. This argument went on all the time but we had our own pride. Since we were the only Brigade at that time, we formed a trainees' disciplinary committee and prescribed corporal punishment to trainees who were lazy to work or misbehaved in any way. We wanted to succeed and we wanted people to admire us. We were really the pioneers and after our Brigade, others followed quite quickly.

There were forty of us on the project. Our course lasted for three years and after about two years twenty trainees dropped out of the training scheme. Money was the problem. They began to resent working for no pay, so in 1967 a bonus scheme was introduced to encourage students to stay the course and take the trade test. We were given R1.00 to R2.00 a month, depending on the profits made from the building we did for people. It had always been the most bitter pill that we did not get enough money for our labour and yet this problem was solved in a natural way. By 1973, the training programme had expanded and it became more and more difficult to cover costs. The bonus scheme was dropped completely, for practical reasons. No money. The Brigades just managed to cover their costs. But by that time people had begun to look at the Brigades in a new way — there was more eagerness to acquire knowledge, rather than to be paid for it. In fact, students themselves now pay a registration fee of R10.00 a year and we are swamped by letters of application to join the Brigades.

A letter we received from an applicant wishing to enter our advanced course is an example of the new spirit in the Brigades. We have an advanced building course attached to the Builders' Brigade. The advanced course is to give men a higher grade trade test and also to train them as local building instructors, once the services of overseas volunteers are no longer available. By the time young men take the advanced course, they are already married and have families, so we allocate them R30.00 a month for the duration of their studies. This also means that we admit a limited number of applicants. So, we received this letter of application for the advanced course from one of our former trainees. We rejected him on the grounds that we had our quota of trainees for the year and could not pay him that R30.00 a month. He wrote back: 'Please, please accept me. I'll do without the R30.00. When you are thirsting for knowledge, there's nothing that matters but getting that knowledge.'

Political independence is a boon to our country. So far, our independence cannot be compared to the turmoil and coups that have taken place in the rest of Africa. Everything is peaceful here and people have so much to do. I don't know what we would do if things were otherwise. We are an unarmed people. We don't even have spears.

The Textile Brigade

There is a magic in seeing the whole production line — from the stately, imported Angora goats who supply the mohair wool for the brilliantly

160

woven mats, shawls and blankets, in the Serowe Textile Workshop. The Angora goats are precious and beautiful, and they deserve a note all to themselves. They are very tall, for goats. They have masses of long, soft, silky-white hair falling down to their feet; they look like animals from outer space. When they first arrived in Serowe, people screwed up their eyes anxiously and asked: 'What sort of animal is that?' Angora goats take their unusualness a little too far, to the point of killing each other so I have observed. All the local goats go in for head-bashing games. They give each other a quick bash now and then, but mostly they are preoccupied with grazing. Angora goats, who live under privileged conditions and are given concentrate as supplementary feed, spend hours slowly and patiently bashing each other's skulls until they bleed. They are an experiment. They are mated with local goats at the Brigade farm, to produce a kind of crossed mohair wool.

The goats are sheared at the Brigade farm and the raw wool is brought to the Textile Workshop where it is washed in Teepol, a chemical detergent. The greyish wool is then dyed in brilliant colours — deep purple, midnight blue, red, orange and brown, and these dyed wools are then woven in original combinations to form designs for mats, shawls and blankets. Supplementary orders of mohair, karakul and merino wool are supplied from South Africa. Mats are usually a combination of mohair and karakul; blankets are usually mohair mixed occasionally with merino wool; and shawls are entirely of mohair. Real wool is twice the price of nylon and other simulated wool fibres on the market, and therefore the articles produced by the Textile Brigade are very costly. Always lingering in the finished article is the faint smell of the goat and that might be a fascination in itself, to own something 'real' in this age of plastics and chemicals. People with money and tourists usually make the Serowe Textile workshop their favourite shopping centre.

The Textile Brigade has also experienced job creation problems. It originally had three departments — a weaving department, silk-screen printing, and a dressmaking department. The weaving department trainees had the most difficulty finding jobs on completing their course; they had been given a skill but there were no weaving industries to absorb them. The first graduates are now working in shops, doing work unrelated to their training. As one trainee said to me in despair: 'If we do not find work after training, it is of no value.' The training programme in the silk-screen printing department has ceased and today it is a small business co-operative enterprise which employs its trainees. Most of the girls in the dressmaking department, on completing their course, can set up in business on their own. Most parents can afford a sewing machine and indeed, dressmaking is one of the most popular private trades for women in Serowe — what the trainees say they have is skill, at factory level.

The equipment used for producing woollen articles in the weaving department ranges from simple frames to very complicated hand-operated looms.

*

Ndoro Sekwati

Age: thirty-four

Occupation: instructor in weaving department

In the old days all that the young girls could hope for was marriage and all women had to know how to plough. There was no other life for women, outside of that. Ploughing was something we started from birth with our mothers. We all went to the lands with them every rainy season, and when we were about sixteen we started to help with the work, using the plough which is pulled by oxen and broadcasting the seed over the land. We never got any money out of it, only food, and there were many years when the land produced no crops. There was money in cattle but women seldom looked after cattle; the cattle always belonged to and were cared for by the men in the family. You can say that this is the history of our women right from the olden days; they have no other history. Many women still live like this but the one big change that has taken place is that marriage has now become a thing of the past. Women are no longer certain of marriage but they still have children and have to support them. When life is like that, any education or new skill that can be taught is sacred to us. I think it is mostly the young who have this feeling for education and new ideas. In my village ward we have only three young people who are well educated and most of our old people have had no education at all.

In 1967 I was just about to take my primary school leaving exam and was expecting a child at the same time. This interfered with my studies and I could not go on to secondary school. A woman in the village spread the news about the opening of the Textile Workshop and as I had nothing to do, I came and joined as a weaver. Many other girls joined for different reasons — they had either failed the primary school

162

leaving exam or failed to get entry into secondary school. So, I was one of the first trainees then and our training course lasted for two years. We learnt everything. We started off with the raw wool — washed it, carded it, spun it and dyed it. From there we moved on to weaving carpets and tapestries on the looms. We still stick to this method of learning to this day — all trainees have to learn all the skills concerned with weaving a carpet — but in the near future we may have an outside group of people to specialize in washing, carding and spinning the wool, to save time.

Originally, we paid no school fees but we received a bonus of 15c per foot of weaving we did and 15c for spinning two pounds of wool. Now the girls pay R12.00 per year for training and the bonus payment has ceased.

We have three departments in the Textile Workshop — weaving, dressmaking and silk-screen printing. Of all our departments, only the dressmaking department equipped our trainess with a skill they could use outside the Brigade. It's easy to set up in business as a dressmaker and some of our trainees are now attached to shops; they make dresses which are sold in the shops or they set themselves up as dressmakers in their own yards.

For our weaving and silk-screen printing trainees, there is no employment at all outside the Brigade. Some of the first group of trainees were absorbed by the Brigade — I became an instructor in 1972 and ten others were given employment. The rest just went to find employment as shop assistants and primary school teachers. The problem is that most trainees cannot set themselves up as weavers and silk-screen printers because the equipment is too costly. The silk-screen printing department had to close down its training scheme due to this and employ all its trainees. The weaving and dressmaking departments are the only departments that now take in new trainees.

This state of affairs created a lot of frustration among the trainees in the beginning because they spent two years learning a skill that could not be put to use. In spite of this, many girls did not regret the period spent in the Brigade. They would have joined anyway, out of curiosity, just to see if it would help them or not. Young people in Serowe are very attracted to something new.

The Printers' Brigade

Jack Turner

Age: thirty-eight
Occupation: printer

SIR, YOU'RE STANDING ON SACRED GROUND. THIS IS A PRINT SHOP proclaims a big green poster on the walls of the Serowe Printers' Brigade workshop. I asked Jack Turner, in charge of the project, where it came from and he replied that it was sent by a ticket printer in Fort Smith, Arkansas. The words implied that a print shop was a defender of truth and freedom of thought. Rather an ambitious poster for, as yet, the Printers' Brigade has not had much truth to defend and a small newspaper, *Mmegi Wa Dikgang* (*Reporter of News*) which they ran alongside the job printing business, had to close down due to financial burdens and lack of qualified staff. The printing office is in the Swaneng Hill Secondary School grounds. In size it is about 14ft by 16ft, with the printing machinery crowding out the walking space.

The most striking thing about Jack Turner is the sheer pleasure of his company. He is a quiet, orderly man, with a routine. Everything — people, friendships, politics — has a place in his world and his politics are perhaps the best expression of his personality. I once asked him who he'd vote for President of the U.S. and he replied: 'I wouldn't vote for an out and out radical. I've always been middle-of-the-road.' Then he held up his hand and screwed his face thoughtfully. He didn't mean he was a conservative, more likely a liberal, and he shook his head again, finding it difficult to define. Perhaps he hasn't yet found a politician in his own image who could make a world for everyone.

*

I come from Clearwater, Florida. My wife and I applied to the United Methodist Board of Global Ministries and asked for an assignment to work in a developing project, in Africa. It took them a year to find somewhere for us to go and eventually the United Methodist Board linked up with the Botswana Christian Council who said that Pat van Rensburg needed a printer at Swaneng; so that was how I came to Botswana. Oh, at first we didn't know where we were going! We received a letter saying I'd been sent to Swaneng. I looked Swaneng up on the map and there was no place like that in Botswana. I wrote to the mission and they couldn't find it either. I wondered where I was going! We had to write to the Botswana Christian Council to find out that Swaneng was in Serowe.

My motivation was purely a response to the Christian gospel, ministering to others, and also a strong commitment to help others to help themselves. There were additional motives; a desire to travel for personal enrichment — to broaden one's outlook on life. My first impressions of Serowe were a surprise. It was a year of drought. It was October 1971, very dry with absolutely no leaves on the trees. My wife and I came from Palapye at two in the morning. Someone gave us a lift into Serowe, so we saw the village for the first time in the dark — the rubber hedges, rondavels and the maze of pathways. We wondered how someone could go into this because it was so completely confusing. Waking in the morning filled us with awe; everything was stark, rocky. We'd just come from a country where everything was green.

Before I came I'd read accounts of people working on printing projects in Africa — mostly reports by missionaries — so I knew about problems of paper supply, training of unskilled personnel, etc. I found the project partly started and most of the basic equipment was already there. Shortly after I advertised and selected three printing trainees. The major hurdle we had to face at the beginning was the financial set-up. There was a balance of R200 in an account, plus a very modest supply of paper. That meant that we had to operate on a very minor scale till such time as we could accumulate enough capital to operate on. The original intent of the project was to start a local newspaper. 'War on Want' had given the basic equipment — a used offset press, camera and paper cutter. With these limited resources it was extremely difficult to start a newspaper because no one would want to advertise in a paper which was not widely read.

We hired a high school graduate as our first editor and started the newspaper 'on a shoe-string'. The paper was called *Mmegi Wa Dikgang* which means *Reporter of News*. We received lots of help from Swaneng Secondary School teachers. The people of the school looked on the project as something they could jump in and help with. The English teacher provided traditional stories and another teacher actually supervised the journalistic efforts of the students. In many ways it was like a high school newspaper. We applied for and received financial assistance from the agency for Christian Literature Development, in London. After many interesting experiences where we were all learning together, we felt that the financial burdens and technical difficulties of establishing a newspaper without a full-time trained journalist, were too difficult. We decided to stop the newspaper until a qualified journalist was available.

We had always done a certain amount of job printing side by side with the newspaper, so we turned all our resources in that direction. Mr Mathware, who had been hired as our business manager for the newspaper, also worked as a job printing salesman. Job printing is now our major emphasis and contributes significantly to the needs of a rapidly developing country. We do printing for mining companies, local government offices, merchants and church organizations. We also print adult literacy booklets — we needed to do more of this type of work, that's why a newspaper was so badly needed — to work in with adult literacy. It was also much easier to fit job printing into the cost-covering concept which Brigades adhere to. We are perhaps a semi-Brigade in that we are not primarily a training institution. We are very much a technical Brigade and as such more suited to operate on a commercial basis. One of the things clearest in my mind is that education is insufficient in a developing country; you must have job creation. The Brigades experiment has proved that only in the building sector are jobs available after training; a number of Brigades like the Farmers', Tanners', Textile workers', in turn face Brigade leavers' problems, while initially those Brigades were started to solve the school leaver problem.

We can see a real potential in the Printers' Brigade for creating jobs requiring a degree of technical skill. I personally feel our work generates self-esteem. The Printers' Brigade will provide a strong base for re-establishing a newspaper at a later date. The printing employees — I don't call them trainees any longer — are paid a salary ranging from R20 to R34 a month; rather good wages in this economy. The Swaneng project presented the right kind of atmosphere for me to create an independent, self-supporting project.

24
Swaneng Consumers' Co-operative Society

Motusi Seretse

Age: thirty-nine
Occupation: manager of Swaneng Consumers' Co-operative Society Stores

'Good morning, brother. Good morning, brother,' says he. To this charming greeting he adds a short bow, a big friendly smile and a brief lift of his soft brown felt hat. Motusi Seretse is of medium height, stout, with a big, full booming voice. His personality and brotherliness towards his fellow men seems a natural part of the constant bustle and air of prosperity which surrounds the co-operative stores. Everything about him, and the concepts of the stores he manages, are so good that people tend to say: 'Oh Motusi, he's one of the best managers of co-ops in Botswana, you know.'

Often, the Swaneng Consumers' Co-operative Society Stores are so crowded, it is impossible to get served. The stores are owned by the members, and membership at present stands at about 5,000. They get their rewards in very tangible ways. As they shop, they are given bonus stamps, the equivalent of the goods they are purchasing. At the end of each financial year these stamps accumulate into savings which are then distributed among the members in the form of a chit with which a member may purchase goods in the store, or in cash.

*

I was born in Serowe and attended primary school here. Moeng College, which Tshekedi built, had just opened and I completed my primary education there. I went on to high school but mid-way, after completing three years, I became ill. I suffered from anaemia and this interfered with my studies, so I left school. I lived for a few years at my father's cattle-post.

The management of the Swaneng Co-op Stores was my first job. We started with a small store in 1965 outside the village. This store was founded by Pat van Rensburg. His idea was to give village people cheaper goods at wholesale prices. Our first order of goods was made with a loan of money from the members; a group of members contributed R10 each. This was done deliberately so that members could feel they were building the store from its beginnings and that it would be communal property. Other capital was raised from members' share fees. The share fee was then 50c, now it is R2.00. Within a year the shop was paying for itself and we could repay the loans given by members. We also called our first annual general meeting for members and paid out a bonus of 5 per cent on members' purchases. It was this bonus payment which established the co-op stores as a success in Serowe — at the end of our financial year the members receive their bonus in the form of savings and they can either take it in cash to pay school fees or spend it again in the store. I know that people understand that the co-op store belongs to them. At our annual meeting all the books are presented to them and they stand up and ask detailed questions about how the business is managed.

After two years, we, as well as paying members' bonus, had accumulated a small reserve fund. Then we borrowed R3,500 from the Co-op Development Trust and in 1967, used this to build a self-service co-op store in the central part of the village. Because of its central position, this store turned out to be more successful than our first store. We paid back the loan to the Co-op Development Trust; we paid members' bonus as usual every year, then, over a period of six years we accumulated a reserve fund and unallocated surplus of R44,000. Then, with the permission and agreement of the members we started an extension to the self-service co-op store, a co-op bottle store and butchery, and a co-op hotel. The extension to the self-service co-op cost

168

R4,600. The buildings of the hotel, bottle store and butchery cost R40,000.

We do quite well. Let me give you some examples of our trade for the year 1972:

Sales	R188,150.00
Net profit	R 20,269.00

The bonus paid out to members was $7\frac{1}{2}$ per cent of the sales which was R14,111.00. The remaining R6,158.00 became our unallocated surplus plus our reserve fund which we use to expand the co-operative movement in Serowe.

25
The Boiteko Project

Introduction

Boiteko can be roughly translated as 'many hands make light work' or the idea of a group of people getting together and sharing everything with each other. *Boiteko* is a village, self-help, development project. Like most Swaneng projects, it was initiated by Pat van Rensburg, who at one stage became fascinated by the ancient African system of exchanging goods through bartering. He wrote a number of papers beginning: 'Before the white man came to Africa, African peoples had a system of exchanging goods, without money.... ' Indeed, a lot of business in Serowe is still conducted along those lines, where about two to three cows may purchase a ploughing implement or a bag of sugar and corn.

Then, a British volunteer outlined to Pat van Rensburg the work of a compassionate British industrialist, Robert Owen, during the industrial revolution in England. Robert Owen, reacting in 1820 against the exploitation of workers, built a shop to which members brought goods which they had made themselves, in exchange for a paper currency of their own. After a while, Robert Owen's system collapsed because the members purchasing goods had fixed tastes and set ways, and did not like the range of goods available in the store. Local dealers soon moved in buying up all the popular lines and the co-operative collapsed. But like Robert Owen's project, the *Boiteko* project at first revolved entirely around a shop we had built. It was thought that the employment situation was different in Botswana; that *Boiteko* members had no fixed tastes or set ways and that a co-operative store could be made workable with a range of goods the members had produced themselves. We also printed our own paper money called *Dirufo*, which means 'sharing', and which acted like a work-chit to enable us to purchase our own goods in the store. Six *Dirufo* were equal to thirty-six hours of work. This was the beginning of the *Boiteko* project. Ever ready to set pen to paper, Pat van Rensburg wrote:

> And when we build dams or dig wells or erect buildings or make gardens for our own benefit, must we expect payment from each other? Can the poor support the poor with money? No. But the poor can support each other with work by co-operating together. This is what the people of *Boiteko* are proving. They make goods and they can exchange them, without money. They help each other to make gardens, to build dams, to dig wells and to erect buildings. The gardeners feed the wool-spinners and leather-workers; the builders, the well-diggers and the dam-builders. The leather-workers shoe them all . . .

After about three months, the system collapsed entirely. We had said, or rather Pat van Rensburg had said, that we were going to be an economy of our own and our exports would not exceed our imports (we could not produce sugar, tea, powdered milk, sorghum and mealie meal, all of which *Boiteko* members needed and these goods were purchased with aid money). No proper tally was kept and one day we ended up with a bill of R2,000 for imports. In a paper on the failure of the *Dirufo* system, Pat van Rensburg wrote: 'When the store was opened, I succumbed to the temptation to please *Boiteko* members and reward them, and to attract new members by providing a wider range of goods in the store than we had produced or in fact could afford. I succumbed to the temptation to take short-cuts, and capital was pumped into building and equipment.'

Our shop was closed, the *Dirufo* system of exchange scrapped, and out of the one hundred members who had joined, only forty remained. The early idealism was replaced by down-to-earth money-earning. Each work group on the project takes its goods into the village of Serowe and at the end of every two weeks, we meet at what is called a 'shares meeting'. All the money earned is put into a communal bowl, for equal sharing among the members. It is very experimental, more trial and

171

error than anything else. The wonder of it is how eager and prepared very poor people are to share everything with each other — some work groups like the pottery house and the stone masons have higher earnings than the others and often tend to carry everyone else on their backs. Like all the other projects, new skills and new ideas invade people's lives. The poor and illiterate are slowly building up their own economy where no one is exploiting them and they control their own affairs. It is a common sight at *Boiteko* to see a member pick up a garment or an article and say, with a very learned air: 'Now what are my production costs? How am I going to price this article?'

Boiteko Pottery

Peter Hawes

Age: thirty-five
Occupation: manager of *Boiteko* pottery

My wife and I come from the north Midland part of England, and before we became involved in the *Boiteko* pottery we were both teachers at Swaneng Hill School. My wife had done a little pottery at college in England as part of her arts course and Pat van Rensburg asked her to start a pottery brigade. She didn't feel she could organize it and asked me to join her. I'd never done any pottery before. Except for what my wife, Christine, knew all my preparation for the pottery came out of books.

We started the pottery with a grant from Norway. It was R3,500 — that was for building, equipment and our salary for the first year. *Boiteko* was just about to open at that time, so instead of becoming a brigade, we became a part of village rural development. I combined several designs together from books for the kiln, and I found an old potter's wheel at Swaneng School and out of this I produced a design for a potter's wheel from bits of an old tractor, a lorry engine's fly-wheel, and the fly-wheel from a corn grinder. I'm not very expert. I fudge around — the potter's wheel often didn't work very well! I had to spend hours seeing what I had put in the wrong way.

This could be said about the roof of the pottery house I helped put up too. I was, as usual, trying to save money. I worked with another semi-skilled man. We set up the main beams on which the thatch would rest. We had two main trusses tied up with ropes, and we were pushing up the corner poles to meet the trusses. We pushed a little in the wrong way. One beam swung round, caught all the rest and all the roof beams spun around and crashed to the ground.

In setting up the pottery workshop, we did, as far as possible, try to use local materials. Most of the clay we use is local clay; and for making a slip, an outer decoration, we use imported white clay from Rhodesia. Initially, we had made enquiries from traditional women potters, from the geological department, and the clay we use at present is a mixture of the sandy-red clay which the traditional potters use and a 'fire clay' from the Morupule coal mine which has just been opened, a few miles from Serowe. This 'fire clay' is white and like china clay — it stops the traditional red clay from cracking when it dries and stops it from cracking when it's fired in the kiln.

We found it more difficult to use local materials for the glazes because this mixture, which is largely traditional clay, won't fire quite to stoneware temperature, so we have to buy fluxes which will make the glaze melt. But we do make our own feldspar from a local granite. With this feldspar we blend local sand and sometimes limestone to make our own glaze. We also have tried to use Botswana's ores for colouring the glazes. But these are generally from hundreds of miles away and organizing supplies has proved almost impossible.

My work has taken me out a lot into the Botswana bush. I like going with an object in mind, as an excuse. I've chopped my own wood for the kiln. We always went with a lorry-load of people and camped out. The spot where we find our clay, Kutswe Hills, is particularly beautiful with tall, fresh trees and far away from everything. An old woman took us to Kutswe the first time and she told us the custom was that we had first to make an offering before we took this gift from the earth. We had to throw down a green branch of a tree in a simple ceremonial way.

My aim was to start a small local industry. The pottery sells to the richer people in Serowe — mostly white people. In the last year, the slightly rough pottery that we make has proved very popular with our customers. It is a little disappointing that local people do not buy our pottery. Probably they like the factory-made articles in the shops, the thin china tea sets, and people from Europe, who have had too much of that, prefer our rough articles. We generally make things for domestic

173

use — cups, bowls, plates, casseroles and coffee pots. We also try to encourage traditional potters by buying the things they make and re-selling them, and also to lessen their labour by providing them with clay and firing their pots in our kiln. The young boys who lived at the cattle-post had a tradition of making clay cows. All Batswana men have this skill and the workmanship is often magnificent, nearly always powerfully life-like. We glaze and fire them.

Boiteko Women

'I wish they did learn more to spin and weave, but they mostly string beads....' During his visit to England in 1895, Khama the Great was interviewed by a lady journalist for the *Christian World* on the position of women in his country, and the above remark was one Khama made in response to her query as to whether women were making good progress in his country. Khama no doubt referred to the ordinary mass of village women for whom then no careers and skills were available. Today, seventy-nine years later, the women of Boiteko reply . . .

*

Mmatsela Ditshego

Age: twenty-four
Occupation: *Boiteko* potter

I trained as a nurse for two years and left because of ill-health. It was thought that I could not manage the duties of a nurse. I had no employment for a year then I read an advertisement about the start of *Boiteko* pottery. It was my first time working with clay. I'd seen old women in the village making traditional clay pots but I had never done anything like that myself.

I like being a member of *Boiteko* because while acquiring skill as a potter, I also learned how a producer's co-operative was organized. I was on the first committee that was formed to look after the affairs of *Boiteko*. The committee was composed of one person from each work

174

group — one from pottery, garden, tannery, weaving, sewing and so on. We each reported the problems of our work group and the committee would decide how these problems would be solved. The committee had to meet once a week, every Thursday, but if a serious problem arose during work hours, we could meet at any time. We'd keep minutes and then report our decisions and problems to a general meeting of all *Boiteko* members before the share-out of money. We have no manager for *Boiteko* so this was a way for all members to participate in organizing *Boiteko*.

There are mostly girls in the pottery. We worked with a few men in the beginning, but they left. We collected locally all our material for the pottery, except the glaze and about once a year we'd all go out camping at Kutswe with Peter Hawes and his wife and collect a truck-load of clay. We do a wide range of work — we had to learn all the steps necessary to produce a glazed pot. Over a month I would have done the following jobs: we take the clay and soak it in water. After soaking, we mix two or three different types of clay together, then sift it to remove the big stones, then grind the clay in the ball-mill, then tip it out of the ball-mill and pour it into barrels by the bucketful. Then we sieve the clay again with a finer sieve. The clay has to dry out a bit before it is ready for use. We don't immediately use the newly prepared clay. We use clay that has been standing for about two or three weeks. It is easier to work with clay that has been standing for a bit; if the clay is too wet, the pots will collapse. Before I throw the clay on the wheel, I knead it for five to ten minutes to get all the air out and if I am making a number of pots, all the same size, I weigh out the clay in equal parts. After about a year at *Boiteko* pottery, I started making my own designs for pots. Customers would often re-order the same design if they liked it.

The range of goods I have made so far are cups, plates, bowls and storage containers. I throw about sixty items a day on the wheel. That is not the end of my work. I decorate the pots with a slip of wet, coloured clay, squeezed out of an enema tube. Then the pots go into the first firing. All pottery girls help to fire the kiln and we take day and night duty. The kiln has to be slowly brought to a temperature of one thousand degrees centigrade. When the pots come out of the kiln, they are dipped into glaze and then go in for a second firing for twenty-four hours, up to a temperature of one thousand, one hundred and eighty degrees. We work out our own production costs for the goods and price them.

I think my work at Boiteko is more valuable than working in a factory. I visited a factory at Bulawayo. The people working there were limited to the job they were doing. A glazer was glazing all the time. A potter never moved away from the wheel, and the person who was firing the kiln just fired the kiln all the time. I have had to learn everything, from digging out the clay to sticking on the price ticket. I think of myself as a skilled person.

Abotseng Olefhile

Age: fifty-nine

Occupation: *Boiteko* weaver

In our custom, it was the duty of women to stay home and plough. And if a woman was not married, the work of her life, and her lands for ploughing, was given to her by her parents. Things began to change once the men left the country and began to seek work in South Africa, and South-West Africa. At first, during Chief Khama's times, only men were allowed to travel on the trains. He forbade women to travel on the trains. I think it was too dangerous and it was also not proper in custom for women to move far from home. It was only during Chief Tshekedi's time that many of us started to take the train to Johannesburg. The husbands began to demand that their wives accompany them and once both husband and wife were settled, they would also invite relatives and friends to join them and seek work too and that is how many women began to leave the village. But we could never just do as we please. Our every movement was controlled. When we wanted to leave, our parents took us to Chief Tshekedi, who wrote out a note which we took to the police camp, and we were then given a permit to allow us to go for work.

My first experience of employment was in Serowe when I worked for one and a half years for Sister Haile at the L.M.S. mission maternity clinic. I had attended school for five years, up to Standard Three, when my mother took me out of school to help her with the ploughing. In those days parents didn't care about education like they do now. One day it was heard that Chief Tshekedi was looking for a girl to assist Sister Haile, and my parents who were well-known to the chief offered me. It was a small maternity clinic of three rondavels with two beds in each rondavel and patients could stay at the clinic for two or three days. We used to deliver about four to six babies a week, mainly because women never gave birth regularly to children like they do today and partly because many women feared to attend the clinic. In custom a woman had to breast-feed a child until it was three years old and during that time she was not supposed to become pregnant.

Before Sister Haile opened the clinic, all the babies used to be delivered by the grandmothers and mothers according to Setswana custom. So the clinic was a very new thing and different from the ways of our grandmothers. In our mother's custom we were never allowed to lie down during delivery. They made a high seat of folded jackal skin upon which you sat upright with your legs apart and back resting against the wall of the hut. And so you pushed the baby out. In Sister Haile's clinic, the women lay down for delivery. Many women feared to follow this new way, though I think it's better.

Sister Haile paid me thirty shillings a month. It was a lot of money at that time! With a salary like that in those days, you could buy a blanket, shoes and dress all at once, but not today. I was taught everything and how to deliver babies so that often when Sister Haile left Serowe to visit women in other villages, I worked alone. I never really liked the work because I was always afraid of the women older than myself. When they came in for delivery they would start shouting as soon as they saw me there. I was very young then and they would shout that according to Setswana custom they could not expose their 'special parts' to such a young person. Sister Haile used to say: 'All right then. If you don't want Abotseng here, go and deliver your own baby.'

That would calm them down but I was never happy. I was relieved when the hospital opened and Sister Haile's clinic was transferred to the hospital. It also meant that my work ended, so I left Serowe to find work as a housekeeper in Johannesburg. I was only there for three years but I did not like it. Again I became afraid. People were just killing each other in Johannesburg. I returned to Serowe because I prefer our peaceful life of ploughing and looking after our things at the cattle-post. That was what I did all the time until I joined *Boiteko* where I do weaving.

I know how to weave after three years and I like the idea of *Boiteko* because it was something people started on their own but *Boiteko* only provides me with just enough money to buy soap. It takes me about a week to weave a blanket on the frame and three days to weave a carpet on the loom. The sales from a single woollen blanket or carpet is about R65.00. But I never see that money. At the share-out I take home only R3.00. The weaving group is one of the highest earners in *Boiteko*, next to the pottery and builders, and we spend all our time carrying on our backs groups like the sewing, kitchen and garden, whose earnings are either absent or very low. There are six of us in our group and if we shared our earnings only among ourselves, we would take home enough money to support our lives. All I can say I have gained from *Boiteko* is the skill to produce a blanket, carpet or shawl, right from the time the wool comes off the sheep — I do everything; card the wool, spin it, dye it and weave it — but I don't get rich. It isn't the sort of skill I could take home and do in my own yard and pick my life up a bit. It's too complicated and has to be done in a place like *Boiteko*. But what I complain about is the way *Boiteko* is organized. We share the money equally among all the members while the group earnings are not equal.

Epilogue — A Poem To Serowe

Oh, never a doubt but, somewhere, I shall wake,
And give what's left of love again, and make
New friends, now strangers ...

Rupert Brooke: 'The Great Lover'

*

These I have loved:

The hours I spent collecting together my birds, my pathways, my
sunsets, and shared them, with everyone; The small boys of this village
and their homemade wire cars; The windy nights, when the vast land
mass outside my door simulates the dark roar of the ocean.
— And those mysteries: that one bird call at dawn — that single,
solitary outdoor fireplace far in the bush that always captivates my eye.
Who lives so far away in the middle of nowhere? The wedding parties
and beer parties of my next-door neighbours that startle with their
vigour and rowdiness; The very old women of the village who know so
well how to plough with a hoe; their friendly motherliness and insistent
greetings as they pass my fence with loads of firewood or water buckets
on their heads; My home at night and the hours I spent outside it
watching the yellow glow of the candle-light through the curtains; The
hours I spent inside it in long, solitary thought.
These small joys were all I had, with nothing beyond them, they were
indulged in over and over again, like my favourite books.

Appendix

The Founding of the British Bechuanaland Protectorate, 1885-95

Since time immemorial, people have referred to themselves as Batswana, people of the Tswana grouping of tribes, but during the colonial era they were known as Bechuana and their land as, Bechuanaland. This appears to be an English mispronunciation and mis-spelling of the proper name. This error was corrected at independence and the country became known as Botswana, the land of Batswana people. Before the era of colonial invasion the lands of the Tswana tribes extended as far south as the Vaal River and included the lands of the Barolong and Batlhaping tribes. They were many small clans living under independent chiefdoms.

Botswana cannot be viewed outside the context of southern African history as a whole with which it is deeply involved. There are many categories of horror that one has to deal with when considering southern African history during its earlier period — the settlement of the Dutch at the Cape in 1652, the sudden eruption of tribal violence in the early nineteenth century known as the *Mfecane* or period of intertribal wars, British imperialism and Cecil John Rhodes. Botswana was a cross-road where all three factors met. A period of 200 years lapsed before white settler penetration from the Cape into the interior took place and more relevant to the earlier history of Botswana is the *Mfecane*.

The *Mfecane* began about 1816 and raged on into the 1830s. It is a complicated story of intertribal warfare which roughly assumed the following pattern: three Nguni chiefs, Zwide, Dingiswayo and Shaka (of present-day northern Natal) began reversing the old system of small scattered settlements and creating loose confederations of people with standing armies. Zwide built one such on the northern side of the Mflozi River; Dingiswayo on the southern side. Both Zwide and Dingiswayo then attacked Matiwane, chief of the Ngwane. Matiwane, when faced with warfare from such powerful enemies, asked a neighbouring tribe, the Hlubi, to take care of his cattle. When danger of warfare was over Matiwane asked for the return of his cattle but they had been stolen and appropriated by the Hlubi. This was the start of the widespread devastation of the tribal wars. Matiwane then attacked the Hlubi and drove them from their ancestral home, settling his people in their area near the Drakensberg mountains. The Hlubi, under their chief, Mpangazitha, fled over the Drakensberg mountains into the Transvaal highveld and attacked the Batlokwa, appropriating their cattle and grain and driving them from their home.

The three tribes, the Ngwane (dislodged from the Drakensberg area by Shaka Zulu), the Batlokwa and Hlubi, devastated the Transvaal highveld and Caledon valley, the home of the Sotho tribes. The eruption engulfed east and south central Africa. Nguni tribes collided into Sotho tribes who collided into Tswana tribes. War, and it seemed unending, became the order of the day. It was a period of terror with the daily rhythm of ploughing, cattle-herding and hunting completely disrupted. Many chiefdoms lost their entire ruling families and disappeared. Human bones littered the land. Desperate bands of homeless people turned to cannibalism in order to survive.

Two waves of this tribal violence swept through Botswana: one, a Sotho group, the Bafokeng or Makololo, under their chief, Sebetwane; and the other, an Nguni group, the mighty military army of the Ndebele warriors under their leader, Mzilikazi. It is said that the Makololo, before settling in the plains of the Zambezi River, scattered the Bamangwato nation in all directions, and the Ndebele warriors from their base at Bulawayo continued to raid and ravage the land for the next fifty years. The Tswana tribes were in utter disorder. From this disorder, the Bamangwato were the first to re-emerge as a stable nation. Out of these troubled times emerged some outstanding men with powers of leadership and the ability to reunite the people. In the pre-*Mfecane* days the small clan-based tribe was the order of the day. Now began a new era of nation-building, not only to reunite the small clans, but also to absorb the many bewildered and wandering refugees, disrupted by the tribal wars.

Three men are significant in the later development of Botswana history — Sekgoma I (the father of Khama III), Sechele of the Bakwena, and Moshoeshoe of the kingdom of the Basotho people. Their histories mingle and intermingle.

Sekgoma I was the son of Kgari, said in legend to be one of the great chiefs of the Bamangwato — kind, just and courageous in warfare. Unfortunately, Sekgoma was the son of an inferior wife, Dibeelane. He was to suffer from this sense of insecurity all throughout his rule. The heir-bearing wife, Bobjwale, bore Kgari a son named Khama II. Kgari was suddenly killed in a tribal war about the year 1826. When Kgari was killed, his cousin, Sedimo, acted as regent during Khama II's minority. As Bobjwale was the senior child-bearing wife, Sedimo entered her hut to raise seed to the dead Kgari. She bore him a son who was named Macheng. According to Tswana custom, Macheng was thus in direct line to the chiefship after Khama II. Khama II duly succeeded Kgari as chief of the Bamangwato but it was during his rule that the tribe was scattered in all directions by the Makololo. Khama II had a short reign of about two years. He was unpopular, unmarried and died about 1835 of an unknown cause. In about 1835, Khama II was succeeded by his half-brother, Sekgoma I, who represented the era of nation-building and a return to stability. Bobjwale and her son, Macheng, the rightful heir, fled Bamangwato country to take refuge with the Bakwena. Sekgoma established the tribal capital at Shoshong and generously admitted into the tribe many refugees displaced by the *Mfecane* wars, as well as smaller tribes like the Baphaleng, Botalaote, Monwatlala, Bakhurutse and Bakalanga, who sought his protection.

Sechele was the son of Motswasele II of the Bakwena tribe. He experienced much tribulation in his youth as his father, Motswasele, was publicly assassinated by the tribe in about 1823, due to his bad conduct of tribal affairs. A royal relative, Moruakgomo, then ruled the tribe and forced Sechele, his uncle Segokotlo and his brother, Kgosidintsi, to flee to the Bamangwato for protection. Sechele spent his youth wandering from place to place. In about 1829, he attempted to reunite the Bakwena tribe but was not successful as the tribe was split among the many factions who had fought for power after his father's death. It was only in 1853 that he succeeded in uniting the dissenting factions under his rule and bringing stability to his people. Relevant to the history of the land was that Sechele of the Bakwena built up diplomatic links with the Basotho king, Moshoeshoe. They were related in the customary way in that they had the same totem, that of Kwena or the crocodile. Moshoeshoe's small clan was known as the Kwena of Mokoteli. Such relatedness is described by the saying: 'Cousin, we are all swimming in the same river.' It was an invaluable link at a time when black people had no sense of national consciousness to unify them in their struggle to defend their land.

Moshoeshoe was, in his time, the grand lord of southern African politics. From his stronghold, Thaba Bosiu, he spun out all the new shapes and changes that were to vitally affect the destiny of black people in southern Africa. He held court every day and received ambassadors from all corners of the land, advising their leaders of the changing balance of power, the slow encroachment of white settlers and the manner in which this encroachment should be dealt with. Yet Moshoeshoe's beginnings were humble. Before the *Mfecane* triggered off a series of catastrophes that caused bloodshed and complete disintegration, his world was a small isolated society of mixed farmers and hunters organized into small chiefdoms, living in scattered village settlements of about 50 to 400 inhabitants. Moshoeshoe was merely the senior son of a village headman, Mokhachane, with no pretensions to the power and grandeur he was to later acquire. During the time of the tribal wars he was first attacked by the Batlokwa tribe at his mountain fortress, Botha-Bothe. Although he and his people survived the attack, the stronghold was found to be too insecure and a more defensible position, Thaba Bosiu, was found.

On the way to their new capital, the Mokoteli clan were attacked by a band of roving cannibals. Moshoeshoe's grandfather, Peete, was captured and eaten by the cannibals. Moshoeshoe proved himself during this time of crisis to be a sane, rational and humorous man. Rakotsoane, the leader of the cannibals who had eaten his grandfather, was captured and brought to Thaba Bosiu for trial. In spite of irate demands from his people that Rakotsoane be put to death, Moshoeshoe spared his life and replied that he did not wish to disturb the grave of his ancestor. His word travelled with lightning speed throughout a country racked by distress, winning him the loyalty and trust of the many fugitives and refugees of the *Mfecane* who turned to him for protection. He built up his Basotho nation from these refugees. He united many diverse people under him, creating a kingdom with boundaries and establishing himself as king over this kingdom. He had hardly begun to build up his new nation, when the Boer Great Trek of 1836 from the long established colony of the Cape of Good Hope, impinged on him and the Boers began to cross the Orange River and appropriate his land.

In early 1833, a friendly Griqua hunter named Adam Krotz visited Moshoeshoe and advised him of the simple form of diplomacy that was later to be of vital importance in the history of a country like Botswana. The Griqua tribes, partly Khoikhoi, partly mixed blood, had already known displacement by white settlers from their lands at the Cape and had resettled on the northern borders of the Cape Colony. Missionaries had helped them bring order to their affairs and had helped them communicate with overwhelming foreign powers who were conquering black people with superior weapons and seizing their land. From this time onwards, Moshoeshoe repeatedly sent out requests to missionaries, with offers of gifts of cattle, to come and live among his people. On the 28 June 1833, two missionaries of the Paris Evangelical Mission, Eugene Casalis and Thomas Arbousset, arrived in his kingdom. Not only did they write Moshoeshoe's diplomatic correspondence during the troubled times that lay ahead. They also recorded the history of his people and the founding of the Basotho nation during the *Mfecane*.

British rule at the Cape and the Great Trek. From small beginnings in 1652, the refreshment station for ships at the Cape had expanded into a large colony which was administered by the Dutch East India Company until it was declared bankrupt in 1794. In 1685 French Huguenot refugees who had fled to Holland during the massacre of St Bartholomew, arrived at the Cape to reinforce the Dutch settlers. The settlers at the Cape created vast agricultural estates, using the labour of slaves imported from tropical Africa, Madagascar and Malaya, as well as that of the indigenous peoples, the Khoikhoi. In 1806 the British took control of the Cape. The sea route around the Cape was of strategic importance to Britain as she was involved at that time in the conquest of India. The interior of Africa was not her concern.

However, there was much in British imperialism that was attractive to black people. British imperialism was commercial; its humanitarian side was represented by the Anti-Slavery Society, the Aborigines' Protection Society, the missionaries and other philanthropic bodies in England. Their voices were always raised in defence of the 'rights of the natives'. In 1833, the Anti-Slavery Society succeeded in persuading the British Government to abolish slavery throughout all its colonies. In 1833, the missionary, Dr John Philip, persuaded the British administration to raise the status of the indigenous inhabitants, the Khoikhoi, to the level of the white settlers. By the enactment of Ordinance 50, the Khoikhoi, except those who were slaves, were allowed freedom of movement, permission to own land and made the equal of the whites before the law. In 1834, by an act of the British parliament, all slaves at the Cape were emancipated but, to ease the transition to freedom, slaves were required to serve as apprentices for four years.

The settlers deeply resented the British decision and were determined to leave before the expiry date and take their slaves with them. In their manifestos of 1836, they stated that the proceedings were shameful and unjust. They did not so much object to the freeing of slaves, but that slaves would be placed on an equal footing with Christians. This was contrary to the laws of God and the natural distinction of race. It was intolerable for them to bow down before such a yoke. The Dutch or Trek Boer was to maintain this attitude of uncompromising inequality towards black people for the next three hundred years.

The tribes of South Africa fared badly with their only alternative, British imperialism. The tribes of Griqualand West were the first to experience British protection. Griqualand was divided into Griqualand East under the Adam Kok line of chiefs, and Griqualand West under the Waterboer line of chiefs.

Prior to the discovery of diamonds in 1866, Griqualand West was a desolate, unwanted corner of the earth where the Griqua tribes could live in peace. The area around present-day Kimberley was inhabited by Chief Nicolaas Waterboer and his people. They were living on diamond resources, present in quantities not found elsewhere on the earth's surface. The newly established Boer Republic of the Orange Free State immediately claimed the land between the Orange and Vaal Rivers to be theirs; the Transvaal Republic claimed the triangle between the Vaal and Harts Rivers. Chief Nicolaas Waterboer, who claimed the whole area, sought British protection rather than be under Boer rule. In October 1871, Griqualand West came under British protection. The land was annexed in such a way as to make it a possession of Great Britain. Griqua people found that the diamonds did not belong to them but to the white prospectors who alone had licences to mine or deal in diamonds. They found their land appropriated on all sides. In 1878 the Griqua rose in rebellion. The rebellion was brutally suppressed by Sir Charles Warren. Vast herds of cattle and numberless wagons were captured from the rebels and the spoils distributed among Warren's men. In 1880, Griqualand West was incorporated into the Cape Colony. With the incorporation of their territory, the Griqua tribes became a landless proletariat.

Moshoeshoe of the Basotho kingdom fared no better. In his appeal for British protection he stated: 'If I obtain an agent I will be under the Queen as her subject, and my people will be her subjects also, but under me. What I desire is that the Queen should send a man to live with me, who will be her ear and eye, and also her hand to work with me in political matters. He should be a man who would be fully trusted by everybody and he must know our ignorance and our ways.'

A hard and bitter struggle followed before Moshoeshoe was able to obtain this form of British protection that would leave his people largely independent and in control of their own affairs. By the time it was offered in 1884, Moshoeshoe's kingdom had become a land that could

185

be traversed in one day. The rest, including the green and fertile Caledon valley, had been seized by the Orange Free State Boers.

In 1838 the Trek Boers crossed the Orange River in organized parties with numerous wagons, large herds of cattle and vast flocks of sheep. They were stock farmers intent on appropriating the best springs and pastures for themselves. They recognized no black political ruler as having any authority and hated the missionaries who served them. At that time Moshoeshoe was the most powerful ruler on the southern high veld. His people numbered about 40,000 and their lands reached as far south as the junction of the Caledon and Orange Rivers and as far north as the source of the Caledon River. The first treaty signed by the Cape Governor, Napier, in 1843, acknowledged Moshoeshoe's claims. A succession of treaties signed with various British governors at the Cape gradually reduced his territory in favour of Boer encroachment. Conflict, war, raids and counter-raids resulted as neither Boer nor Sotho peoples would recognize the boundaries.

In 1848 British authority was extended from the Cape to the Vaal River by Sir Harry Smith with the creation of the Orange River Sovereignty. This was to protect the rights of all hereditary chiefs, and the rule and government of Her Majesty's subjects in their interests and welfare. This policy was reversed in 1852 when Britain recognized the independence of the Transvaal Republic at the Sand River Convention, to be followed in 1854 by the establishment of the Orange Free State and the abandonment of the Orange River Sovereignty. With the withdrawal of British influence in the area, Moshoeshoe and his people were left entirely at the mercy of the Boers. War broke out between the Orange Free State and the Basotho kingdom and in 1867, the Orange Free State emerged as the victor.

To save his country from complete dismemberment by the Orange Free State Boers, Moshoeshoe repeatedly requested British protection. In 1868, a tentative form of protection was offered but in 1871, after the death of Moshoeshoe, Britain incorporated his land into the Cape Colony. The Cape Government mismanaged the territory and in 1880 passed a law depriving all black people in South Africa of the use of firearms. Basotho people resisted successfully and the Gun War, which lasted eight months, cost the Cape Government £5,000. In September 1883, Basotholand was dis-annexed from the Cape Colony and on 18 March 1884, declared a British protectorate under direct rule of the Queen. Moshoeshoe set the precedent for the creation, a year later, of the British Bechuanaland Protectorate in 1885. He also set the precedents followed by Khama III of the Bamangwato. He prohibited the sale of land. He prohibited the sale of intoxicating liquor to his people.

Khama III or Khama the Great; John Mackenzie and the founding of the British Bechuanaland Protectorate (1885 to 1895). There are two images of Khama III, chief of the Bamangwato. There is the image of Khama, the traditional ruler, known only to his people and this is a history full of conflict and domestic quarrels; with his father, Sekgoma I, his brothers, his half-brothers and his own son, Sekgoma II. There is the image of Khama, the diplomat and delicate negotiator with the British for the right to retain the land for his people. This image, known only to British administrators, missionaries and many European travellers, was always written of in superlative terms. To them, he was a man who could do no wrong, the most remarkable African of his time and the great convert to Christianity.

Indeed, Khama's conversion to Christianity bears all the signs of deep sincerity. Missionaries of the London Missionary Society, like John Mackenzie and Elizabeth Lees Price, who served at Shoshong during this early period, recorded in their journals that Khama hovered around them continuously, anxious to learn. He questioned them earnestly on the value of human life and other moral issues which Christianity raised. In the first years of his reign in 1876, Khama enhanced the standing of the Bamangwato tribe by introducing reforms into traditional customs and ceremonies. Many of the great traditional ceremonies like rain-making, and *bogwera*, the initiation ceremony for men, required that blood should flow, often human blood. These ceremonies Khama made open and public, at which a missionary officiated.

The struggle to establish the British Bechuanaland Protectorate moved in two phases. The preliminary work was done by the missionary, John Mackenzie; the rest by Khama. John Mackenzie was to emerge as one of the most political-minded of missionaries of his time but during his early service of ten years among the Bamangwato, like Casalis and Arbousset before him, he recorded the history of the tribe in his book *Ten Years North of The Orange River*. He also, incidentally, established Khama's reputation internationally with his dramatic account of Khama's stand as a Christian in conflict with his 'heathen' father, Sekgoma I. But this first work of Mackenzie has a wide range and reach. It begins at Cape Town and travels up the westward side of southern Africa, along the wagon route opened up by missionaries and traders as far north as Matebeleland. It describes the lives of the people along this route, whether Boer or tribal man, with objective sympathy. This wagon route or 'missionary road' to the north was to be of strategic importance once the Scramble for Africa began in the 1870s.

In 1876 John Mackenzie was transferred from Shoshong to the Moffat Institution at Kuruman, in southern Bechuanaland, to be principal of a bible school that would train African evangelists to preach the word of God to their people. Kuruman was situated in Batlhaping country and since 1817 had been the main station of the London Missionary Society. Mackenzie immediately became embroiled in the struggles of the Batlhaping and Barolong tribes to save their land from being seized by the Transvaal Boers. Their lands adjoined the Transvaal Republic and by this time Boer land-grabbing activities had become voracious in the extreme.

The system whereby a Boer might acquire new land had become exceedingly simple. A new settler seeking a new farm would ride out beyond the limits of known habitation and seeing a portion of land that pleased him would note the natural features in order that he might define it. He would then go to the nearest *landdrost* or magistrate and stake his claim, whereupon the magistrate would hand him a certificate of ownership. The law of the Boer Republic limited the ownership of land to 6,000 acres. It did not matter that the tribes had lived in this area for generations. They were evicted. Those who had nowhere to flee were required to be labourers on the land that was formerly theirs. The southern Tswana tribes were totally disrupted by this activity.

In 1875, the Transvaal Republic annexed the lands of the Batlhaping tribes on the excuse that it had been ceded to them by a Tlhaping chief, Botlhasitse Gasebone. Sir Henry Barkly, then British High Commissioner at the Cape, anxious to avoid conflict with the Transvaal Republic, accepted the annexation. In 1878, the Batlhaping tribes rose in rebellion against the plunder of their lands by the Boers and murdered a farming family named Burness. All whites in the area fled to the Kuruman mission for protection. The mission was beseiged by the tribes for two months and Mackenzie was in charge of the beleaguered mission until a contingent of volunteers was sent from Griqualand West to relieve the mission. A general uprising throughout the land of the Batlhaping people was soon crushed by Sir Charles Warren. In the rebellion, Chief Botlhasitse Gasebone was one of the ringleaders.

This incident swayed Mackenzie towards political involvement in the affairs of southern Africa. In late 1878 he met the governor of the Cape,

188

Sir Bartle Frere, in Kimberley. Frere asked him to become Commissioner for Bechuanaland. The London Missionary Society, whom Mackenzie served, refused to approve the appointment. They suggested that Mackenzie resign from the Society in order to work with the Administration. A second incident, the seizure of the Barolong lands by the Transvaal Boers in 1882, propelled Mackenzie into action. Power struggles had developed between Chief Mankurwane of the Tlhaping and a neighbouring Korana chief, David Mosweu, as well as between two Barolong chiefs, Montshiwa and Moswete. Volunteers from the Transvaal Republic enlisted on the sides of Mosweu and Moswete in return for promises of land. Thus the countries of Mankurwane and Montshiwa were plundered and the Boers now founded two Republics, that of Stellaland in the heart of Mankurwane's country, and Goshen, in Montshiwa's country. The Republics of Stellaland and Goshen now lay across the 'missionary road' into the interior.

In July 1882, Mackenzie returned to England on missionary furlough, determined to arouse British public interest in Bechuanaland and action to restrain the land-grabbing activities of the Transvaal Boers. All the southern Tswana chiefdoms had appealed for British protection and Mackenzie firmly believed that British imperialism represented justice for all; the only way to save the lands of the southern Tswana tribes was to make southern Bechuanaland a British colony under direct rule from London. Mackenzie addressed meetings of philanthropic bodies throughout the land and endeavoured to get influential persons in government interested in his cause.

To the British Government Mackenzie seemed to be the man most needed at that time. Due to his long period of service in southern Africa as a missionary and the success of his campaign to enlighten the British public about events there, Mackenzie was offered a government post as Deputy Commissioner to southern Bechuanaland to establish a British protectorate over the area. On 10 March 1884, Mackenzie formally resigned from the London Missionary Society. But the situation was much more complex than Mackenzie's public campaign on behalf of the Batlhaping and Barolong tribes.

The least concern of the British Government was the plight of black people. The British Government was worried about German activity in South West Africa. As far back as 6 March 1878, Britain, intent on holding most of the sea ports round the coast of Africa, annexed Walvis Bay and a coastal strip of thirteen to eighteen miles surrounding it. Beyond that, the British Government disclaimed all responsibility for the territory or the people outside the Walvis Bay borders. From 1883 German influence began to make itself felt in South West Africa. On 29 May 1884, the British Government formally agreed to the annexation of a portion of South West Africa by Germany.

There was unease in government circles, both in London and the Cape Colony, about Mackenzie's appointment. On his arrival in the troubled area Mackenzie's activities instantly alarmed the Transvaal Government and the Government of the Cape Colony. He immediately set about establishing a British title over Stellaland and Goshen. Then, on 3 May 1884, Chief Mankurwane, whose land had been seized and renamed Stellaland, signed a treaty with Mackenzie ceding powers of jurisdiction in his country to Mackenzie and the British Government. Mackenzie now announced to the Stellaland Boers that he would be setting up a land commission to investigate land claims; 427 white farms had been carved out of Mankurwane's country. If all these claims were acknowledged the indigenous people would be left homeless.

To the north, war raged between the Barolong and the intruders of Goshen. Chief Montshiwa had not so long ago attacked the Goshenites, destroying the homes they had built on his land. Mackenzie's arrival was greeted with acclaim by the Barolong, and on 22 May, Chief Montshiwa signed a treaty placing his country under the rule of the Queen. Mackenzie announced that he would uphold all the land claims of the Barolong. He further decided to sign treaties of British protection with the many small independent Barolong chiefdoms. As soon as Mackenzie left Montshiwa's country, the Barolong were attacked by the Goshenite Boers. Mackenzie requested of the British Governor and High Commissioner at the Cape, Sir Hercules Robinson, a reserve force of a thousand men to help him bring order to the territory. This request was turned down.

The Transvaal Government, angered by Mackenzie's activities, sent a delegation to the Cape. The delegation included Paul Kruger, the head of the Transvaal Government. They demanded Mackenzie's removal. In late July 1884, Mackenzie was recalled and replaced by Cecil John Rhodes.

Cecil John Rhodes was at that time member of the Cape Assembly for Barkly West. Rhodes had already made his fortune on the Kimberley diamond fields by buying up all the smaller claims and amalgamating them into the de Beers Company, of which he was the major shareholder. He represented the unity of English and Afrikaner interests at the Cape. Rhodes immediately set about undoing the preliminary work done by Mackenzie. He recognized all Boer titles to farms and he forced Chief Montshiwa to cede his lands to the Goshen Republic, except for a small reserve where he might live with his people.

In August 1884 Germany finally annexed all the coastline of South West Africa, excluding Walvis Bay, and announced a protectorate over the land. Correspondingly, Paul Kruger published a proclamation annexing Goshen to the Transvaal Republic. The Transvaal Vierkleur flag was run up in Goshen. This created panic in the British parliament. It was feared that if Kruger pushed his boundary of the Transvaal Republic to the German border, Britain would forever be excluded from the road to the north. The cabinet decided to send Sir Charles Warren with 4,000 British troops to assert British authority in the area.

Mackenzie's services were needed again. He was asked to join the Warren expedition due to the speed with which the protectorate was to be announced to the tribes; Mackenzie's presence in the expedition would thus give credence to the British claim of protection. On 11 March 1885, the Warren expedition arrived at Mafeking. Germany was formally notified that Bechuanaland and Kalahari, as limited by an order in council of 29 January 1885, were under British protection. The extent of British protection was abruptly moved up from the Barolong lands to latitude 22 degrees north and longitude 20 degrees west. Latitude 22 degrees north marked the northern-most boundary of the Transvaal Republic and cut through the middle of Bamangwato country. It was Britain's intention not to grant protection to the whole of Bamangwato country but only to extend British authority abreast of the Transvaal to prevent any link between that country and the German protectorate of South West Africa. Bamangwato country was to act as a buffer zone up to latitude 22 degrees north.

Khama had sought British protection since 1876 and he graciously welcomed the Warren expedition. When presented with British protection up to latitude 22 degrees north, he objected, stating that his country reached as far north as the Zambezi River. Of the three Tswana chiefs who qualified for British protection in 1885 — Khama of the Bamangwato, Sechele of the Bakwena and Gaseitsiwe of the Bangwaketse — only Khama produced terms by which British protection was acceptable to him and his people, set out in a lengthy document dictated in Setswana and translated into English by Mackenzie. On 12 May 1885, Sir Charles Warren declared Bamangwato country a British protectorate.

It was an evil deal. Britain had no intention of honouring obligations and responsibilities. A partition was now made of the lands of the

Tswana tribes. The lands of the Barolong and Batlhaping tribes, south of the Molopo River, which contained the Stellaland and Goshen farms, were set up as the Crown Colony of British Bechuanaland. This section was annexed to the Cape Colony in November 1895, against the wishes of the tribes. The northern section, the British Bechuanaland Protectorate, was eventually to be administered by Cecil John Rhodes and his British South Africa Company. Mackenzie was used by the imperial power and once his usefulness was over, he was discarded. Mackenzie and the Tswana tribes were mere pawns in the game.

Cecil John Rhodes and the British South Africa Company. In May 1885, Cecil John Rhodes resigned as Deputy Commissioner to Bechuanaland and was replaced by a personal friend, Sir Sydney Shippard. Like Mackenzie, Rhodes was an imperialist but the two men differed in their interpretation of British imperialism. Mackenzie's vision of a British-controlled southern Africa grew out of his concern for the indigenous people and he felt that Britain was the only power that could ensure justice to the true owners of the land. He was defeated in this major concern. While Rhodes had dreams of British expansion throughout the continent of Africa, he profoundly distrusted the tendency of the British government to be influenced by the many philanthropic groups that operated in England. Rhodes believed that the unification of southern Africa had to be achieved by the government from Cape Town, while Mackenzie saw it being implemented by direct rule and responsibility from London. Seizure of black people's land and exploitation of their labour and resources were the major aims of Rhodes.

Rhodes' dreams from 1885 onwards now centred on the conquest of the legendary Mashonaland. For centuries a myth had been built up about the country due to the habit of Shona kings and chieftains trading with a small animal horn filled with gold dust. Spread far and wide in the still unopened interior, the legends grew and grew. Mashonaland was thought to be the original source of King Solomon's mines, the great gold-bearing lands of the south and it was even wildly stated that the gold grew up the trunks of trees.

In traditional oral history, Mashonaland was also a legend to the tribes of southern Africa. For centuries, Shona people had had vast, stable dynasties, ruled in the earlier period under the Mwenemutapa line of kings, and in the latter period under the Changamire line of kings. The stability of the Shona kingdoms attracted many small breakaway clans from all parts of southern Africa who sought the protection of the Shona kings. They were allocated a vast belt of land to the south of the Shona kingdoms and over the centuries a new nation was created, the Bakalanga, a mingling of many tribes.

About 1837, the Ndebele general, Mzilikazi, with his army of warriors, carved his way northwards and massacred the Bakalanga nation, scattering the survivors in all directions and settling on their lands. His system of government was aggressive and military, and from that time onwards and for the next fifty years, the tribes had always to be on the lookout for the Ndebele warriors who raided, stole cattle and killed people. Missionaries like Mackenzie wrote harrowing accounts of their aggressive exploits and recommended their dismemberment as a nation.

In 1870 Lobengula succeeded his father, Mzilikazi, to the throne. His kingdom commanded the approaches to the north, and from 1887 onwards Lobengula's court at Bulawayo became the focus for political intrigue and white concession hunters begging to explore his land for gold and diamonds.

On 11 February 1888, the Assistant Commissioner of the Bechuanaland Protectorate, John Moffat Smith, under instructions from the Deputy Commissioner to the Bechuanaland Protectorate, Sir Sydney Shippard, and the Governor of the Cape, Sir Hercules Robinson, signed a treaty with Lobengula by which he promised to cede no land or concessions without prior approval from the British Government.

On 20 September 1888, Charles Dunell Rudd, an agent for Cecil John Rhodes, arrived in Bulawayo and presented Lobengula with a complicated concession. The verbal explanation offered to Lobengula did not tally with the contents of the document. The Rev. C.D. Helm of the London Missionary Society and John Moffat Smith, who aided in translating the document, favoured Rhodes and disliked the Ndebele nation partly for their warlike activities and partly because they proved difficult to convert to Christianity. Verbally, Lobengula was informed of the usual arrangement applicable to elephant hunters, that ten men would arrive in his country, prospect for gold and then leave. The document actually dealt with the colonization of Mashonaland, the granting of an exclusive mining monopoly and all powers to work it. An agonizing delay of one month followed during which Lobengula hesitated to sign the document. On 16 October, Sir Sydney Shippard arrived to tip the scales in favour of Rhodes. To Lobengula, Shippard was an old friend. Since 1885 a lengthy correspondence had ensued between Shippard and Lobengula mostly about a boundary dispute the latter had with his neighbour, Khama. Shippard now carefully explained that Britain had two main interests — to preserve peace between Lobengula's country and Khama's country, and to protect both countries from invasion by the Transvaal Boers. But it was also known, he said, that Britain had a bad name in South Africa for betraying the interests of the natives.

Strangely reassured by these words, Lobengula's attitude changed and on 30 October 1888, he signed the concession. Lobengula had been tricked into selling his whole country and that of Mashonaland to Cecil John Rhodes.

On 29 October 1889, the British Government granted Rhodes a royal charter to exploit the Rudd concession on the grounds that a business company administering Mashonaland would relieve Her Majesty's Government of diplomatic difficulties and heavy expenditure. The royal charter gave birth to a new company, the British South Africa Company. The Company was empowered to colonize and govern a vast area of south-central Africa. A clause in the charter provided for the eventual transfer of the British Bechuanaland Protectorate to the British South Africa Company.

Events moved swiftly after that. A telegraph line was built to the northern borders of Bechuanaland. A force of 500 police and 200 pioneer settlers moved secretly towards Mashonaland. The hunter and explorer, Selous, carefully led the pioneer column in a wide circuit around Matebeleland and safely to the Mashonaland plateau.

The confusion of events which led to the Ndebele war of 1893 are almost irrelevant. A few clear threads are evident. The myth that Mashonaland was paved with gold was quickly exploded. There was no gold there worth mining and the Company's shares were falling. It was still thought that a ream of gold ran through Lobengula's kingdom, Matebeleland. In 1893 war was deliberately provoked with the Ndebele nation.

In August 1893 the Company started enlistment in South Africa for an armed force to march on Bulawayo. Khama's help and co-operation were needed for the recruits to pass through Bechuanaland. False rumours were spread to him by Company agents of an imminent Ndebele attack on his capital. Not since 1863 had the Ndebele attacked the Bamangwato but Khama accompanied the expeditionary forces as far as the borders of his land. Having undertaken only the defence of his land, Khama abruptly withdrew.

The war was brief. On 25 October the bulk of the Ndebele warriors were massacred near Bulawayo with the newly-invented Maxim gun which fired 620 rounds a minute. Lobengula fled. Two ambassadors whom he sent to make peace with the British were shot dead. The

Ndebele army was broken and Lobengula is said to have died during his flight into the bush. Their land and cattle were seized by the Company who now allocated farms and gold claims to their own people.

With the conquest of Matebeleland, Rhodes was free to turn his attention to the transfer of the British Bechuanaland Protectorate to his Company. Towards the end of 1892 Rhodes made an offer of an annual subsidy of £50,000 to administer the Bechuanaland Protectorate. No specific promise was immediately given by the British Government about the Protectorate. There was confusion for the first time in the Colonial Office and government circles as to whether the transfer of the administration of the Protectorate should be done by an arbitrary act of the British Government, or whether those powers of government should be acquired by the Company through concession, agreement, grant or treaty from the chiefs. It had always been an arbitrary act on the part of the British Government but now the person of Khama, chief of the Bamangwato, loomed large on the horizon. His name repeatedly appeared in official despatches. He was recognized as a faithful friend and ally of the British Government and by their own definition, a man of great integrity and enlightenment. To betray his trust would be a breach of faith the British Government would not for a moment entertain. It was impossible that Khama would agree to the transfer of his territory to the British South Africa Company. He had requested direct rule from London.

On July 9 1895, Rhodes asked the newly appointed Secretary of State, Joseph Chamberlain, to hand over the Bechuanaland Protectorate to him. A counter-petition was immediately sent by chiefs Khama of the Bamangwato, Sebele of the Bakwena, and Bathoen of the Bangwaketse to Chamberlain, requesting that their countries should not be handed over to the Company and that their people might continue to be protected by government from London.

In August 1895 the chiefs, Khama, Sebele and Bathoen, accompanied by the missionaries, W.C. Willoughby and Edwin Lloyd, sailed for England to protest to the British Government against the transfer of their territory to the Company. No black man then had such a wide appeal to the British public as Khama. Not only was he respected in government circles, but coinciding with his visit to England was the publication of *Twenty Years in Khama's Country*, being the letters of the missionary J.D. Hepburn who had served in Khama's country for that period. Once again there was a superlative account of Khama's character, his management of tribal affairs, opposition to the traffic of liquor through his country and the genuine unfoldment of the Christian faith 'in darkest Africa'. It was sold out on the day of publication and immediately went into a second printing.

All the doors of the many philanthropic groups were quietly opened to Khama by John Mackenzie. Mackenzie had retired from government service in 1891 and resumed his position with the London Missionary Society, serving at a mission station, Hankey, in the Cape Colony. On hearing of Khama's proposed visit to England, Mackenzie wrote to all the former champions of his cause — the directors of the London Missionary Society, the secretaries of the Anti-Slavery Society, the Aborigines' Protection Society and the Native Races and Liquor Traffic Committee — requesting that they receive his former pupil and assist him in every way. The Native Races and Liquor Traffic Committee were Khama's ardent admirers. Thus were ranged the many humanitarian groups against powerful, corrupt, ruthless business interests as represented by Rhodes.

On 11 September, the three chiefs had an interview with Chamberlain. Chamberlain, who was already in league with Rhodes, advised the chiefs to come to terms with the Company, stating that they would still be under the rule of the Queen since the Company derived its authority from the Crown. He then went on holiday.

The philanthropic societies clamoured to see the chiefs. They addressed crowded meetings over the length and breadth of England, Khama particularly speaking on the land question. He explained that if the Company took their lands his people would be enslaved to work in the Company's mines. Moreover, his people subsisted on the land and took all their food from the land and they feared that they would lose these benefits. He further protested against the arbitrary decision of the British Government to transfer the Protectorate without prior consultation with the chiefs.

On 6 November the chiefs once again met Chamberlain. A great agitation had been raised in Britain by all the philanthropic groups in favour of continued British protection over Bechuanaland. Before this agitation the Company surprisingly seemed to give way. They were disposed through the Company's secretary, Rutherfoord Harris, to make large and liberal offers to the chiefs of their own land, conceding to all that the chiefs requested concerning self-government, hunting rights and the prohibition on intoxicating liquor. They only requested that a strip of land, ten miles wide, running along the old 'missionary road' be ceded to the Company for the extension of the railway from Mafeking to Bulawayo. The chiefs would continue to enjoy British protection with direct rule from London. A hut tax would be levied to be paid into the coffers of the imperial Government. Satisfied with this arrangement, the chiefs sailed home.

But the wheeling and dealing continued in the background. The stage had been set for a larger drama. By 1894, after his successful conquest of Mashonaland and Matebeleland, Rhodes was forced to acknowledge that the country had no gold potential. In 1886 gold, once again present in resources not found elsewhere on earth, had been discovered along the Witwatersrand in the Transvaal Republic. John Hays Hammond, an adviser to Rhodes, suggested the seizure of the Transvaal goldfields. Rhodes had been premier at the Cape since 1890 and the position was aggravated by the attitude of Paul Kruger, the president of the Transvaal Republic. Rhodes had struggled to create free trade between the two Boer republics of the Orange Free State and the Transvaal and the two British colonies of Natal and the Cape. Kruger resisted these trends by raising the tarif on the railway line to the Cape.

The second aggravation was the discontent of the *Uitlanders* or outsiders, a large mining community of alien white miners, many of them British citizens who had flocked to the Transvaal and developed the mines. They were almost relegated to the status of black people; they were landless; they were allowed to make money and pay tax to the Transvaal Government but they could not wield power. During a brief visit to the area Rhodes had experienced a demonstration by the *Uitlanders* of their discontent. He made a wrong assessment of the situation. The *Uitlanders* had prospered financially under Boer rule. The Boers knew how to exploit the black man and extort cheap, almost free labour from him. The planned overthrow of the Transvaal Government needed both the support of the *Uitlanders* and the British Government. The Bechuanaland Protectorate was to be the launching ground of the raid on the Transvaal Republic by Leander Starr Jameson, the administrator of Mashonaland and Matebeleland and a personal friend of Rhodes.

During the absence of the chiefs in England, Rhodes announced his intention to transfer the lands of Ikaneng, chief of the Bamalete, to the Company. Chief Ikaneng was subordinate to and living on the lands of Chief Bathoen of the Bangwaketse, now in England with chiefs Khama and Sebele. Shippard, the Deputy Commissioner, was instructed to inform Chief Ikaneng that the Protectorate would eventually be transferred to the Company. Chief Ikaneng was at first hesitant, stating that he preferred to live under British protection. Shippard replied that the British Government could no longer afford to maintain the territory. Also, a railway line would be built as far as Gaborone by the Company and the Company needed a camp site to protect the line. Shippard, after his ten-year service in the Protectorate, was regarded as a trusted friend of the Tswana tribes. On 30 September 1895, Chief Ikaneng placed his mark on a document offering a portion of his land for the building of a camp site. The chief intended to grant a camp site and nothing more, but Shippard's report stated that the lands of the Bamalete had been transferred to the Company.

On 2 October 1895, Chief Montshiwa offered Shippard a farm for the building of a Company camp site but it was stated in Shippard's report that the lands of the Barolong had been transferred to the Company. On 10 October 1895, by the High Commissioner's proclamation, the so-called ceded territories became Company lands and Leander Starr Jameson became Resident Commissioner of the territory. On 28 December 1895, Jameson, with 600 men and the tacit support of the British Government, invaded the Transvaal Republic from the vantage point of the camps built on Bamalete and Barolong lands. He failed to get the support of the *Uitlanders* in Johannesburg who were in no mood for an uprising. Instead, he was met by a strong Boer force and surrendered on 2 January 1896. Rhodes lost the support of the Cape Afrikaners and resigned as Premier.

On 3 February 1896, an embarrassed British Government proclamation postponed the transfer of the British Bechuanaland Protectorate to the British South Africa Company. The lands of chiefs Ikaneng and Montshiwa were returned to them. The failure of the Jameson Raid confirmed the independent existence of the British Bechuanaland Protectorate under direct rule from London. In 1966 it became the independent state of Botswana. Botswana has experienced a history without parallel in southern Africa. If the indigenous people had lost their lands, they would have lost everything and become slaves and a source of cheap labour to any white exploiter at hand. Of a country totalling 220,000 square miles, 112,503 square miles remained under the ancient traditional African land tenure system. The 104,069 square miles ceded to the British Crown still remained effectively under the traditional land tenure system. Of the remainder, 7,500 square miles were used by European business enterprise on a rental and lease basis.

Bibliography

Books

Mary Benson: *Tshekedi Khama – A Biography* (Faber & Faber, London, 1960)

Anthony J. Dachs (ed.): *Papers of John Mackenzie* (Witwatersrand University Press, Johannesburg, 1975)

John Flint: *Cecil Rhodes* (Little Brown & Co., Boston, 1974)

J.D. Hepburn: *Twenty Years in Khama's Country (Being the Letters of the Rev. J.D. Hepburn to his London Missionary Society Headquarters)* (1895; reprinted by Frank Cass & Co., London, 1970)

Una Long (ed.): *Journals of Elizabeth Lees Price* (Edward Arnold, London, 1956)

John Mackenzie: *Ten Years North of the Orange River: A Story of Everyday Life and Work Among the South African Tribes, from 1859 to 1869* (Edmonton & Douglas, Edinburgh, 1871)

J.D. Omer-Cooper: *The Zulu Aftermath* (Longman, London, 1966)

Isaac Shapera: *A Handbook of Tswana Law and Custom* (Oxford University Press, London, 1938)

Anthony Sillery: *Founding a Protectorate* (Mouton & Co., London, 1965)

Anthony Sillery: *John Mackenzie of Bechuanaland: A Study in Humanitarian Imperialism* (A.A. Balkema, Cape Town, 1971)

Leonard Thompson: *Survival in Two Worlds: Moshoeshoe of Lesotho* (Oxford University Press, London, 1975)

Patrick van Rensburg: *Guilty Land: A Semi-Autobiography* (Jonathan Cape, London, 1962)

Monica Wilson and Leonard Thompson (eds.): *The Oxford History of South Africa*, Vols. I and II (Oxford University Press, London, 1969)

Papers

Botswana Government Information Service magazine, *Kutlwano*, Vol. XII, No. 10, for extracts from 'Things are Happening'; Vol. XIII, No. 1, for extracts from 'Why Marry?' by C.G. Mararike

Quentin Neil Parsons: 'The Words of Khama', *HAZ*, No. 2, 1972 (Historical Association of Zambia)

Quentin Neil Parsons: 'The Image of Khama the Great', *Botswana Notes and Records*, Vol. 3, 1971 (The Botswana Society, Gaborone)

Patrick van Rensburg: 'Brigades: Some Constraints and Experiments', unpublished paper circulated among volunteers

Patrick van Rensburg: 'Education and Training in Relation to Rural Development', unpublished paper circulated among volunteers

Unpublished sources

Quentin Neil Parsons: 'Khama III, the Bamangwato and the British, with Special Reference to 1895–1923' (Ph.D. thesis, University of Edinburgh), 1973